Praise for Gabriel Roth's
# The Unknowns

## One of the Top 10 Books of 2013
—Janet Maslin, *New York Times*

"If only all social misfits were as stealthily charming as Eric Muller, the nerdy narrator of Gabriel Roth's sparkling debut novel. Mr. Roth's remarkably funny, tender book is much more than one code-writing kid's success story. As its title indicates, *The Unknowns* is about how Eric grows up trying to fathom those things he doesn't naturally understand. Mr. Roth writes in a gently self-mocking, utterly disarming style that gives *The Unknowns* an unusual type of tension."
　　　　　　　　　　　　　　　　　—Janet Maslin, *New York Times*

"Smart, funny, and emotionally layered, Roth's debut explores the eternal struggle between intimacy and autonomy."
　　　　　　　　　　　　　　　　　　—Andrew Abrahams, *People*

"*The Unknowns* is wonderful—a wry, ironic novel about the perils of contemporary romance, where you can collect intimate details about people you've never met, but still not know the truth of somebody you want to love."
　　　　　　　　　　　　　　　　　　　　　—Scott Turow

"For lovers of Nick Hornby and Joshua Ferris, this debut novel is the smartest, funniest, and most emotionally astute book about the gauntlet of contemporary relationships I've read in years."
　　　　　　　　　　　　　　　　　　—Megan Abbott, *Glamour*

"Roth cracks the code of the male ego and nerd culture in his meditative and absorbing debut.... A convincingly introspective narrative that traces the masculine rationale, Roth's novel reinterprets love in the digital age."
　　　　　　　　　　　　　　　　　—Jonathan Fullmer, *Booklist*

"Very funny.... Roth is at his finest in flashback chapters that depict Eric as a painfully hopeless adolescent."  —*The New Yorker*

"Eric's analytic mind, so useful in the world of computers, hinders his human interactions in the real world, especially with the fairer sex.... He perceives dating with an omniscience reminiscent of Neo from *The Matrix*.... *The Unknowns* crackles with commentary, one part post-structuralism and one part observational comedy, on how we interact in 2013."  —Nicholas Mancusi, *The Daily Beast*

"Gabriel Roth is a natural. This is a very assured first book—fast, funny, full of snappy dialogue, and never losing its poise even when it's glancing into the abyss. I think he's a find."
—Sebastian Faulks, author of *A Possible Life*

"This is an impressive and scarily assured debut—and really funny."
—Harry Ritchie, *The Guardian* (UK)

"Terrific."  —Daniel Roberts, *Fortune*

"It's a kick getting inside the head of this highly observant, self-conscious—and funny—narrator."
—Laurie Muchnick, *Bloomberg News*

"Roth's novel explores love from the point of view of someone who has spent his whole life thinking logically, solving problems and living analytically. It's an excellent setup for the drama and comedy that comes out of falling in love, especially for Eric because it's way beyond his comfort zone."
—Tony DuShane, *San Francisco Chronicle*

"Gabriel Roth's *The Unknowns* is a remarkable and assured debut novel, poignant and funny, and one of the most enjoyable books I have read all year."  —David Gutowski, Largehearted Boy

"I adored *The Unknowns*." —Susan Cain, author of *Quiet*

"A geek-com of frequently Woody Allen–esque brilliance.... Gabriel Roth is a genuinely exciting talent." —Stephanie Cross, *Daily Mail* (UK)

"Gabriel Roth's Eric Muller had me from the first obsessive aside, but I soon found myself watching through half-covered eyes as he made a bungle of every goddamn thing. I loved and cringed at every moment." —Ben Shrank, author of *Love Is a Canoe*

"*The Unknowns* is a confident novel that manages to be both funny and sad." —Ben Lawrence, *Telegraph* (UK)

"*The Unknowns* feels at first like a very great and very funny coming-of-age novel, about a high-school loser destined for Internet riches. But then suddenly you realize you're reading something much more powerful: a beautiful and painful story about the dangers of learning too much—and about how little we can ever really know about other people." —Ben H. Winters, author of *The Last Policeman*

"An incisive debut novel.... Roth deftly illuminates the origins of Eric's exacting personality." —Patrick McGinn, *Paste* magazine

"Richly imagined and deliriously funny, *The Unknowns* ponders the unponderable and comes up with a surprisingly sweet coming-of-age story." —Georgia Rowe, *San Jose Mercury News*

"Thoughtful.... This is a debut novel by a skillful young writer." —Kerryn Goldsworthy, *Sydney Morning Herald*

# The
# Unknowns

A Novel

## Gabriel Roth

BACK BAY BOOKS
LITTLE, BROWN AND COMPANY
New York   Boston   London

Copyright © 2013 by Gabriel Roth
Reading group guide copyright © 2014 by Gabriel Roth and Little, Brown and Company

Back Bay Books / Little, Brown and Company
Hachette Book Group
237 Park Avenue, New York, NY 10017
littlebrown.com

Originally published in hardcover by Reagan Arthur Books, July 2013
First Back Bay paperback edition, May 2014

Back Bay Books is an imprint of Little, Brown and Company, a division of Hachette Book Group, Inc. The Back Bay Books name and logo are trademarks of Hachette Book Group, Inc.

The publisher is not responsible for websites (or their content) that are not owned by the publisher.

The Hachette Speakers Bureau provides a wide range of authors for speaking events. To find out more, go to hachettespeakersbureau.com or call (866) 376-6591.

Library of Congress Cataloging-in-Publication Data

Roth, Gabriel
  The unknowns: a novel / Gabriel Roth.—1st ed.
    p. cm.
  ISBN 978-0-316-22328-7 (hc) / 978-0-316-22330-0 (pb)
  I. Title.
  PS3618.O858U55 2013
  813'.6—dc23                                            2012027289

10  9  8  7  6  5  4  3  2  1

RRD-C

Printed in the United States of America

*For Tali*

# The
# Unknowns

# 1

I need the absolute control over my optic blasts that my ruby quartz visor affords me.

—Scott "Cyclops" Summers, *X-Men* 136

IT'S IMPORTANT TO CHOOSE the right moment to arrive at a party. You want to get there after the vertiginous first hour, when the early arrivals stand awkwardly around the kitchen, but in time for the next phase, when the noise level reaches some threshold and triggers a feedback loop and everyone starts raising their voices to be heard. At such a moment it's possible to imagine that this party will live up to the promise inherent in the notion of a party.

But as I step through the door of Cynthia's apartment at 10:32, it's clear that tonight that promise will go unfulfilled. A voice barely carries down the empty corridor from the kitchen, mingling with the faint jangle of a boom box. In the nearest room a few sad coats are piled on the bed. Tonight people will stand around drinking beer from plastic cups, talking about their bosses or their dissertations, before going home to masturbate.

I add my jacket to the heap and proceed to the kitchen, carrying a gift wrapped in brown paper and a six-pack of bottled beer. With so few guests it will be harder to hide, to lean against the wall as if waiting for someone. At a crowded party you can make three slow circuits of the premises, turning sideways to slip past the people in line for the bathroom, and then leave without self-reproach. The fewer guests, the more you're implicated in the event's success or failure.

3

Cynthia emerges from the kitchen at the sound of my footsteps. "You made it!" she says, as though I'd done something more hazardous than ride in a taxi.

To extend the moment alone with her before the introductions, I steer her into her bedroom and present the wrapped box. I have been rich for a little less than five months. She peels the tape off, then unfolds the paper as though preserving it for later use. When she sees that it's a camera she makes an enthusiastic noise, but it takes her a second to recognize the brand and assimilate the specs and understand that it's a better camera than she'd first thought. "Wait, this is too much," she says.

After all of Cynthia's benevolent interventions into my life, an expensive piece of consumer electronics is not an extravagance. But nothing about being rich is as simple as you might imagine.

"Hey, I can afford it now," I say.

She frowns and then, reading my face, takes on the appearance of a woman seized by inspiration. "Oh my God, I know what I'm going to do," she says. "I had this idea at work: I'm going to start a photo series of the pills my clients have to take. Like, one shot for each dose, which is five or six a day, and then at the end the patient's face. But the pills in super-close-up, so you can see the textures, because some of them are capsules so they're smooth and red and blue like rockets and others are tablets so they'll have this grainy organic texture like a sand sculpture." This hypothetical project began as a scheme to justify the gift, but now she's caught up in it.

Cynthia decided she was a lesbian about six months ago. It wasn't without foreshadowing: she has pictures of Claire Danes up on her wall, and she's told me about jokey little crushes on women, and once she said she regretted sitting out the dorm-room experiments of sophomore year, which made me sorrier than ever that I didn't go to college. And now, even though she's turning twenty-five and it's embarrassingly late, she's coming out. A shorter haircut seems imminent, as does sex with a woman. A week ago she made out with a twenty-one-year-old named Ayelet.

"So is she here?" I say.

"I don't think she's coming," Cynthia says, setting the camera on the bed. "It's pretty mellow so far. A lot of people are out of town."

"That's what you get for being born in December."

In the kitchen I can identify two of eight people. Cynthia's roommate Gretchen, who is thin and pretty and not interested in me, is talking to a bald man in suspenders. And standing by the fridge with two women is Justin. Justin is a firefighter; he rides in the truck and everything. He went to college with Cynthia, then moved out here to go to grad school in urban planning, and then right after the terrorist attacks last year, when America was going through its little love affair with firefighters, he quit school and signed up with the SFFD and now he walks with the quiet confidence that comes when you stare death in the face every day and save innocent lives and think of yourself without hesitation as a man. Justin is also taller than I am. He greets me as I put the beer in the fridge, and then he introduces me to the women he's talking to, and I make the first in a series of mistakes that will lead me, standing in a taqueria some weeks hence, to pray that I have not been recognized.

I shake hands with them from right to left, calibrating my grip to coed handshake strength. The one on the right is Lauren: nice curly blond hair, a big bulbous nose, bad khaki pants that she probably wore to work. Sweet, shy, works in some kind of helping-people job, a little insecure about her weight, a couple of flowy Deadhead skirts in the back of her closet. And on the left is Maya. Small body, small features, chestnut hair in a shaggy bob, neolibrarian glasses. A subtle smile at the corners of her eyes that says *I see through you entirely and find you benign but a bit ridiculous.* Girls spend years working on that look without reaching Maya's level. Anything I might say to such a woman would be a line, and would hang curdling in the air on leaving my mouth, so I open a conversation with Lauren.

"How do you know Justin?" I say.

"We used to volunteer at the *something something* Homeless *something* together," she says as I calculate a follow-up question.

"Used to?" I say. "What, did you decide to stop wasting your time helping homeless people?"

A smile. "No, I went to Latin America for a year."

"Oh yeah? Where in Latin America?" I ask, because it would be rude to say what I'm really thinking, which is *What is it with you white girls and Latin America?* The Latin America phase that Bay Area girls go through in their early twenties, their attempts to transcend their whiteness via Frida Kahlo and salsa dancing, has always puzzled me. As Lauren begins the familiar litany—Ecuador, Costa Rica, "the D.R."—Maya and Justin head out the door to go have sex in the bathroom or something.

"How do you know Cynthia?" she asks me.

"We went to high school together," I tell her. "I knew her when her name was Cindy and she was dating boys." I should mitigate the joke about wasting her time. "So do you work in homeless services?"

"I work at a nonprofit, but it's mostly policy around housing issues," she says. "What about you? What do you do?"

This is a difficult one, because right now I don't do anything, and what I used to do was a combination of computer programming and business, which Lauren would find arcane and distasteful, respectively. There are women who would be interested to learn that you've made a lot of money, but they don't live in San Francisco, work at nonprofits, and travel around Latin America. So I say, "Oh, I started an Internet company," and shrug to acknowledge the fact that, in the Bay Area in 2002, this is a cliché.

She asks about the company. "It's a consumer profiling system," I tell her, hoping this dry phrase will prompt a subject change, but she's tenacious.

"Assume you're talking to a fourth-grader," she says.

"We give you special offers, like a discount at an online store or something," I say. "And in exchange, everything you do on the Internet—everything you read, everything you click, everything you buy—is tracked and stored and put in a database. Not your email, obviously, or your banking, but all your public activities online. All that data could be compared with the data for millions of other people, and from there you can be categorized as, let's say, Espresso Granola, or, uh, DIY PYT."

"Whoa," she says with a theatrical shudder. Now I seem slightly scary. That's not a bad thing, necessarily, especially when you factor in the acronymic compliment, but I should balance it with some self-deprecation.

"So I built a program to gather and keep track of all that stuff," I say. "And then I sold it to a bigger company, and now I bore unsuspecting women at parties who have the misfortune to ask me what I do."

I'm watching her responses closely throughout. Visibly paying attention is crucial, especially when you're talking about yourself and thus at risk of appearing *not* to pay attention. When I was maybe thirteen I heard my mother on the phone with her friend Stacey, talking about the latest of her post-divorce near-boyfriends, each of whom had some insurmountable flaw (no job, drank too much, participated in Civil War reenactments). My mom, defending this guy, said, "I know, I know, but...he pays attention to me." I remember hearing Stacey say, "That can go a long way" (although obviously that part is an invention of memory; they were on the phone), and my mother saying, "Exactly."

But I'd like to check on Maya in case there's an opening, and I can't just look over Lauren's shoulder, or I'll be one of those guys who look over your shoulder while you're talking. I'm getting worried, because this conversation is going pretty well, and if it lasts much longer Maya will be off-limits. (I'm assuming their friendship contains a tacit noncompete clause.) "I'm going to get a drink," I say. "Do you need anything?" She's hardly touched her vodka and cranberry, so I'm free to head to the other end of the kitchen and glance at the people milling in the hall. The population has increased, but not to the Malthusian degree it would take to make the party memorable. Gretchen is leaning against the sink talking to two women with their arms around each other's waists. They look like some complicated riff on butch/femme stereotypes: one wears a slip dress and too much makeup, the other a baseball cap and low-slung jeans, but the former is large and hirsute while her partner is waifish and delicate and kind of stunning. It's hard to tell if the arrangement is deliberate irony or just an unusual intersection of body type and sexual self-identification. Of the new arrivals, the only one I recognize is a coworker of Cynthia's who once started a conversation with me about hip-hop. (He liked certain kinds of hip-hop but not other kinds.) I'm standing at the little bottle-crammed table pouring Coke into whiskey when Maya is suddenly next to me.

"Could you fix me a gin and tonic?" she asks. The proximity of her body is overpowering.

"Sure," I say. There must be more to say than that, although I can't think of what it could be.

Maya says, "Thanks," rotates 180 degrees, and goes back to talking to Justin. When I hand her the drink a minute later she takes it without even interrupting her conversation to say thank you—a kind of antiflirting and hence a kind of flirting, an effortless triangulation, arousing hope and jealousy in us both. Well played, Maya.

And I'm still left with no one to talk to except Lauren, and every minute I spend talking to Lauren takes me further out of the game vis-à-vis Maya. I scan the room as if I'm looking for someone specific who was here a minute ago. Lauren is examining the Magnetic Poetry set on the fridge, the special Lesbian Pride edition, half words like *dyke* and *cunt* and *partner* and *dog* and the other half prepositions. Gretchen is smashing a bag of ice against the counter to break it up. Maya is laughing at Justin, who appears to be doing an impression of Lenny from *Of Mice and Men*. Cynthia's voice comes from down the hall, and something characteristically trusty about its timbre makes me regret getting her the camera. It is at this moment, as I stand alone in my friend's kitchen, my right hand fingering a little Ziploc bag in my pocket, that I conceive my ill-fated plan.

Inhale, exhale, commit.

I return to Lauren and pick up where we left off. *See, I just went to get a drink.* I break out some intermediate-level tactics: Asking a Question That Refers to Something I Learned About Her Earlier; Suggesting We Continue the Conversation Sitting Down. We move to the grubby couch in the living room, which is not as comfortable as it looks because the cushions are fifteen years old and have had the buoyancy squashed out of them. The party has finally overspilled the kitchen, and guests stand in clusters around the swept-out room. Lauren and I sit at forty-five-degree angles and turn our heads the rest of the way to face each other. I don't do anything sexually assertive like holding eye contact or casually touching her arm. I watch closely for signs that her interest is waning. I tell her the How I Was Unfairly Accused of Making Obscene Phone Calls story, probably my number one anecdote: funny, raunchy but not dirty, unbraggadocious. I wait for her post-anecdotal *No way! Really?*s to dry up, and then I pull the trigger.

"Hey, I don't know if this is something you're up for," I say, "but I've got some Ecstasy with me." That's bold enough, and I pause to let it register, but it's only step one. "And I was wondering if you guys"—I incline my head toward the kitchen to indicate Maya and Justin—"would be up for doing some."

"Oh my God, I don't know," she says. "I mean, I haven't done it in a really long time."

"All the more reason," I say. Do I sound like I'm pressuring her? Pull back. "Listen, if this isn't a good night for it, that's cool. But if you guys feel like it, we can hang out and do it here, or we can go back to someone's house, or whatever." Like a salesman I stop talking and let her dismiss her remaining objections herself.

"I think I want to do it," she says, and how could she not? Everyone loves Ecstasy. "But I have to talk to Maya."

"I've totally got enough for those guys," I say. It would be great if there were a way to exclude Justin from the invitation, but I can't see one that doesn't push the sleaze factor, already dangerously high, into the red. "Go talk them into it."

I stay on the couch and watch through the kitchen doorway as she engages Maya and Justin in a little huddle. I'm hoping to see a flash of excitement on Maya's face; what I see instead is Lauren explaining something and Maya touching her arm and nodding. "It's fine," Maya says twice. Justin looks over at me with a vaguely cynical expression.

And now Lauren is heading back toward me with a nervous grin, alone, and five minutes later the two of us are in a taxi, hurtling up to the Richmond, where she apparently lives, and I'm leaving the party with a girl but it's the wrong girl, and I'm unsure whether I should be feeling remorse or triumph.

There's a right way to do these things. At the corner store I purchase two large packs of sugar-free gum and two large bottles of Gatorade. We sit at her kitchen table, clink glasses of water, down these little aspirinlike tablets. Lauren lives alone, so there's a cat, which is going to set off my allergies in about forty-five minutes. On the walls are paintings by talentless friends; black-and-white photos, presumably by Lauren herself; Kodachrome snapshots of her parents in their youth. I conceive the idea of an exhibition of parental photos from the walls of girls' apartments, a show that would be situated somewhere between found art and ethnography. Maya does not appear in any of the pictures. I am trying hard not to get hung up on Maya and how she's occurring without me right now. If the world would just freeze whenever I'm not around, I'd be less worried about missing something important.

We make a kind of prelapsarian small talk.

"Do you do this kind of thing a lot?" she asks me.

"What *kind of thing* are you referring to?" I have my teasing face on.

"Oh, going home with strange girls and taking Ecstasy," she says.

"Are you a strange girl, then?" It's almost too easy.

"I've done it three times," she says. "And the first time I only took half, so it doesn't count."

"So tonight you'll have to take two to make up for it."

She laughs, like that's preposterous. "No, to make up for it I'd only have to take one and a half."

"You're not adjusting for inflation."

I'd be more anxious if we were about to have sex. It's certain that the next few hours, at least, will be very pleasant. I'm greedy for it already, smiling hard and getting an anticipatory buzz, even though it's only been five minutes and the drug has barely made it to my stomach lining. But I'm impatient, and I don't want to be sitting in this wooden chair anymore. The apartment is tiny; I leave the kitchen and I'm in the bedroom. Sometimes you just have to accept these things.

In the cab I had worried about her CD collection, and a close examination bears out my fears. It's frustrating, because I've got my iPod right here, and if I had a Y-cable I could hook it into her little bookshelf stereo. (Then I'd have to reposition the speakers to achieve a proper left-right spread.) For the fiftieth time I consider carrying a Y-cable around with me, and for the fiftieth time I realize how lame that would be, and I am momentarily paralyzed, stretched across the gulf between my life's twin goals: experiencing uncompromised happiness and not being a loser. I sneeze.

At some point I have become aware of my heart beating and my blood pumping, and I feel a twinge of admiration for my body, which somehow keeps functioning through everything, although I so rarely stop to enjoy it. And I realize I'm really glad the evening is going this way: I can't think of a better outcome than making a new friend, a really nice girl, and getting to hang out with her and do Ecstasy.

"You know what we should do?" I tell her. "We should take our shoes off."

"My shoes aren't bothering me at all," she says.

"And yet once you take them off you will be astonished at how much comfort is available simply by removing your shoes." I am sitting on the bed, hungrily removing my shoes.

She is playing. "What if I'm more comfortable with my shoes on?"

"I suppose there is the remote possibility that you are more comfortable with your shoes on," I say, "although I don't believe it for a second. But I seem to have acquired some kind of neurotic fixation on you experiencing the state of shoelessness right now, and so it wouldn't be inaccurate to say that your shoes are making *me* uncomfortable."

"What a terrible situation!" she says, and for a moment it looks as if she really does think it's a terrible situation. "Incompatible desires! What should we do?"

"I will propose a solution," I tell her. "It requires that you do me a small favor. You remove your shoes—no, you don't even have to put in the legwork—*legwork*, ha! Anyway: I will remove your shoes for you. You will spend thirty seconds assessing the resultant sensation. If at the end of that trial period you wish to return to your previous shoe-clad state, I will gently replace the shoes, and my mind will rest easy in the knowledge that you are enjoying your personal optimum comfort state as regards footwear. If, on the other hand, you decide that you prefer to go without shoes, I will do a little dance of vindication."

"That could work," she says, sitting down next to me on the bed.

"This way, neither of us will have to sacrifice comfort, physical or psychogenic, for more than an instant."

"That's a great plan," she says.

I get up off the bed (just standing is extremely enjoyable, and I sit back down and stand up again so I can experience it for a second time) and crouch at her feet. She's wearing some kind of black dress shoe. I cradle her foot by the ankle, fiddle with the buckle, slip the shoe off. I repeat the process with the other shoe. I place the shoes carefully next to the bed, side by side, then stand up.

"Oh wow," she says. "That's really comfortable."

Lauren reclines, moving all of her limbs at once as if swimming through some viscous medium. Something is happening. She opens her eyes and sees me smiling down at her and she smiles back. She looks lovely. I lie down next to her and start stroking her neck. It's awesome to be stroking her neck. I'm seeing her hair with a kind of hyperclarity that reminds me of something I can't place. I look at her face, and suddenly the Ecstasy is doing what we pay it to do. We kiss for a while, gently, like deer. The part of my brain that compares whatever's going on in real life to whatever might simultaneously be going on in some parallel universe has shut up. And now we're naked, and there's these breasts right in front of me, these things that have no purpose but human comfort, and the skin of her neck is so soft, and her pubic hair grazes my leg. Thanks to the Ecstasy my penis is resolutely flaccid, but I know she understands this. She gives it a tender look, as though it's her newborn baby. It feels like we're both bouncing now, like we're moving up and down in giant arcs, like we're floating in space. We lie there awhile.

"God, it's been such a long time since I've felt close to anyone," she says.

"I know," I say. "I'm so glad you were up for this."

"I almost didn't, you know. I was like, *Who is this guy, I've never met him, Justin hardly knows him, I shouldn't go and do drugs with him.*"

"You were just being sensible."

"I was being scared. I go around being scared all the time. I'm usually scared to be naked with boys."

"Everybody is."

"Really?" She seems surprised by this, as though it's never occurred to her before.

"Absolutely. Everybody is." This seems true as I say it. "We spend all this energy hiding ourselves, and then when we're having sex or whatever, we're supposed to be naked with each other, but we get so scared, and then we're more wrapped up and guarded and closed off than ever."

"I'm so scared that I make it like I'm not even there at all," she says. "I just remove myself, mentally. But that's what sex should be about. It's about being close to each other." She's running her fingers through my hair.

"It's not about having an orgasm," I say.

"Orgasms are nice, though."

"They certainly are. But it's—do you want to have an orgasm right now?"

"No." She's beaming.

"Can I tell you something about having orgasms?"

"Yeah."

"I've never told anyone this in my entire life." It's true. I haven't. Why not?

"Tell me." She nods rhythmically. She really wants to know.

"Every time I have an orgasm with another person, every time, it doesn't matter who she is, right before I come I hear these words in my head."

"What are the words?"

"*I love you, Mom.* Every time, just like that. *I love you, Mom.*"

She looks like she's just been given a Christmas present. "Really?"

"I spend my whole life being ashamed of that."

"There's no reason to be ashamed!"

"I know! I know!"

"Because it's a good thing in you! It's a good feeling!"

"It's love!" I tell her, and I've figured it out for the first time. "It's just love! It's all the same thing!" And I get up and start dancing, naked, while she stares at me, her pupils wide as saucers.

Four hours later the tide is going out. I'm pacing the room and starting to narrate.

"So I'm getting a little cold, so I'm going to put on my T-shirt and my boxers now, if that's all right with you. Wait, where did they...oh, here's my T-shirt, it got lost under the comforter. And I'll bet—yup, here's the boxers, right next to it. There we go. You know, until I was about twenty I bought all my T-shirts in extra-large because on some unconscious level I think I thought I was going to grow into them."

"God," she says, "my stomach really hurts."

"That sucks. Do you have any Pepto-Bismol? I don't really get stomachaches. There's stomach people and head people, apparently, and I'm a head person. I feel stuff in my head. Maybe I should put my pants on too. I feel weird walking around your apartment in my underwear."

We spend another hour waiting out the symptoms—her stomach, my jaw, my monologue—and then I make well-I-should-get-going noises, patting my pockets for my keys and wallet and phone.

We hug goodbye at the door, a quick chest press, a take-care-of-yourself hug. Neither of us mentions seeing each other again.

It's just after dawn and everything looks weirdly bleached out, as if the color saturation hasn't caught up to the brightness. I have chemical energy to burn off, so I start walking home through the unfamiliar neighborhood, past stuccoed seventies houses and Chinese seafood restaurants. I feel like shit but I'm glad to be alone, in a place I have no reason to be, at a time when I shouldn't even be awake. The cold feels good, and I've got my coat. I shouldn't have told her about the thing.

I'm in no shape to think about this. I'm just going to walk off the rest of this buzz, go home, get some sleep. Tomorrow I'll do the math, figure out what happened, what to do next.

I shouldn't have told her about the thing.

I get home circa 6:40 a.m. and crawl into bed and put a mask over my eyes. The mask is made of soft foam lined with sateen, and its eyepieces bulge convexly to prevent eyelid contact, which can disturb REM. The mask usually helps me sleep, but this morning there is no sleeping because of the adrenaline racing up and down my spine. My friend Danny claims to have consumed pure MDMA, uncut with amphetamines, manufactured by a CU-Boulder chemistry Ph.D. If I'd taken that I'd be asleep now, although it wouldn't have kept me from humiliating myself with a stranger. Responsibility for that error lies with the Ecstasy itself, which suppresses faculties of self-consciousness and shame that, although harsh at times, serve a vital regulatory function and shouldn't be artificially disabled for the sake of some momentary intimacy with a girl who isn't even the girl I was pursuing. Is Maya going to hear about what happened? Are Lauren and Maya on the phone together right now? By turning my head hard to the left and peering out through the narrow gap between the mask's edge and the right side of my nose, I can see the bedside clock, according to which it's only 7:33. They're not on the phone. Lauren is lying in bed, trying to lower her heart rate by force of will, thinking about the weird guy she brought home who seemed sort of charming at first and gave her drugs and got her naked and then instead of fucking her took the opportunity to unburden himself of his infantile peccadillo.

Lying here is bringing me no closer to sleep. I should get up, pass a few hours in vigorous exercise, flush the speed from my bloodstream, return to bed around ten, sleep through the day, wake up in the evening and get some breakfast and then stay on a nocturnal schedule, eating lunch at three in the morning, taking vitamin D supplements to substitute for sunlight, never seeing another human being except the clerks working the night shift at the twenty-four-hour Safeway, until one night I run into Maya in the cereal aisle—I'm holding Honey Bunches of Oats, she's holding Special K—and the two of us leave the supermarket together and drive to the top of Twin Peaks to hold hands and watch the sunrise.

Giving up, I remove the mask and emerge from the bedroom into my apartment's vast living room/kitchen/dining area. The light through the casement windows is lurid and exhausting, and when I reach the couch I collapse on it and gaze out at the skyline. When I bought this place the view of downtown seemed a thrilling prospect, but four months later it looks like something off a postcard. I'm wearing the same underwear and T-shirt I had on last night, now sour-smelling and soft, and the couch's coarse fabric is slightly rough against my bare legs. I'm aware that there's something I'm trying to forget, and the awareness prompts me to investigate, and then I remember last night's indiscretion and my brain winces and tries to vomit. I go to the fridge for a Gatorade, and keeping my balance requires more concentration than usual. I drink half the Gatorade standing by the fridge with the door open so the cool air prickles the hair on my legs. Is there a way to ensure that I never see Lauren again? She's probably just as embarrassed as I am. Obviously she's nowhere near as embarrassed as I am. She's probably embarrassed, although not as embarrassed as I am, and wants to forget the whole thing. Or else: over the next few days our five-hour artificially instigated love affair will tug at the back of her mind, and she'll decide the only way to scratch the itch is for the two of us to meet for coffee and review our feelings about the events in question and start erecting a mandatory friendship. She could get my email address pretty easily. I shut the refrigerator door and flip open my laptop, which is sitting on the granite surface of the kitchen island. Once it wakes up and finds the wireless connection I refresh my email, but of course there's nothing from her, only an invitation to speak on a couple of panels at the Digital Future Conference in March. She won't email today—she'll give me a few days to contact her first. I set the email client to alert me when a new message arrives and wonder if there will be any girls at the Digital Future Conference. Where is Maya right now? It's 8:12 on Saturday. She's asleep in Justin's bed, her head on his shoulder in the morning-after composition familiar from American cinema, a sheet draped over her to hide her nipples from the camera. I can't remember the specifics of her face, just hair and glasses and an expression of compassionate skepticism. The newspapers are waiting downstairs, and the crossword would occupy me for half an hour. I put on the pants I wore last night and then ride barefoot down to the lobby in the nearly silent elevator. When I bought the apartment I decided I'd take the stairs every time, to build some exercise into my routine, but I'm always in a hurry or tired in a way that justifies taking the elevator, or else I've just done something noble and thus deserve to take the elevator as a reward. I am aware that these are excuses that prevent me from gaining the health benefits of taking the stairs, and I've started trying to tell myself I should take the stairs anyway, even when I'm feeling rushed or exhausted or virtuous, but this particular unslept serotonin-starved humiliated morning is clearly not the morning to abjure the elevator at last. The newspapers are just outside the building's frosted-glass front door, the *Times* in its blue bag, the *Chronicle* in yellow. As I stoop to pick them up I wonder if Maya is sending me an email asking if I want to hang out sometime. I recognize the absurdity of this thought and try to dismiss it, but I nevertheless return to the elevator at a faster pace and am disappointed when the doors don't open as soon as I press the call button. I shuffle from foot to foot on the cold painted concrete, waiting.

Eventually the metal doors part and reveal the family from the third floor, a young couple with a two-year-old and an infant and a big Akita. I'm standing closer to the elevator doors than is customary, and I must look pretty bad. The mother flinches protectively toward the boy's stroller.

"Papers," I say, displaying them, and try to smile reassuringly.

When I get back to the apartment I drop the papers on the island and glance unstoppably at the laptop's screen, where nothing has changed.

In the bathroom I clean up, gargle, assess the situation. Looking in the mirror is always disappointing—it's strange that something can be *always disappointing;* you'd imagine that eventually you'd adjust your expectations downward to the point where they're congruent with reality—but today it's even more disappointing than usual. My skin is ghastly pale, and my hair has flattened and swollen in random whorls and eddies. The real problem, though, is not these contingent features but the face itself. When we say someone has a big nose, we're usually talking about the third dimension, the degree to which the nose protrudes into the outside world. My nose, in contrast, is big in the first two dimensions, the x- and y-coordinates. (This corresponds to greater negative space in the nostril area as well.) But my nose is just the most dramatic symptom of a deeper problem: there isn't enough room on my face. When I was a boy my features could coexist in peace, but as I emerged from puberty they began to manifest expansionist aims and struck out into the neutral territory between them. I am surveying the battlefield when a chime sounds in the other room, and hope spikes into my heart, and I defer the brushing of my teeth and exit the bathroom to check my email.

I haven't spoken to my father since I left Denver more than three years ago, and I thought we were both committed to falling out of touch. But there it is: *B_Muller@spencercollege.edu.*

Eric, Im going to be in San Fran next month. Thought we might get together if your free. Got something BIG to spring on you. I'll be the the 7 to the 16, hope that's good for you. Barry (dad).

Sic passim. His signature takes up seven lines and lists his job title, employer, mailing address, and phone number, none of which has changed in a decade.

I spend most of the following weeks surfing the Internet to no purpose. I wake in the early afternoons with no memory of any dreams. I compose a brief reply to my father, suggesting that he call me when he arrives. The program coordinator for the Digital Future Conference emails again, and this time I accept the invitation. In the evenings I rotate my three most reliable culinary options: the hamburger place, the burrito place, and spaghetti. Christmas and New Year's occur without me.

I'm not sure exactly how much time has passed since my last unwise attempt at social contact, but the number of days modulo three must equal two because I'm getting a burrito. The taqueria is painted in kindergarten shades of red and yellow, and the jukebox plays Mexican pop music at an excruciating volume, and the lighting makes everyone more animated than usual. I walk up the aisle toward the counter and there, at a table on the left, is Maya, and my heart is suddenly audible to the entire restaurant. She's listening intently to a pale, pierced girl who is talking loudly and gesturing with her hands. Does Maya see me? I lock my eyes on the far wall and walk past her, trying to maintain a natural pace and gait. The possibilities start branching: Either she saw me or she didn't. If she saw me, did she see me see her? If she saw me see her, does she think I didn't recognize her? Is it possible she doesn't recognize me? And this: *What does she know about me?*

The guy taking the orders calls me *amigo*, which he only started doing a month ago and which usually makes me feel good but not today.

I've never been able to figure out how much girls tell each other. I used to assume that information is a status symbol in GirlWorld, and so anything you tell a girl will be displayed like a piece of jewelry. But I've come to think it works more like money, something to be judiciously invested for maximum returns. If I'm right, Maya doesn't necessarily know about my, what, my *Oedipal thing*. Let's say she doesn't. Let's say she thinks I'm just some guy she met at a party, and I sit down and eat a burrito with her and her friend. The next time Maya sees Lauren she says, *Guess who I ran into at El Submarino the other night?* and when Lauren hears this she smiles cryptically and says, *Oh, what was that like?* in a funny tone of voice that prompts Maya to start saying *What? What?* until, after demurring for a suitable interval, Lauren tells Maya what I told her about ejaculating and the voice in my head and *I love you, Mom,* and first shock and disgust ensue, and then eventually hilarity, and by the end of the conversation I have become an anecdote to them, a strange, sad boy-man they once met who disguises his creepy little perversion behind reflexive flirting, and just imagining that makes me want to kill myself.

So while I wait for the line cook to assemble the burrito I stare fixedly at the refrigerators full of soda and beer. The sodas are imported from Mexico; they are made with cane sugar rather than corn syrup and bear stickers warning that they're not to be sold in the U.S. Finally the cook calls out, "Forty-four, *cuarenta y cuatro!*" and I'm clutching my burrito and chips and heading for the door. And then there's that business of pretending you haven't seen the person without making it look like you're ignoring her. It's impossible to know how successful this deception ever is. You don't know if she genuinely doesn't know you're there, or if she sees you but thinks you don't see her and prefers not to announce herself, or if the two of you are collaborating on a little play in which you pretend not to notice each other. Accurate data is almost impossible to come by, and in its absence I have the feeling of flying blind into a whirlwind. Of course, I could just talk to her. Even if she knows. I could say hello and introduce myself to her friend and start talking to her and see what happens, and if she gives me a knowing look and says, *I heard you and Lauren had quite a time the other week,* I could smile and say, *Yeah, we had a time.* My eyes are fixed dead ahead and I'm standing too straight, in a way that feels unnatural and probably looks stupid. I could just sit down next to her. Instead I walk past her, through the door, out to the sidewalk, and think, *I've made it.*

# 2

If they're so smart, why don't they figure out how popularity works and beat the system, just as they do for standardized tests?
—Paul Graham, "Why Nerds Are Unpopular"

NICKY BOONT AND I were making an adventure game: lines of text on the screen that said things like *You are in a dungeon filled with skulls. There is a door to the north and one to the east.* Together we made elaborate maps of underground architecture, wrote adjective-studded descriptions of caverns and weapons and monsters, cultivated the pseudomythological backstory. Every school day we met at lunch in the computer room, an L-shaped cubicle that had been freed up when the office supplies were moved to larger quarters. There we catalogued each object the player might find in the dungeon—weapons, keys, potions—and every action he might perform.

When I walked in, Nicky's chair was turned away from the Commodore 128 toward the door, his legs crossed professorially. His pale hair was cut in a perfect bowl that made him look like a mushroom. "We need a hide command," he said by way of a greeting. Theoretically we'd finished the actions two weeks earlier.

"You mean like hide yourself, or hide an object?" I asked. It's hard to develop an entire syntax when you don't know words like *transitive* and *intransitive*, but that was the project we had assigned ourselves.

"Both, obviously," Nicky said, in a way that suggested he had only been thinking of one or the other. "It has to be hiding in a specific place. Like, you can't hide in an empty room."

Jeremy Glissan snorted without looking up from the other machine. Jeremy was a more experienced programmer than either of us, and had a more powerful computer at home, and he helped us by pointing out our stupidest potential blunders.

My interest in the game had, perversely, increased a month earlier when I had discovered girls — *discovered* in the sense of *realized that they maybe had magic powers of some kind*. I had known Bronwen Oberfell forever, literally: our mothers were pregnancy friends. I was at her house, where there was a garage and a garbage disposal and stairs. My mother and Bronwen's mother Stacey were smoking in the kitchen, and Bronwen and I were in the living room eating spaghetti and watching *Fame*. It was easy to make me happy when I was twelve: a bowl of spaghetti and an episode of *Fame* would do it. I happened to notice Bronwen's profile as she looked at the screen. I thought, *She's got a really small nose*. And then, *Hey, actually, she's really pretty*. And then: *Oh wow*. And a bowl of spaghetti and an episode of *Fame* would never again be enough to make me happy.

In the days that followed this revelation I started to imagine showing the game to Bronwen, seating her at my computer and inviting her to enter the subterranean tomb of Morbius the Vengeant. From over her shoulder I watched her type the simple commands that led her into our world, leaning gradually forward in her chair until her nose was almost touching the monitor. I saw her horror at the appearance of the skeleton army, her frustration with the rapidly multiplying Furbles, her determination to capture the treasure interred with Morbius's corpse. No artist ever had an audience more exquisitely responsive than I had in Bronwen Oberfell, and no artist has been more gratified than I was when, after vanquishing a dozen foes, after solving increasingly devilish puzzles and evading artfully designed traps, after achieving the center of the Maze of Mithraeth and collecting the priceless Jewel of Bora-El, Bronwen (who, sitting at the computer, was somehow wearing a chain mail bikini) turned to look at me, as if for the first time, with the light of adoration in her eyes.

So: what if, at some point during this magical journey into danger and love, she felt the need to conceal herself, or to stow some precious object out of sight? It turned out there were a lot of parameters involved in hiding. Size, for instance: a loose stone in the wall would make a good hiding place for a key, but not for a person. Multiply that by 134—the number of verbs in the Tomb of Morbius lexicon—and that was eighth grade. It wasn't that we were unpopular, Nicky and I; it was that popularity wasn't a property of the object class to which we belonged.

And the earth continued in its endless laps around the sun, and middle school waned, and the first hairs sprouted around my genitals, and I worked on the game, nursing the idea that it would make Bronwen love me. Lying in bed clutching my growing-but-not-yet-fully-functional penis, I turned the fantasy over in my mind, adding details, refining the characterization. Each twist in the program's design, each new puzzle and contrivance, was tested against Bronwen Oberfell. Sometimes the dream would be interrupted by an error message, and I would get out of bed and look over the code. I caught a few bugs that way.

"So I understand congratulations are in order," my dad said when I arrived for one of my biweekly visits. "You got into that junior high school." After the divorce he'd moved into a tiny furnished apartment near the college where he taught. It was meant to be a stopgap place, until he found somewhere more permanent, but six years had passed and he was still there.

"High school, Dad," I said, unrolling my sleeping bag on the pleather couch. "I'm about to turn fourteen."

"Are you sure?" he asked. "I got a letter from them..." He began to leaf through a pile of paper on his desk, the one containing W2 forms and notices from the DMV. "Here it is: *Congratulations on your child's admission to Dr. Martin Luther King Junior High School.*"

"That doesn't mean it's a junior high school," I said. "It means it's a high school named after Dr. Martin Luther King Jr."

"Well, I'm sure you're right," he said. "You must be getting pretty smart if you're passing that test and everything." He walked over to the corner where the fridge and stove were, where the floor was linoleum instead of carpet. The first time I saw my dad's apartment, when I was eight, I learned that the word *kitchen* is functional rather than ontological, although I wouldn't have put it like that at the time. He rifled through the TV dinners in the freezer and took out one for me: meatloaf and mashed potatoes, the variety I'd named as my favorite six years earlier. By now I was a little sick of meatloaf and mashed potatoes, but I never said anything about it, just like I never said I hated being at my dad's house. Saying it would have raised questions I didn't want raised, like *How incompetent was my dad anyway?* and *Did my mother maybe appreciate the chance to spend every other weekend without me?* So I ate the meatloaf, although I had eaten it so many times that I had begun to identify the constituent parts of its flavor and texture—the meaty roundness, the sugar, the fatty gloss that held the slice together—and to imagine them as individual powders and solutions in jars on a shelf in the Stouffer's lab.

In the first year after the divorce, Dad had occasionally and with much fanfare planned outings to minor-league baseball games or the science museum. It was an Abilene paradox: each of us would have preferred to stay inside, but we went on these awkward excursions in deference to what we thought were one another's wishes. Eventually he got me a Nintendo, and now we rarely left the apartment.

After dinner I was in the middle of a particularly deep game of Arkanoid when I became aware of him lurking in the doorway. He obviously wanted to say something, which made it impossible to concentrate. When the ball split into three I made the beginner's mistake of trying to follow them all, instead of picking the two that were furthest out of phase and abandoning the third, and lost my last life.

He was leaning against the doorframe with a shy, hopeful expression, like he wanted to ask someone to dance. In the past few years he had become pear-shaped; all the substance had drained out of his head and shoulders and settled in his hips.

"Wanna see something?" he said.

Spread out on the table in the living-room area were a bunch of typewritten pages, pencil sketches, legal documents. "I'm starting a business," he said. There was a quality in his voice I'd never heard before — pride, maybe.

He wanted to walk me through it, so I let him. He'd been looking at some beverage-industry case studies for a class he was teaching when he had this eureka-type vision: in a moment of hallucinogenic omniscience, he saw the entire structure of the industry laid out in front of him, like a beehive in cross section, and he could perceive wormholes and inefficiencies that were invisible to normal men. Everyone knew the big soda companies were just selling sugar water, that Coke's vaunted "secret formula" was a load of marketing hooey — over the past five years they'd gradually replaced the cane sugar with high-fructose corn syrup (cheaper, thanks to sugar tariffs and corn subsidies), and not one of fifty million Coke loyalists had noticed the difference. The conventional wisdom held that it was all about advertising: *branding,* they were calling it now, linking your product with youth and fun and sexual fulfillment and tagging the competitor, by implication, with death. But ignore this newfangled persuasory superstructure; focus on the nuts and bolts. What does the beverage industry *do?* What is its business? *It trucks sugar water around the country.* Production costs are marginal; the main ingredient is good old $H_2O$, cheaply available on demand anywhere — and yet bottlers spend billions driving it to stores. Listen: Put a machine in the supermarket that adds syrup and carbon to tap water. Make the soda at the point of sale, like restaurants do. You're selling the exact same product, and your prime costs are lower than the big boys' by more than 30 percent!

He gazed wistfully into the middle distance, and it was clear that this was what he'd been looking for his entire life: the main chance, the shortcut no one else had seen.

"So you're going to start a soda company?" I asked him.

"We're going to launch it locally first," he said. "Use Denver as a trial market. Once it catches on here, we can attract some investors, maybe go public. And then we take it national."

I imagined America putting down its Coke and drinking instead from a can with my dad's face on it. *Barry-Cola*, it said on the can. I laughed.

Dad looked hurt. "This is going to be paying your college tuition," he said, and I felt bad.

"I don't think I get it," I said, although this was not true. "How do you lower the costs?" And so he told me again.

When she picked me up on Sunday night, my mom was in one of her wanting-to-talk-about-Dad moods. "So what did you guys do?" she asked me. I never told her the truth: that I had played Arkanoid and Super Mario Brothers and Castlevania III and maybe Excitebike, although Excitebike was kind of juvenile, while my dad watched golf on TV, each of us with the shades drawn to keep the glare of the afternoon sun off our respective screens. There was something about the way men behaved without women around that I already knew to be ashamed of.

"The usual," I said.

She pulled onto the freeway. My mom gets anxious when she has to merge into traffic; her impulse is to slow down, which is not a helpful impulse in a merging situation. When she was securely in the middle lane, she looked at me out of the corner of her eye. "So," she said, "are there any girlfriends around?" She was trying to sound casual. At first I thought she was talking about me, partly because the pursuit of a girlfriend was a problem I thought of as specific to me, and partly because the idea of my dad with a girlfriend was almost inconceivable.

"I don't think he has time for a girlfriend," I said.

"Oh yeah?" she said. "What's keeping him so busy?"

I didn't want to tell her about the soda thing. I didn't feel like hearing my mom laugh at my dad when I was the one who had to go spend every other weekend with him. "I think he mostly works on articles," I said. Dad had once had an article in a journal of management theory.

That seemed to work. We were going home, and I started to feel better. I would still have to do my homework, which I always brought to my dad's in a backpack and then neglected until I got home Sunday night. But at least I'd be in my own room, with my mom lying in bed on the other side of the wall reading one of her thick paperbacks, listening to a tape of the music she liked, the Carpenters or America or Bread.

In an attempt to provide a family atmosphere, my mom had arranged for us to go out to dinner with the Oberfells once a month. At the restaurant I always chose the seat farthest from Bronwen, to disguise my interest. This typically put me next to her brother Pete, a pale, fearful nine-year-old.

Bronwen's father Gary was talking about the challenges his dental practice faced. "There's just too many dentists in the area," he said. "I don't know how we're all supposed to make a living." Gary had massive hands, and watching him bring his cheeseburger to his mouth was disturbing.

"Well, *we're* not going to any of these other dentists, that's for sure," my mom said. "Two sets of teeth you can count on."

"Most of them are Chinese," Gary said. "Or, you know, Oriental somehow."

"Did you see about the babies in Kuwait?" my mom said, following an associative trail that I chose not to pursue. "Where they took them out of the incubators and left them to die on the floor? I think that's so terrible."

We ate in silence for a moment: one table at a Denver-area Denny's paying its own small tribute to the memory of the dead Kuwaiti babies.

Eventually Stacey decided to move things along. "So what's your favorite class in school, Eric?" she asked me.

"Math," I said.

"Eric spends a lot of time playing with his computer," Mom said.

"Wow!" said Stacey. "A computer?" She gestured to her offspring. "These guys don't even know the first thing about computers," she said. "Apparently we're all going to have to know about them soon, though, right?"

I was familiar with the computers-are-the-unstoppable-wave-of-the-future rhetoric she was referring to, and I hoped it was true, but I suspected it wasn't, because besides me and Nicky and Nicky's dad, nobody seemed to *like* computers very much.

"Computers never fixed anybody's teeth, that's for sure," Gary said.

"Tell them what you're making," said Mom.

This was difficult. If I were to reveal even a bare outline of the game now, when it was only half completed, my plan to seduce Bronwen would lose the element of surprise. But after all those hours imagining her reaction, polishing the gemstone of my fantasy, the possibility of arousing her interest was irresistible.

"We're making an adventure game," I said, my voice rising nervously. "Me and my friend Nicky. It's called Tomb of Morbius." I risked a glance at Bronwen, who was pouring ketchup on her hash browns.

"Wow!" Stacey said again. "A computer game! Doesn't that sound cool, Pete?"

"I guess," Pete said. Bronwen put the ketchup down and addressed herself to the eggs.

"Pete really likes computer games," Stacey said. "Pac-Man he likes, and that other one . . . what's that one you like called, hon?"

"Street Fighter," said Pete.

"Street Fighter," Stacey said. "We went to the bowling alley for his birthday and he didn't even want to bowl, he just wanted to play Street Fighter the whole time."

"I got the sixth-highest score," Pete said.

This was all going wrong. "Our game's not like an arcade game," I said, trying not to sound indignant. "It's an adventure game. It tells you where you are and what you can see, and you type in what you want your character to do."

"Oh, it sounds great!" said Stacey. She was a nice person, but she was maybe more appropriate for younger children. "I'm sure he'd love it! Wouldn't you like to see Eric's computer game?" she asked Pete.

"I guess," he said.

"Great!" said Stacey. "Maybe he could come over this Saturday and see it! What do you guys think?"

Pete and I both looked down at our plates. No food cools more quickly than French fries, or suffers more from the cooling. Bronwen asked the waiter to refill her Coke.

Afterward we went out to the Oberfells' station wagon, Pete climbing into what we all called, by long-standing custom, the very-back. I was in the middle of the back seat, with my mom on one side and Bronwen on the other; when we turned right I was rocked toward her, and when we turned left she was rocked toward me, and I could feel her arm touching mine through our jackets. I kept returning to my Bronwen-plays-Tomb-of-Morbius fantasy, but now

I had to route around her little brother. What if Pete returned home raving about the game? *It was so fun! There were all these awesome dragons and monsters…* Unlikely: Pete's usual demeanor was near-catatonic, and even if the game roused him to uncharacteristic heights of enthusiasm it was hard to imagine this having much effect on Bronwen. And what would Nicky say when he learned I'd agreed to show our secret project to a nine-year-old?

What he said was, "You *told* them about it? What the fuck did you do that for?"

"I didn't want to," I said. I was sitting on the desk, my feet dangling. "My mom brought it up."

"How did she know about it?" he said, and I felt found out. I had given her daily reports on our progress.

"Look, I didn't mean for it to go like this," I said, trying to sound more reasonable than I felt. "But so on Saturday Pete is coming over to see it."

Nicky's eyes, small to begin with, narrowed to slits. "What, we're just going to show it to some—some kid?" he said. "Before it's done and everything?"

"It could be like beta testing," I said. "Give us a sense of how it's working." After eighteen months building a byzantine structure that had been seen by no one but me and Nicky, I was hungry for an audience, even an audience consisting of Pete Oberfell.

The computer room was located near some nexus of the school's plumbing system, and conversations there were accompanied by muffled gurgles and flushes. Eventually Nicky sighed histrionically. "All right," he said.

"So, uh, we're going to need to merge the code again," I said. Combining my sections of the program with Nicky's was a tedious process.

"I'll bring my stuff in tomorrow," he said. "You're merging them on your own."

Friday night I stayed up late, drinking Cokes from the fridge and integrating the two sections. When I finished it was almost three. I lay in bed, buzzed on caffeine and crashing from sugar, excited in spite of myself that I was about to see someone actually playing Tomb of Morbius. I slipped into a well-worn mental rut: when Stacey brought Pete over, Bronwen would be with them. *I figured I might as well come along,* she would say, a glint of curiosity in her eye. My hand slipped into my pajamas with a new urgency. Bronwen was playing Tomb, looking at me, kissing me, and now we were naked, on my bed, and the feeling in my body was like moving deeper and deeper underground, one level after another, further than I had ever been. I kept going, and Bronwen was on top of me, kissing me, and I kept going deeper until suddenly I was filled with light and I felt something bigger and better than anything else I have felt before or since, and it seemed like it was going to last forever. And then there was semen to clean up, and I felt strange and proud and exhausted.

I was woken by my mom turning off the TV in the living room. Stacey and Pete were at the door a moment later. We ate hot dogs and potato chips for lunch, and then my mom wanted to sit in the living room with Stacey and smoke and drink white wine, so she said, "Do you guys want to go and play on the computer?"

I led Pete into my room, briefly afraid we'd find a little puddle of semen on the bed in the shape of his sister's initials. "The game isn't done yet," I said. "And you're probably going to think it's pretty lame — it doesn't have graphics or a joystick or anything."

"OK," he said, too young to know how you're supposed to respond when people criticize their work in front of you.

I loaded the file and we waited while the floppy drive whirred. Pete, sitting at the keyboard, kicked his legs rhythmically. And then the screen went blank apart from the introductory lines that Nicky and I had written more than a year earlier:

Many centuries ago, there lived a fearsome warrior-king known as His Almighty Magnificence Lord Morbius the Vengeant. After pillaging and laying waste to four continents, Morbius was finally defeated—but before his demise, he buried his legendary treasure in a fathomless dungeon. Generations of warriors have entered the dungeon, searching for the treasures of Morbius...but none have returned.

Now you stand at the gateway to the dungeon. Will you enter?

Pete looked dumbly at all this text. It was clear that he wasn't reading any of it.

"So, uh—do you want to go into the dungeon?" I asked him. His eyes widened in fear. "In the game, I mean," I said. "Just type *YES*."

He still looked suspicious, but he pecked out *Y-E-S* with his index finger. I reached over and hit the Enter key.

As you step inside the dank tunnel, you hear a crash. A portcullis has slammed shut behind you.

Pete began reading the words out loud, slowly, one by one. "What's a p—a port—?"

"A portcullis. It's like a metal gate, Pete," I said. "So you're in a dungeon, and you're looking for the treasure. Do you want to keep going into the dungeon?"

"OK...," he said.

"Type *GO ON*," I said.

He pecked out the letters and hit Enter, and new text appeared. *"You are a faggot,"* he read with surprising fluency. *"You like sucking cock."* I looked at the screen, and there it was, right underneath Pete's *GO ON: You are a faggot! You like sucking cock!*

"Wait, that's wrong," I said.

Pete was looking at me with frank hatred. "I am not a faggot!" he said. "You're a faggot! And this is a stupid game!" He jumped out of his chair and ran crying from the room.

When I emerged, Pete had his arms around Stacey's waist and his head pressed against her stomach as she stroked his hair. "I really don't know how that could happen," my mom was saying. "I think the computer must be broken."

"We're going to be leaving," Stacey said. "Margo, I'll call you later. And as for you" — she looked coldly at me — "I thought you were more mature than that." She slammed the front door behind her, although it was too lightweight to slam very well.

Instead of going to the computer room on Monday I stood in the yard and watched kids kicking a ball around. There were sweatshirts on the ground to mark the goalposts, and for a while I stood near them on the chance that someone would kick the ball to me and I could tap it in, but there was always a cluster of people surrounding the ball, moving around the pitch like a cloud, and Thomas Lagos, who was playing goalie, told me to get out of the way. Nicky found me on the sideline.

"So did it work?" he asked.

"Yeah, it worked," I said. "Nice job. Now fuck off." The obscenity sounded small and desperate.

"OK, OK," he said. "It was just a joke."

"Really funny, Nicky," I said. "Everyone thinks I'm a child abuser."

"So they found out the truth, did they?" he said. When I didn't laugh, he said, "Well, you shouldn't have gone around talking about the game. So now we're even."

"We will be even when I've torched your house," I said. I turned around and walked toward the school building, telling myself not to look back. I looked back anyway. Nicky smiled at me.

What I really wanted to do was write some code. It was the first time I turned to coding for solace; it might have been the first time I ever needed solace that my mom couldn't provide. In the decade since I walked away from Nicky Boont, who was a dick but who was also my only friend, I still haven't found anything that keeps anxiety at bay as reliably as coding: the possibilities and ramifications branch outward to colonize all of your available brainspace, and the syntax of the language gives direction to your twitches and impulses and keeps them from firing off into panic.

In the computer room Marc Uriel was playing chess, the only computer game allowed during school hours, and Jeremy was hacking out something thorny-looking, so that was both machines taken. I took some scrap paper from the tray and found a pencil on one of the desks—I like coding on paper, you really have to concentrate—but I didn't know where to start. I could have kept working on Tomb of Morbius by myself, but I couldn't see any point. I looked over at Jeremy Glissan, the programming wizard, with his downy upper lip and his Eastern Bloc wardrobe and his nonexistent social life. I saw for the first time how much had gone on outside this room while Nicky and I were struggling with a persistent bug in our initialization subroutine, how Bronwen Oberfell was at that moment standing in a hallway in the high school three blocks away, leaning against a row of lockers, playing with a ringlet, talking to a sophomore boy about some topic unrelated to the recursive descent of the parse tree or evil warlocks with secret vulnerabilities to weapons made of bronze. Something to do with music or clothes, maybe? Or who was having a party, who was going out with whom? Other people found computers arcane, when to me they were transparent. For the first time I recognized that I was in an analogous position: some people found social life as obvious as I found computers, and those people weren't stuck here in a windowless room with no friends. And that's when I set out to hack the girlfriend problem.

# 3

Otherwise you'll find that your hacking energy is sapped by distractions like sex, money, and social approval.

—Eric S. Raymond, "How to Become a Hacker"

THE GROTSCH BUILDING LOOMS over the Mission like a relic of a previous civilization: once a pickle factory, now a square stone memento of a time when San Francisco hosted economic activity beyond symbol manipulation and beverage service. The city's current inhabitants, with their gift for cheerful irony, rent it out for photo shoots and weddings. This month the Grotsch has been hired by a gang of planners and architects and urbanism geeks, grad-school friends of Justin's, to host an exhibition called BayTopia. Cynthia has persuaded me to accompany her to the opening. The volume of space above us makes the conversations sound farther away than they are, and the air has the seedy smell of wet coats. We will find Maya here, supposedly.

In the middle of the floor is a scale model of the peninsula, with crude cardboard buildings on carefully modeled topography. Fantastic elements are painted bright colors: elevated bike paths that stretch around the neighborhoods, public parks and pools on the roofs of high-rises. On the walls are maps displaying census data in colorful and supposedly revelatory ways, but the daylight from the high windows doesn't quite illuminate them properly. Justin is talking to a pale man who seems to be explaining something very intensely. Many of the men here have a Nordic aspect, and the women are disproportionately short. And there's Maya, off to the side, talking to a tall girl in a puffy jacket. Although my instinct is to hide from her, I make myself catch her eye and stage a moment of recognition, raising my chin in the universal sign for *What's up?* At first she's not sure who I am. Then she smiles back, casually but still enough to make me worry I'm going to explode.

"Don't turn around," I say to Cynthia. "Now: I need you to talk to me for the next five or ten minutes."

"I really want to see her," Cynthia says. "I've forgotten what she looks like."

"In a minute. Just chat with me in a friendly but not flirty way."

"I feel like a spy," she says. "OK, chatting, chatting. Spy in the house of love. What's that from? Hey, I should go say hi to Justin."

"That presents me with a problem," I say. "If we go say hi to him together then we've become a couple, doing things in unison. But if you go say hi and I don't, then I'm standing awkwardly on my own."

"I'm really seeing you in action," she says.

"OK, OK, let's go talk to Justin." I glance over at Maya, which is an error, but she doesn't notice.

Cynthia pulls Justin away from his companion and hugs him. I hover while they catch up, trying to look like I'm part of the conversation. Eventually he turns to me. "How's it going, Eric?" he says.

"Not much," I say. I always get the easy ones wrong.

"Cool, man, cool," he says. "There's some wine and stuff over there."

And so I set out toward the buffet table, a journey that takes me directly into Maya's line of vision. The floor is shiny cement, very hard, not comfortable to walk or stand on for long. Overriding my inclinations I look straight at Maya and smile in the hope of projecting the exact opposite of what I'm feeling. People say *It's all about self-confidence,* but they don't say why, and so for a long time I rejected this truism. Why should self-confidence, of all qualities, be the key to attractiveness? The answer is that sexual selection is distorted by information asymmetry. The first time she sees you, she doesn't know if you're a potent, generous alpha male or a guy who spends all day getting into edit wars on Wikipedia. But you know, and the self-valuation you display is her best clue. But knowing that confidence is valuable doesn't help you acquire it—it just pushes your confidence toward the closest extreme. Confident people know they have an advantage and become more confident; insecure people know they have a handicap and become less confident. It's a virtuous or vicious cycle, depending on which side of the zero intercept you start from. I've arrived at her conversation, and she turns to look at me with that amazing unsurprisable expression, and again I'm sure she knows everything there is to know about me.

"What's up?" she says. "Eric, right?" The fact that she remembers my name must be a good sign, unless she remembers it from talking to Lauren on the phone the day after I met her. *I love you, Mom.* Jesus.

"Yeah, Eric," I say. "And you're Maya." It comes out as a statement of fact.

"How's it going?" she says. "This is the lovely Rebecca Grady." The lovely Rebecca Grady smiles sardonically at Maya and makes a curtseying gesture. She is in fact not unlovely; she looks a lot like the actress Helen Hunt, who is of only average loveliness for a TV actress but certainly 98th-percentile by civilian standards. It's a shame for Rebecca Grady that Helen Hunt became recognizable, because now instead of her beauty what you see is her resemblance to Helen Hunt. We stand there for a minute in this awkward triad. I don't have any Maya-specific conversational hooks, so I ask how her weekend is going.

"I've been chained to my desk," she says. "This is the first time I've left the office since Wednesday."

OK, we're going to start with a work conversation. "What do

you do?" I say, shifting my feet slightly so I'm facing Maya four-square instead of splitting my focus between the two of them. It's a little rude to Rebecca Grady, but it has the advantage of diminishing the chances that I'll end up going home with her and making ill-advised confessions.

"I'm a reporter," Maya says. She names one of the local alternative weekly newspapers: left-wing politics in the front, phone sex ads in the back, record reviews in the middle. A month ago, feeling rich and lonely, I called one of the phone sex numbers and made it as far as entering my credit card number, although as soon as the person answered I got embarrassed and hung up.

"So what's the story that's kept you chained to your desk?" I ask.

"Big dull investigation," she says. "Frisco Tow, the company that tows your car when you park in a bus stop. Graft, corruption, the usual."

"You're a muckraker. You rake the muck."

"I do. I've been raking muck for three weeks straight. It gets kind of messy. How about you? You do some kind of Internet thing, right?"

Christ, how does she know? "Yeah, I make software," I say, because I've tried all the synonyms and that one is the least bad. "So how did you get started with the raking of the muck? Were you a freelancer?" The fact that she has made no move to include Rebecca Grady in the back-and-forth qualifies as a good sign.

"No, I got hired right out of college as an assistant administrative assistant," she says. "There's a lot of turnover. Did you study, like, computer science?"

"No, I, uh, I didn't go to college," I say. "I learned on my own, basically." This information can be presented as a badge of shame or a badge of pride, depending on nuances of tone, expression, and gesture. Shame is never attractive, and pride raises the possibility that I don't know anything about anything except computers, so I aim for neutrality, although this risks sounding defensive.

"Did you not want to go, or you couldn't afford it, or what?" she says. I have told maybe one hundred people that I didn't go to college, and they were all wondering the same thing, but she's the first to come out and ask.

"I really wanted to go," I say. "It's a—well, it's a medium-length story."

Maya gives me a go-ahead nod, and Rebecca Grady, demonstrating that there is more to life than failure and humiliation, slips over to the buffet table to refill her wine and dip a baby carrot in hummus. I almost thank her.

"I was set to go to college," I say. "I'd been accepted by Stanford. And then my dad lost all his money and there was no way my mom could pay the tuition. So I got a job doing computer stuff, and I was going to apply to the University of Colorado, and then my friend Bill asked me to come out here and do a startup with him."

"Damn," she says. "That's great." I'm not sure what part of it is great; I suspect she means that it's more interesting than she had anticipated.

"So what about you?" I say. "Where did you go to college?"

"No, we're not switching back to me yet," she says, and I feel like I've caught an eighty-yard pass on national television. "What does your startup do?"

"We built a web service to track and synthesize people's buying habits," I say, "and then we sold it to a bigger company so they could run it into the ground."

"And what was your role?"

"I designed the interface," I say. "I built some of the back end, too. Are we switching back to you yet?"

"Not yet. How did your father lose his money?"

"He started a stupid business and put everything he had into it and burned through it in about two years."

"Were you worried about the same thing happening to you?"

41

*Terrified.* "I tried to learn from his mistakes. We did everything as cheaply as possible. No company cafeteria and no pinball machines and no advertising budget. And we spent other people's money."

"Smart!"

"Thank you. We are now officially done with me and moving on to you. Do you like being a reporter?"

"Yeah, basically. I mean, day to day I hate it, it's one heartbreak after another, but it's the right thing for me to be doing. I like asking questions."

"I'd never have guessed." *Look! I am teasing her affectionately!*

"I like getting to the bottom of stuff. It's just my nature."

Probably time to pull out before I mess up somehow; I'm almost in a position to ask for her email address, even without a pretext. And then I feel a dark shadow across my soul, and before I have consciously registered any specific sensory evidence I am aware that someone is approaching from behind me and that this person's presence is a very, very bad thing. And then I'm turning fifteen degrees to the right, and my smile freezes into a terrified rictus, and there is Lauren.

She's still dressed as if for work, even though it's Sunday. We all say polite things to one another, and Lauren and I ask each other how it's going as though we had an interest in each other's lives, but there's no sign she's any happier to see me than vice versa. I wish Cynthia and I had a special signal transmitter where I'd push a button and she'd hurry over and say *We really need to get out of here if we're going to get to that other thing on time.* The task now is to find out how much information has passed from the girl on the right, with whom I have disgraced myself, to the girl on the left, with whom I am in love.

"So how do you guys know each other?" I say as casually as I can manage, i.e., not very.

"We went to college together," Lauren says.

"Lauren was my WPC," says Maya, smiling. "That's *women's peer counselor.*"

"See, this is the stuff I missed out on," I say to Maya, picking up a thread from earlier and thus exiling Lauren to the conversational margins. "I never had a WPC."

"What, because you're a man?" Lauren asks.

"Uh, no, because I didn't go to college," I say. "I have a whole list of things people talk about that I don't get. *The dining hall* is one. Also something called *discussion sections,* for which no one has ever done the reading."

"It seems like you have a pretty good sense of it," Maya says. "You didn't miss much."

"Really? You wouldn't say *My college years were the best years of my life,* or *God I miss having all that time just to read and hang out and do theater*? Because lots of people say stuff like that."

"I would basically say that," says Lauren. "If I didn't think it might sound insensitive."

"Mine wasn't really like that," Maya says, and Lauren's face shows a sudden flush of sympathy. I get the impression I'm not supposed to ask, so I don't.

"I think we've got to get out of here," I say, gesturing at Cynthia on the other side of the hall. A thin woman in suit trousers is giving her a tour of the exhibits. "But, hey, great to see you again." I throw this out to the pair of them, let them take what they want from it, and head over to grab Cynthia like a life raft.

When I get home, the two kids from the high school are sheltering in the doorway of my building. They wear the kind of sports gear that is never worn for athletic activity and sit on the stoop, him reclining against her chest. In the way of teenagers, they are strange-looking. She has olive skin and a widow's peak, and the blue rubber bands in her braces make her mouth look like a marionette's. His cheeks are carpeted with gemlike pustules. They spend their afternoons sitting in the doorway in the rapture of adolescent love.

Inside, it takes less than a minute to find her paper's website, and from there to discover that her last name is Marcom: glamorously alliterative, like Greta Garbo or Lois Lane. Her stories fall into the investigative genre she described and speak in the reflexively cynical voice of the alternative press. My whole life I've ignored city politics, the province of idealists and racketeers, and as I survey Maya Marcom's work my inattention seems juvenile, unserious, a failure of citizenship. I consider reading her entire oeuvre and constructing a list of questions for use during future conversations, but that would be too much. Instead I scan the archive for something intimate, an unjustified opinion or a sentence in the first person, but whether from heavy editing or an instinct for privacy her prose is an impersonal fortress of elegantly presented research. At the bottom of each article is a link to her email address at the paper, which I protectively store in my mail client's address book.

I leave it there until Tuesday evening, when I should be preparing for dinner with my father. I'm wearing my most obviously expensive shirt, made of silk so slick and luminous it looks like a cliché. Since I last saw my father I have purchased an adult wardrobe, and I want him to know this, but some archaic guilt or fear has me frozen in front of the mirror reconsidering the shirt. To escape this loop I turn to my laptop, which is sitting on my bed, its weight causing a sinkhole in the duvet. This is the time to write her. Emailing the day after our conversation would have been too eager, obviously, but waiting three days would suggest too sustained an interest.

*We'd just finished with me, but we were interrupted before we got to you.* Refers to a shared joke; alludes gently to the Lauren embarrassment; invites a response. *Please now tell me three things I don't know and wouldn't guess about you.* Gimmicky, sure, but that's the point: the obviousness of the gambit, the absence of any pseudoplatonic justification for contacting her—these convey boldness, decisiveness, as though I'm in possession of a natural confidence that obviates the need for ruses and stratagems. If she's not interested, she won't respond, which would be disappointing but not humiliating, and disappointment is within my risk-tolerance profile. I have no idea how anyone managed to have sex before email. I hit Command+Shift+D and cast this latest plea for affection out into the world, and then I finish buttoning my expensive shirt and call a cab to take me to meet my father.

He's chosen an absurd fusion restaurant that I suspect he learned about from a magazine. I find him sitting at the bar in a golf shirt, drinking the closest thing they have to a Budweiser, gazing around uncomfortably. When he sees me approaching he looks relieved, and his handshake is gentle and sincere.

"How are ya?" he says. "Good to see ya!" His hair is markedly grayer than it was, and so is his skin, and rather than allow his expansive belly to flop over his belt he's hiked his pants up to his navel.

"Yeah, you too," I say.

He looks toward the door and fails to catch the eye of the hostess. "I'll just let her know we're all here," he says, the *all* making me wonder if he's brought someone else. On my seventeenth birthday he took me to a steakhouse where, to my surprise, we were joined by a nervous middle-aged woman, an archivist at the college, who he was apparently dating.

But the hostess leads us through the crowded dining room to a small table for two, one of a long row against the restaurant's rear wall. All the other tables are occupied. Along the banquette sits a line of women facing their male counterparts. The walls are brushed metal, and the trebly din of reflected conversation is massive and complex.

The hostess pushes our table to one side to open a path to the banquette, but the diners are tightly packed and the guy next to us has to stand and move his chair to allow my dad to squeeze through. When he lowers himself onto the cushioned seat his hips practically touch the women on either side.

"So," he says when he's settled. "Mr. Dot-Com Startup! The boy genius himself!" I sit there and take it. "Maybe you should be teaching me, huh?"

"I don't know," I say.

"So what was it like?" he says. "Must have been pretty exciting, huh?"

Writing and fixing code for sixteen hours a day was, in fact, exciting, but the excitement was of a kind that's hard to see from the outside. "It was a lot of work," I say. "But we got to make our own hours and wear jeans and drink as much soda as we wanted."

This seems to satisfy his expectations. "So how come you didn't do an IPO?" he says.

"We looked at it," I say. "But we got a good offer, and it seemed like the product had more value to a bigger company than it had on its own."

He bats this assessment away with the back of his hand. "They're going to ruin the culture that made your startup so dynamic!" he says.

I don't think he even knows what our software does. "No, you're probably right," I say.

The waiter approaches our table, introduces himself as Roy, and crouches to tell us about the specials in a rich baritone on which he rightly prides himself. My dad has to lean in to hear him above the ridiculous noise. We order, and Roy goes away, and there's a little pause while Dad smiles nervously.

"Well, so I've got a proposition for you," he says, with the off-kilter enthusiasm of a salesman who has steeled himself to make the call.

"What's that, Dad?" I say, moving the bowmen and the cauldrons of oil into position on the battlements of my heart.

"I can't tell you about it just yet," he says. He reaches down for his briefcase, leaning into the woman on his right, a brunette with a weathered face. "We need to get you under NDA first." He looks around to see if anyone has heard him, then pulls out two pages, laser-printed and stapled, a generic nondisclosure agreement he got off the Internet. He reaches into his pocket and proffers a fat fountain pen. How is it that of all the men in the world my father is this one, grinning and waving his pen at me in a restaurant? I don't want to sign this piece of paper; I want to be excluded from my dad's confidence. I search it for an excuse to decline, maybe a clause giving him the rights to everything I've ever made in perpetuity. But it's just an NDA. I take his fountain pen, struggle to get the ink flowing, and scrawl my name across the bottom. When I hand it back I feel like I've just signed something more significant than a pledge of confidentiality.

"So what's the big secret, Dad?" I ask him.

"Well so I'm starting a dot-com company!" he says, smiling as if the happiness of this news is self-evident and universal. I become very aware of the proximity of the people at the neighboring tables.

"That's great," I say, trying my best. "What's it going to do?"

"We're going to sell stereo equipment over the web!" he says. "How about that? Stereo equipment! I know all about that stuff!" I just nod. "Because, see, no one owns that space yet," Dad says. "When you think of buying books online you think of Amazon. When you think of buying toys, you think of Toys.com. But when you think of stereo equipment, who do you think of? No one. Well, that's going to be us!"

"Cool," I say. "Congratulations, Dad. That's great."

"It *is* great," he says. "It's gonna be great. So that's why I'm here." He takes a dramatic pause, enjoying himself, and extends his hand, palm up. "I want you on board!"

I can't think of a word to say to this. Dad remains frozen, hand out, for several seconds, until I become aware of Roy standing behind me with our appetizers. "All right, here we are," he says as he lowers my dad's pan-fried noodles. Dad, his moment interrupted, looks blankly at his plate while Roy sets down my Thai beef salad.

"It sounds like a really interesting idea," I say, stalling. "So how far along are you?"

"We're just in the initial stages right now," he says, uncharacteristically ignoring his food. "Right now we're putting a team together, a really great team. Then we're going to go looking for financing, and then we start development. And I'm seeing you as a key player on the team." He leans in over his noodles and says, in an intimate voice, "How does chief technical officer sound?"

I concentrate on spearing a bite of beef, onions, and lettuce with my fork. "I'm not really looking for a job, Dad," I say.

"Well, I'm headhunting you!" he says happily. "Hey, I'm not just some twenty-five-year-old MBA. I teach those guys what they know, and I know it better than them. I'm building a real company here, a serious company." Finally he grabs a thick clump of noodles in his chopsticks and ferries them to his mouth. "But I need you to make the website, otherwise this won't get off the ground. Now, I could hire some consultant to do it, if you have any idea what these guys cost, but I want to keep the whole thing in the family, you see? I want—"

Something occurs to me. "Dad," I say, "do you even have a domain name?"

"A what?"

"A domain name," I say slowly. "A web address. Like, uh, *stereo dot com* or *audiophile gear dot net*."

"No, we're not at that stage yet," he says, still eating. "See, I wouldn't even know how to do that! This is why we need you on the team! I think *stereo dot com* would be good. It's easier to remember."

The woman next to Dad stifles a smile. When I glance at her she looks away.

"Dad," I say. "Who is *we?*"

"What do you mean?" he asks.

"It's always *We're going to start a company, we're going to make a million dollars selling this and that.*" I'm doing my best to control my voice. "So who's the *we?* Who's in this with you?"

Dad looks at me as though he's never seen me before and he's not happy about what he sees. "I was hoping you would be," he says.

There's a silence, and I realize that Roy will be back soon to clear the appetizers and bring my sea bass, and I can't bring myself to sit here for one more second.

"I gotta go, Dad," I say. "I'm sorry." There are other things I could say, things that include the words *alimony* and *tuition* and *asshole,* but by the time I've thought of them I'm already out on the street.

I am queasy the following day. My dad is fragile, held together with chicken wire and hopeless dreams, and I've just sliced through the whole structure with a Ginsu knife and left it flapping in the breeze. But he walked out on my mom and me, and now that I have become a man I can walk out on him. No reply from Maya. Just after five o'clock, when it's time to turn on the lights, I call my mom and present the events of the previous evening to her as a comedy. I skip the part about walking out, because gestures of confrontation are frightening to my mom.

"When normal men turn fifty they get hair transplants or sporty cars," she says. "Barry gets a dot-com company."

"I know, Mom," I say. "What can you do?"

"You can start by not marrying Barry Muller, is my advice."

"The women of America seem to be taking your advice." I cough. The anti-Dad conspiracy always starts to make me uncomfortable after a few minutes. "So how's it going, Mom? Are you feeling OK?"

"Yes, I'm fine," she says. "One day at a time." I take this to mean she's still off the painkillers. "Eric, I want to thank you for everything. And I'm really sorry for all the stuff I said." Mom has apologized for this "stuff" at least four times, and I have no idea what she's referring to. I'm glad she's clean, but I wish conversations with her didn't inevitably slide into step-nine work.

We wind down and sign off, and I turn out the lights again and stare at the blackening sky and the sparkling bridge. Looking at the city feels different now that my dad is here, as though something of mine has been repossessed. And then my computer pings and the name *Maya Marcom* appears at the top of the stack of messages, and in the preview pane the words:

1. I have a hunting license.
2. I prefer the desert to the mountains or the beach.
3. I'm not telling you this one.

Here's what's going to happen: I'm going to send her another email, using this information as the foundation for a delicate rapport, and then she's going to send me one, marginally increasing the level of intimacy, and then our exchange will culminate with me proposing some kind of date, ostensibly to discuss some of the issues raised in the correspondence but in fact not for that purpose at all. (The sender of the initial email makes the pitch on the third move.) The flirtatious email exchange is the moment at which physical appearance and confidence temporarily give ground to wit, good judgment, and the ability to punctuate. It's the next part that's hard.

I've suggested meeting in a bar on a weeknight. The after-work drink is low-pressure—it gives her a chance to pull out after an hour or two—but it's easy to convert: you can always say *Do you feel like getting some food?* as though food were a personal interest of yours that she might happen to share. My default first date is an uncrowded Valencia Street bar called Lazarus, one block from a medium-expensive neo-Cuban restaurant with the kind of desserts that have names evocative of Catholicism: *sinful chocolate torte, pure vanilla ice cream with virgin peach coulis.* It's the optimum implementation of the specs.

I arrive a couple minutes late, figuring she'll be a couple minutes later. The bar's your standard fake dive, decorated with big forties-style signs advertising discontinued brands of soda and cigarettes. There's only a dozen people here, in three or four platonic after-work groups. I recognize the bartender, Freya: I had a semi-flirty conversation with her once about how she's named for a Norse goddess. A name like Freya is a gift passed down through the decades from a girl's parents to any guy who wants to flirt with her, as long as he's reasonably up on world mythology.

"What's new with you?" she asks as she pulls my beer.

I scan my brain for some piece of news that might be interesting to a near-stranger. "I got a dog last week," I tell her, which works perfectly—prompts some obvious follow-up questions, portrays me as both masculine and nurturing—apart from the fact that it's not true.

"Neat," she says. "What kind of dog?" and we're off. The lying sharpens my wits, and I feel ready to deal with any situation, outsmart any adversary, until Maya walks in and smiles at me, at which point I'm gripped by the fear that I'm about to get thrown out of the bar for being underage.

I greet her without attempting any physical contact, because the available physical-contact greetings at this point are a handshake, an air-kiss, and an upper-body hug, and none of those is a good way to start a date. Instead I pull out a barstool for her, a display of chivalry that I pretend to pretend is ironic. Maya orders a gin and tonic, the same drink she asked me to fix her at the party the night we met.

Her subtle invocation of that night makes me feel like we have a history, and I smile in recognition before it occurs to me that it's probably what she always drinks. Freya, who is a professional, fades discreetly away after pouring, which is a relief, because it would be problematic if the dog thing came up.

"So are you coming straight from work?" I ask her.

"Yeah, I just got done," she says. For three long seconds it seems as though neither of us will think of anything else to say and we will finish our drinks in silence and then go home. "How about you? Do you have a regular schedule, or are you writing your own ticket now?"

"I make my own hours, pretty much," I say. I don't go into what those hours are filled with. Since the sale I have been learning how much dead time a day can hold. At some point I'm going to have to tell her about being rich, but I don't know when: too soon and I'm showing off, too late and I'm hiding something.

I want to ask her a question she hasn't been asked a million times before—otherwise she goes straight to her prepared answer and the two of you are just acting out a script. But obviously you can't ask her a job-interview question like *In a fight between a bear and a shark in a neutral, jellylike medium, who would win?* because then she'll think you're a dork.

"So what's the best story you've ever written?" I ask. It works: she stops and thinks about it, and there's a public answer and a private answer, which is always good. She tells me about the story she won awards for, the one she sends to magazine editors when she pitches them—a two-month investigation into the shady dealings surrounding a lucrative waterfront development contract, involving the ambitious son of a casual-footwear magnate, a mayoral aide, and the aide's partner, who was running for DA. (Even I was vaguely aware of this when it broke: there were headlines in the *Chronicle*, and people lost their jobs.) But then she tells me about the story that meant the most to her, the one that she remembers when she gets discouraged: a story about a Catholic church in Ingleside whose priest made some odious remarks about gay marriage, and the activists who picketed outside the church dressed as nuns.

"It was supposed to be a quickie," she says of the story. "Get a couple of quotes from each side, a photo of these wacky transvestite nuns. But I wound up spending three days talking to people in the congregation, watching them feed soup to homeless people, going to services, understanding what it meant to them to have, you know, guys in nun costumes outside their church every day. And once I'd done that, I had to spend time with the nuns too, and they were the coolest, funniest, most sincere people I'd ever met. Most of them had grown up Catholic and been terrorized by it. And I was so nervous while I was writing it, because all these people on both sides had really opened up to me, had taken me into their lives, and now I was trying to do right by all of them, except they hated each other."

"How did it turn out?"

"I totally obsessed over it," she says. "Right up to the last minute I was adding things and taking things out and counting the number of words quoting each side, trying to make it balanced. I got a little carried away. And then the day it came out, I got to the office and there were two messages. I'm always so worried the day a big story comes out, I dread checking the messages because it's usually someone threatening to sue. But that day there were two messages. One was from the priest and the other was from the head of the protesters, and they both said, basically, *Thank you*."

"That's awesome," I say, because it is in fact awesome, and because I have a huge crush on her and am glad to be able to tell her that I think she's awesome by pretending I'm talking about her story.

"So what about you?" she says. "Do you get obsessed over your work that way? Do you have a, like, a favorite program that you wrote or anything like that?"

The answer to both questions is yes, of course. But the joy of hacking doesn't translate. If she's like most people, computers are alien to her, mysterious electronic totems that require the ministrations of a shamanic caste of surly gnomes who live in the basement of her office building.

"I get pretty deep into it," I say. "And the work I did for the startup, the interface I designed, I'm proud of that. I mean, I think it's a good solution to a particular set of problems. But talking about it gets really boring to a non-programmer."

"You worry a lot about keeping people on your side, huh?" she says.

"What do you mean?"

"If you were to answer my question, what's the worst thing that could happen? I don't think I'd be bored, but what if, worst case scenario, what if I was bored for a minute? Would that be the end of the world?"

I have to think about this. "Well, I don't want to bore you. I mean…" This is hard, because the reason I don't want to bore her is that I want her to like me, and obviously I can't say that directly.

"I know, you don't want to bore me, because you want me to like you," she says. *Whoa.* "But you know, I'm going to make up my own mind about whether I like you, just like you're going to make up your mind about whether you like me. And anyway, liking you is different from liking a TV show. The reason I like people is not that they never bore me. So why don't you tell me about it, and if I don't understand I'll stop you and ask questions, which is what I do all day in my job, and if I get bored I'll try to hide it until we've moved on to something else. OK?"

She drains the end of her drink, sets down the glass, and turns to face me. I look at her, and she looks at me, and that thing happens when you look at each other and realize, *Hey, here we are.* I ride it out, and then I jump in.

I try to describe what it's like to get deep inside a really hard problem: loading all the pieces into my mind, seeing the relationships between abstract concepts as though they were the physical features of a landscape. I tell her about the marathon hacking runs I used to go on, first when I was a teenager and again in the desperate early days of Demo1, spending twenty hours at a stretch making a program more sprawling and complex and powerful but also more elegant, more beautiful. (It feels risky, using the word *beautiful,* but there's no other way to say it.) I try to convey the experience of settling into hack mode, the way the cruft and chatter of consciousness quiet down, stripping away the self's topsoil and allowing the deeper, truer self to emerge. *We are most ourselves when we subsume ourselves in something greater* is a paradox at the heart of every mystical practice, programming not excepted. This experience of logical-reasoning-as-metaphysical-transcendence has been observed in older vocations like chess and mathematics. A mathematician presented with a clever proof, or a grandmaster lighting on a devastating move, might replay the sequence in his head just to savor it, as though humming a passage from a Mozart concerto. I feel the same thing when I read or write a well-constructed chunk of code: this is logic so artful it's indistinguishable from art.

While I put this into words, Maya listens carefully and says "Uh-huh" and occasionally shuts her eyes and nods as if swallowing an idea, in what appears to be a kind of mental note-taking. If she's bored, she's good at disguising it.

"Thanks," she says. "Now I know something important about you."

"No problem," I say. I'm not used to being reassured like this.

"This is going pretty good, huh?" she says. At first I don't understand what she's referring to, and then I get it and I desperately want to kiss her.

"I think so, yeah," I say. "Ha! I've never tried evaluating a date while it's still in progress." By introducing the word *date* I'm trying to match her audacity.

"It's such an artificial thing," she says, resting an elbow on the bar and propping her chin in her palm. "We both know what we're doing, but we're not allowed to talk about it."

"No, you're totally right," I say. "I love it. Listen, if we're going to externalize: you have reminded me of an anecdote. Are you interested in hearing an anecdote at this juncture, or would you rather the conversation progressed in a different direction?"

"An anecdote would be terrific," she says. "Let me order another drink, and then you can tell me the anecdote. Is it funny?"

"Oh, I can't answer that," I say. "Starting an anecdote with *This is a really funny anecdote* would be a gross violation of sound anecdote technique." We are both grinning.

"You're right, you're right," she says, holding up her glass in Freya's direction. Freya gives me an interrogative look, and I respond with an affirmative nod.

"This anecdote falls into the world's-worst-date genre," I say as Freya sets down the new drinks and removes the old, using both hands to perform the operations in parallel on Maya's glass and mine. "It happened not to me but to my mom."

"Before your mom and dad were married?"

"After they got divorced," I say. "I remember when this happened."

"Got it," she says. "OK, go."

"So they'd been divorced for like two years," I say. "My mom was really wanting to start dating someone, and she wasn't meeting anyone through her job or anything, and this was when dating services operated by mail and catered chiefly to the desperate. So she'd asked her friends at work to fix her up, and one day her friend Doreen was all like *Oh my God, I have found the perfect guy for you!*

"My mom is pretty short, and she says that whenever anyone says *the perfect guy for you* they mean *short and divorced*. She meets the guy for dinner, and it's confirmed that these are the only qualities that make him suitable for my mom. And the short thing is only suitable from his perspective, because she doesn't even like short men; she likes tall men, just like everybody else." I can get away with this because of the precise averageness of my height. "She once said that short men get offended when she doesn't want to go out with them, like it's her responsibility to help them breed more short people so that the inability to reach things on high shelves will survive to the next generation.

"Anyway: the guy is apparently completely charmless. He drives her home from the date, and he invites himself in for coffee—as in, literally, he says, *May I come inside for a cup of coffee?* And it's this incredibly complicated moment for my mom, because on the one hand she knows just as well as any other television-watching adult what *coffee* is a euphemism for, but she really wants to be polite—she's a very polite person—and it wouldn't be polite to refuse a cup of coffee to someone who's just bought you dinner. It's like she's trapped in the semantic gap between the literal and the figurative meanings of the word *coffee*. And in the end, she just doesn't have the vocabulary to say no—it's not in her social-behavior repertoire. So they go inside the house, and my mom puts some coffee on and sits down very deliberately in the armchair rather than on the couch next to the guy, and they sit there and wait for the coffee to percolate. And just as she's getting up to pour the coffee, my dad's car pulls up outside, and he gets out in his undershirt."

"Whoa!" Maya says.

"See, after the divorce my mom continued doing my dad's laundry for a while."

"Get out."

"I swear to God."

"After they were *divorced?*"

"She's a soft touch," I say. "He moved into this place without a washer and dryer, and he would bring over his laundry when he dropped me off on Sunday nights. She only did it a couple times before she told him to do his own goddamn laundry." Years later I discovered that there were indeed a washer and dryer in the basement of my dad's building, but I don't get into this, because my father and his character flaws are not the point of the story. "So my mom is asking this guy how he takes his coffee when my dad walks in in his undershirt—you know, like a wifebeater? He's spilled a bunch of tomato sauce on his shirt, and he doesn't have anything else to wear to the class he's teaching tomorrow." I have fabricated this explanation—in fact I have no idea why my dad came over to pick up the laundry instead of waiting until Sunday when he'd be there anyway. Was he really wearing his undershirt? That's how I remember it, but it's possible that I've added that detail when telling the story on some previous occasion. It gives the scene more color, though. "He had called my mom, and she'd said he could let himself in and pick up the laundry, which my mom had folded for him and left in a plastic laundry basket. So my dad lets himself in, and this guy, my mom's date, sees my dad come in the door in his wifebeater and says, *What the hell is going on here?*

"My dad, I should point out, is not tough, but he's big, and he could probably fit this guy in his stomach. He's going over to the guy to introduce himself, and the guy looks at my mom and says, *I don't know what kind of sick arrangement you people have, but I want no part of it!* and walks straight out the door."

Maya laughs at the punch line, but she seems to recognize that the story is not, ultimately, a comedy. She asks a bunch of questions about my parents, which reduce to *Is he really that clueless?* and *Does she ever stand up for herself?* My answers hint at something I realize I want her to know: I'm self-invented; I had no one to learn from. This may be why I told the story in the first place.

When she's out of questions, she sets up an anecdote of her own. "OK, I've got one," she says. "Ready?"

"I am so ready," I say.

\*　　\*　　\*

The rest of the evening glides along as if on rails. At some point we finish the drinks and effortlessly escalate to dinner. ("So are we gonna get dinner?" I say. "Hell yes," she says, and we nod at each other to say *Nice job*.) In the restaurant, as the hostess leads us to the table, I set my hand lightly on the small of Maya's back to indicate that she should go first, and this gentle first attempt at physical contact comes off without a hitch. It's more crowded than the bar, but we're off in a corner and the walls are hung with heavy velvet curtains. We sit down and, perhaps in response to my boldness with the hand-on-the-back thing, Maya throws me a fastball.

"So did you hook up with Lauren?" she asks.

"I did," I say. "I hooked up with her." I can handle this.

"But you didn't want to pursue it?"

"I guess not. I don't think either of us really saw it as something to pursue. Is she...did you talk to her about it?"

"Not really," she says. "I mean, I didn't get the blow-by-blow." She does not grin saucily as she says this.

After the appetizers have been cleared I excuse myself, walk confidently to the bathroom, lock the door behind me, and allow my limbs to go slack, rolling my head alternately clockwise and counterclockwise as the dopamine of infatuation sloshes around with the alcohol in my brain. In the safety of the burgundy restroom, decorated with photographs of tailfinned American cars and decaying neocolonial palaces, I look back in wonder at the past two and a half hours. How did I learn to do this, and will I be able to sustain it when I get back to the table? At any moment the waiter will bring my plate of medium-rare steak strips with onions and potatoes. This infusion of protein and salt is exactly what my body wants; how thoughtful, how prescient of my past self to arrange it! While urinating I look in the mirror on the left wall and only half recognize myself: a smile is organizing my features into their most harmonious proportions, and my usually sallow cheeks are flushed with beer and happiness. I pull off a couple sheets of toilet paper and dab at my forehead to take the shine off, carefully keeping the stream aimed into the toilet bowl.

An hour later, we are figuring out what happens next. Part of me is convinced that there will never be a better time for us to have sex; another part desperately wants to get away before I can screw up. Of course, it's not my decision.

"So," we say to each other outside the restaurant. Then she says, "I should be getting home," and smiles beautifully. "Walk me to my car."

We pass the assortment of pedestrians — after-dinner yuppies, Latino adolescents, homeless alcoholics — who make up the Mission's thriving urban street culture. A bearded panhandler with crimson skin mumbles at us, and some suicidal ebullience tempts me to ostentatiously drop a twenty-dollar bill into his Styrofoam cup, but I don't, because tonight my superpowers are strong enough to defeat even my own personality.

Here's her car. It's a red Acura, old, kind of beat-up, totally unexceptional, except that it's hers and thus imbued with magic. I try to memorize it, as if it were a clue. "So this is it," she says, and I turn to her, heart pounding, and our eyes lock and the world pours itself through a funnel and everything but us is revealed to be an illusion. Neither of us flinches. We hang here long enough to etch the moment onto the surfaces of our brains, so that in every one of the infinite possible futures we will each be able to remember exactly what the other looked like in the moment right before we started kissing, when we had no inkling of the world of trouble to come.

# 4

Much to the surprise of the builders of the first digital computers, programs written for them usually did not work.

— Rodney Brooks, *Programming in Common LISP*

THE DESKS IN MY new homeroom were laid out in a five-by-five
grid, somewhere on which was located the socially optimal spot. My
mother, unsure how long the drive to MLK would take, had erred
on the side of caution, and all but three desks were still available.
The choices of the first three arrivals suggested starkly different
intentions: two girls in ornate sweaters sat front and center, while in
the last row a boy reclined his chair against the wall, his eyes shut.
The boy's haircut was horizontally bifurcated at the level of his ears,
shaggy above and close-cropped below. I considered joining him in
the back row, and perhaps mimicking his insouciant posture, but
that would have drawn too much attention, so I opted for a seat
in the classroom's exact center. Pleased with my choice I settled in,
savored the symmetry of rows and columns around me, admired the
perfect diagonals that stretched from my seat to each corner of
the room. At once my satisfaction spoiled: the midpoint was the *most*
noticeable, the *most* calculated. I snatched my bag and scrambled to a
seat one row back and one column to the left, although no one else
had come in yet. I was happy with this innocuous choice, but I feared
that the boy with the haircut had seen the switch and perceived my
decision-making process at work. In attempting to avoid the appearance of calculation, had I exposed my calculation? I turned back and

glanced at him, and our eyes met. By looking, I had given myself away.

We sat in silence for at least ten minutes before others began to arrive, many in groups of three or four who had carpooled or arranged to meet outside. I tried to believe that they were as anxious as I was, despite the casual way they picked seats, chatted, called out to one another. This kind of information is inherently distorted: we see others from the outside, all smooth surfaces and fixed appearances, and ourselves from the inside, with our subjectivities and histories and bodily fluids.

The room's population self-organized into groups of people who'd gone to middle school together. The only person I recognized from Wilson, April Melkonian, seemed to have no idea who I was. The year before, she had allegedly let Jason Kroll feel her tits for one minute in exchange for writing her nature diary for biology class. All I could see of the girl in front of me was a cascade of brown hair held back by a blue velour hairband. On my right, two Asian boys were telling an Asian girl about going to Wet City and how fun it was. Wet City was a local water park. The seat to my left was still empty.

And then in walked Bill Fleig, and before I knew his name I knew that he was going to sit down next to me and determine the direction of my life for the whole of high school and perhaps beyond, and then he did.

He was almost freakishly tall for a fourteen-year-old, with an overbite so intense his jaw seemed to stop halfway to his upper lip. He peered around the classroom, saw the open seat, then made his way over. He had to kind of fold himself at the waist to fit into the chair, and then he didn't seem to know what to do with his arms; he wound up draping them over the desk. Trying to avoid eye contact I looked down and futzed with my pencil case, which turned out to be my fatal mistake, because it allowed him to see my calculator.

"Is that a Texas Instruments TI-80?" he asked, and I had to acknowledge that it was.

"I had one of those," he said. "Then I got this for my birthday." He handed me his calculator right there in front of everyone. I took it as though it were a fish, looked it over quickly, and passed it back to him. "I'm Bill Fleig," he said, like an adult. "Do you have a computer?"

"Yeah," I said, hoping no one besides Bill Fleig would hear. The girl in front of me, the one with the hair, turned around, and I was afraid she was about to call me a loser. She turned out to have a big nose and cheeks that looked padded with cotton wool, but she was a girl.

To my relief she addressed Bill Fleig. "You shouldn't use a calculator," she said. "You'll start to depend on it, and then you'll never be able to do arithmetic without one."

Bill Fleig had heard this argument before. "I carry it with me, so I won't need to do arithmetic without one," he said. I was horrified but somehow unsurprised that this conversation was taking place near me, as if I were sending out invisible, contagious nerd rays.

"What if you're on a plane and it crashes on a desert island?" the girl asked.

"I'd have it with me on the plane, wouldn't I?" said Bill Fleig.

"You might forget to pack it," said the girl. "Or the battery might run out."

"I'd carry extra batteries with me if I was going on a plane," said Bill Fleig. He spoke in a breathless, hyperarticulated way, as if his lips and tongue were struggling to keep up with the words.

"It doesn't matter how many batteries you have," she said. "They're going to run out eventually, and then you won't be able to do math."

I couldn't stop myself. "Why would he need to do math if he's stuck on a desert island?" I said. It came out too loud, and the Asian guy to my right turned to see what was going on.

"I might need to calculate the angle for a lean-to," Bill Fleig said. "I might need to do long division to figure out how to divide up the food among the people who are on the island with me."

"He might need to calculate where to put up a sundial," said the girl.

"I wouldn't need a sundial," said Bill Fleig, extending his wrist to display a chunky digital watch.

"You shouldn't wear a digital watch," the girl said. "You'll forget how to tell time."

Mercifully, the teacher walked in. She was fat, and I hoped that meant she'd be jolly; it would be nice to have a jolly fat lady for a teacher. "All right, you guys," she said, louder than the situation warranted, since we had quieted down as soon as she walked in. She didn't sound jolly. She called roll, and I got that slight nervous feeling you get the first time they call roll and you don't know who's before you in the alphabet, and you're afraid you're going to miss your name or answer too emphatically or you won't be on the list at all. But she read my name, and I answered fine, and I experienced the tiny sensation of pride and belonging that you get after they call roll for the first time. As we headed out for the first-day assembly, I surveyed the kids in front of me and realized that none of them had ever seen me before. I felt a strange excitement building, the kind stowaways must feel as they watch the coastline recede: my identity was up for grabs.

We must have been the last homeroom to arrive in the auditorium. The student body was catching up after summer vacation, saying *Omigod* and *How's it going?* to the kids next to them, behind them, several rows away. As I looked down at the crowd I was staggered and overwhelmed by the endless varieties of girls: Girls who were going for cute and girls who were going for sexy and girls who were going for normal. Soccer players in shorts and sweatshirts and future English majors in long Laura Ashley skirts. Girls with big breasts who were trying to hide them and girls with big breasts who were trying to show them off. Christian girls in button-down sweaters and nerd girls in overalls and rocker girls in black T-shirts with elaborate heavy-metal iconography. Groups of pretty girls, groups of almost pretty girls, ugly girls in ones and twos. It was an impossibly rich and complex zoology. I froze momentarily, and the people flooding in behind me pushed me forward and I stumbled and nearly fell.

I began by gathering data. Accounting for overlaps, my seven classes plus homeroom contained forty-six distinct girls. I listened for their names during roll and wrote them in a notebook, along with a quick notation indicating something about their physical appearance to remind me who was who. Once I'd got the names I started pruning. I wasn't picky. To the least desirable girls I applied a litmus test: Would I prefer to be involved with her or to graduate high school without ever acquiring a girlfriend? That knocked out seven and left Rita Bambrick, whose head looked like one of the Easter Island statues, on the borderline.

And so I started tracking thirty-nine girls: their friends, interests, cliques, extracurriculars. After two weeks of fieldwork I had compiled a fairly thorough ethnography of the freshman class's female population. I identified the groups, the pairings, the loners, the girls with steady boyfriends and the girls who dated around and the girls who were concentrating on their schoolwork. I rated them on a few crucial axes: studiousness, athleticism, sociability, sexual maturity (at one end of the spectrum was Erica Watterson, who was famous for her promiscuity; at the other was Pamela Beal, who was obsessed with horses), and social status. I was certain that this data would be useful to me, and that when I had accumulated enough of it I would know what to do with it.

As I walked out of history during the second week, Tara

Pulowski fell in beside me. "How's it going, Eric?" she said, and I was thrilled to hear her call me by my name. My left hand instinctively reached behind me to verify that the zipper on my backpack was secure. Inside the backpack was the ring-bound notebook in which Tara's name was written next to the words "curly brown hair" and the glyphs for *pretty* and *rich*.

"So what do you think of this class?" she asked me. I cast about frantically for the correct answer, until she stepped in to help me. "It's OK, I guess, but there's way too much homework."

"Yeah," I said. We were walking through the hallway to the cafeteria, having a conversation.

"So where do you live, Eric?" she asked me.

"Sheridan," I said.

"Neat," she said, waving hello to Becky Busch without breaking stride. "So, I'm running for student council."

"Oh," I said.

"The election's in eight days," she said. "Yikes!" She held up her hands and wiggled her fingers in a little pantomime of anxiety.

"Wow," I said. There must have been a better response but I was unable to imagine what it might be or how anyone might be able to calculate it in the time allotted.

We had arrived at the cafeteria. It seemed that we were about to sit together, and it occurred to me that by the end of lunch I might have thought of something better to say than *Oh* or *Wow*. "So where do you want to sit?" I said. I had neglected to inhale for a few minutes, and my voice came out sounding strangulated and glottal. Tara's eyes scanned the room, then lit up as they landed on Michelle Kessel and Louise Treadwell, over by the big windows.

"So wish me luck in the election, Eric!" she said, then hurried off, smiling and greeting people. I waited in line for lasagna, found a seat alone, and took out my notebook. Next to Tara's name I drew a little asterisk to signify that I had talked to her.

I voted for her, of course. She came in a very respectable third, after Dean Hoestetler, who had locked up the endorsements of the after-school clubs by sending pizza to their meetings, and Heidi Weir, who was immense and wore headgear and was the subject of a sarcastic write-in campaign.

From there my notes on Tara expanded to take up most of a page. After her defeat at the ballot box she began an equally vigorous campaign to become Michelle Kessel's best friend. For almost two weeks she and Michelle and Louise were together constantly—in the cafeteria, in class, going into the girls' bathroom—but Tara's place in the group was never secure. She was more earnest than the others, and she lacked the talent for exclusivity: during her abortive political career she had made too many acquaintances.

And then one day in biology Tara's eyes were puffy and red, and she sat apart from Michelle and Louise and stared straight ahead. Mr. McCallum called on her, and when she gave the correct answer—"To increase surface area?"—Michelle and Louise broke into a laughing fit, pitched just below the threshold of acceptable classroom noise. At the end of class they left without her, whispering. Tara took her time assembling her belongings and walked out alone, her back stiff, like a finishing-school girl balancing a book on her head. I followed her out and caught up with her.

"Are you OK?" I asked her. She looked away, with an expression so vulnerable that, for the first time since Bronwen Oberfell had awakened me to the strangeness and terror of love, I was able to talk to a girl without feeling nervous.

"No, it's fine," she said. "It's totally fine." She hauled a smile into place as if by powerful hydraulics, but as the corners of her mouth reached the apices of the parabola the whole arrangement collapsed and she began to sob. I had never seen a girl cry, but I'd seen my mother cry many, many times, enough that Tara Pulowski's tears were a lodestar. In uncharted territory I could use them to navigate.

"It's all right," I said. "You can tell me about it." I felt a thrill of sincerity as I spoke, as though the feelings I'd had in the past were a child's toys and Tara's grief the first harbinger of adult life. We were standing by the bulletin board, in front of flyers announcing auditions for the musical and meetings of the Italian club. Students flowed past, parting around us, their voices and footsteps bouncing off the cinderblock walls.

"Why are people so mean?" she said, and I had to lean in to hear her. "It's like, how is it that you can feel so close to someone and then all of a sudden find out that you don't really know them at all?"

I had no idea what the answer was, but it seemed that what was called for was wisdom, and so I did my best with what I had. "Sometimes people are really mean," I said. "Some people don't care about anyone but themselves, and are just out to see what they can get."

She nodded at me, her eyes wide. She was waiting to hear what I would say next, and it seemed important that I somehow shift into a higher register. "But sometimes, when people act in a mean way, what it really means is that they're scared," I said. I don't know where that came from. Probably TV.

She took it in humbly, as though it were really valuable. "I want to talk to you more," she said, and inside me something leapt in the air and punched the sky. "But I have to go to math."

"I could meet you after school," I said. It did not occur to me that my mom would be waiting for me after school.

She said nothing for a minute—whether evaluating my offer or lost in her misery I couldn't tell. Eventually she said, "Meet me at the side entrance, by the trash cans." No one would see us down there, which suggested either that she wanted our encounter to be private and intimate or that she didn't want to be seen with me.

She was waiting when I arrived. We walked away from the school, down Randall Street, on a grass-lined sidewalk beside a wide, extravagantly cambered road. A commuter suburb at 3:45 on a weekday is a ghost town. We headed for the little playground two blocks down, its jungle gyms and swing sets hardly scuffed. Families here had their own play structures in their backyards.

"So what happened?" I said.

"It wasn't like this at my old school," she said. "At my old school, people were…there wasn't this *pressure,* you know? Here there's all this pressure to, to hang out with the right people and stuff. I used to"—she paused and looked down—"I used to be really into My Little Ponies, OK? I mean, I know, it's dumb, whatever." I smiled as if to say *It's OK, I know all about embarrassing childhood passions.* "But I had sixteen My Little Ponies and I loved them."

"Sixteen?" I asked, wondering what you could possibly do with sixteen My Little Ponies. Tara looked hurt, and I regretted it immediately.

"Yeah, I know, it's totally dumb," she said. "Whatever. Never mind." She was about to shut down.

"No, I just mean, I never had any My Little Ponies, because I'm a boy," I said. "So I don't know what you'd do with sixteen of them. Like, did they each have a different name and everything?"

"They each had a different *personality,*" she said. "And they liked to be fed at different times."

I had no idea what to say to this, so I kept quiet. We had arrived at the playground, and we made our way across the sand toward the swings, the kind whose seats consist of a strip of black rubber suspended between a pair of metal chains. We sat on adjacent swings and flexed our knees, propelling ourselves into tiny, ironic arcs.

"Anyway, I know it's totally stupid and everything, but I still have them in my room," she said. "And then there was this slumber party and…I can't talk about it."

She was about to disclose something that happened among girls, something that might be important. "No, tell me," I said.

"Michelle and Louise and Emily were all at my house," she said.

There were two Emilys in my notebook, neither of whom had been linked with Michelle, Louise, or Tara. "And I was so psyched that they were there, because it was the first time they'd been to my house, so I was really nervous but I was really psyched too. I made my mom promise to stay out of my room and everything. And we were talking about who we liked, and Michelle said she knew who I liked, and I was all, *Cut it out, you do not!* and she was like, *No, I do, I do,* and I was so worried because I thought she knew I liked Leo Garson." This information appeared with no special emphasis, like a man who brushes past you in a crowd and slides a knife into your stomach. "And then she was like, *And the person Tara likes is right here in the room with us right now!* And I knew it was a total lie, but I started getting really creeped out—like, what if Leo is in the closet, you know, what if they sneaked him in to embarrass me? And then Louise was like, *He's in the closet, and I'm going to go get him!* And I was really freaking out—I mean, I was trying to be all, *No way, whatever,* but really I was freaking out. And then she went into the closet and she came out and she was holding Sparkler, who was like my favorite My Little Pony. And she was all like, *This is who Tara likes, and she—she does it with him every night!* Even though Sparkler is a girl; all My Little Ponies are girls. And I was like, *Don't be stupid, how could you do it with a My Little Pony?* And they were like, *You totally do, here's how,* and they started saying just this really gross stuff? I mean, I can't even say it, is how gross it was. It really made me ill; it makes me ill just, like, talking about it."

She was facing the opposite direction from me now, with the chains of her swing twisted around one another. A couple of stray curls had fallen over her face, and through them she surveyed the monkey bars and the seesaw as though from a great and tragic distance.

"And so now whenever they see me, they just start laughing," she said. "In social studies they passed me a note with a picture on it—it was horrible."

I was slightly shocked at the mature themes that had entered our conversation. I didn't know how a girl might "do it" with a plastic toy, although if pushed I would have guessed that it had something to do with inserting it in her vagina. And I was still reeling from the revelation about Leo Garson, who was in my homeroom and was known for doing a retarded character he called Special Ross. I hadn't expected Tara to tell me she loved me, but I'd hoped I was at least sufficiently on the map that she wouldn't casually tell me she loved someone else.

"They sound terrible," I said.

"They are terrible," she said. "They're so mean."

"So why would you want to be friends with them?"

She looked at me with pity. "Everyone wants to be friends with them," she said.

"I don't want to be friends with them," I said with total sincerity. The cryptic remarks about the My Little Pony had frightened me.

"That's fine for you," she said sadly. "You've got...you've got your own stuff going on." What stuff was she referring to? "But I'm not like that. I wish I could just be like, *Oh, whatever, Michelle, if you're going to be friends with* Louise *then I can't be friends with you.* But, you know, if I tried to be all tough like that, she wouldn't care, she'd just be like, *OK, fine, whatever.* I mean, what am I going to do, be friends with Cheryl Palatino and Emma Price again? I can always be friends with them, they'll be friends with anyone. But I don't want to hang out with them. Why would I want to hang out with them? So I'm going to hang out with nobody." A look of resignation came over her face. It seemed sad, the idea that if Michelle Kessel wasn't going to be your friend there was no one else in the world.

"I should get back," she said suddenly. "I'm supposed to be in yearbook right now."

We began walking back toward school. "You're really special, you know that?" she said. "You're a really good listener. You're a really good person."

"Thanks," I said, and I felt like I might be about to sprout wings and soar above the school, up over Denver and into the mountains. And then we were at the corner of the parking lot behind the school building, and Tara headed off across the lot along the diagonal. I watched her heading for the building's rear door, occasionally raising her hand to wave at a carful of departing kids. I kept walking straight on Randall, alongside the parking lot, beside the school building, and toward the front steps, where my mother had been waiting for half an hour.

"I have no idea what you're thinking" was what she said when I climbed into the car. "Where the hell have you been?"

"I was talking to a friend," I said, feeling somehow self-righteous. "I was talking to a girl who was really upset, and she needed to talk to me." This seemed like a valid justification.

My mom let out a long sigh as she turned the key in the ignition, and I had the feeling that she would have been angrier if she hadn't been so tired. We drove home in silence. When we got home I went straight into my room and took out my notebook. On Tara's page I wrote, *Beautiful and deep. Truly a good person. Likes LG — serious? Too sensitive for the everyday social world — wants to make a deeper connection.* Under Michelle's name, where it said *Lots of makeup* and *Popular*, I added *User*. Under Louise's I wrote *Mean*.

During most classes I split my brain in two: half of me tracked the material being covered while the other half revised and expanded my girl database. The exception was Combined Math, a two-semester dash through geometry, trig, and algebra designed for math-adept freshmen. Only two of the girls in the class were listed in my notebook, and the content consumed all of my attention. The teacher, Mr. Gestetner, was a rumpled man with a genius for exposition: you left his class palpably smarter than you were before. Kids like teachers who are good at teaching, but teaching is difficult, so a lot of teachers settle for being friendly.

Gestetner assigned quizzes every few weeks, with extra homework for anyone who performed unsatisfactorily. We were leaving the classroom after one such quiz when I heard Graham Neale's voice behind me. Graham was the boy from my homeroom with the split-level haircut. In math he sat in the back and didn't volunteer, although when Gestetner called on him he always produced the correct answer with no evident struggle.

"That was brutal," he said over my shoulder.

"Yeah," I said, slowing to fall in with him. In fact I had enjoyed it.

"The number of quizzes in this class is a fucking joke," Graham said, coming down on the penultimate word with savage relish.

"I know," I said. "It sucks." I was trying to use words like *sucks* more. And then I heard a croaking voice calling my name, and Bill Fleig was hurrying out of the classroom after us. From a distance of more than ten years, I can see how he recognized me as a kindred spirit: my dull wardrobe; my habitual look of beatific concentration; my unfortunate haircut, which swooped out from my ears in smooth shallow curves describable by quadratic equations. But at the time it felt like he had arbitrarily chosen to mark me by association.

"Do you know Pascal?" he asked. He had a way of jumping straight to the substance of conversations, treating greetings and pleasantries as noise.

"Nuh-uh," I said as Graham looked on.

"I was talking to Mr. Gestetner," Bill said. "He says he'll teach Pascal classes after school if I can find one other person who wants to do it."

This proposal was not without its appeal. I was frustrated with the limitations of BASIC and eager to become a more sophisticated programmer. But allying myself with Bill, or publicly expressing an interest in computers, would be a catastrophic error.

"Pascal is retarded," I said, proud to be disowning my nerd impulses. And then Graham gave me a quizzical look and I realized my mistake: I should have said, *What the fuck is Pascal?* Instead I had outed myself as someone who had opinions about programming languages.

"So does that mean you won't do it?" Bill asked. "Because if I can't find someone else, Gestetner won't teach the class." Graham was heading off toward his locker.

"Well, boo hoo," I said, and turned my back on Bill Fleig. Feeling defeated, I grabbed my coat and books and made my way out of the building to the school's front steps where my mom would pick me up. Plastic bags and sheets of loose-leaf paper soared and sank in the wind. I waited on the bottom step, at the far left, where my mom always looked for me, and watching the cars I realized: they were all driven by other students. That's when my mom's pale blue Nissan pulled up, and she leaned over the passenger side and waved, and there I was, the only kid at my high school getting picked up by his mom. As I got in, it was as if some adult version of me, someone capable and self-reliant, was watching and protesting: *That's just a kid! That little kid is going around pretending to be me!*

When I started at MLK Mom had, temporarily and with great bureaucratic effort, adjusted her schedule at the doctor's office where she worked reception. We'd anticipated that I would meet other kids who lived in Sheridan and my mom would arrange a car pool with their parents. But I had not yet met any such kids, and if I had I don't think I could have said, *Hey—you live in Sheridan? We should carpool!* Most of the older kids drove or got rides with friends; the younger ones took the municipal bus. But then, most of the kids at MLK didn't live in Sheridan, off the city bus routes.

It was warm in the car. "Hey, sugar," Mom said. She pulled away from the curb, humming with the radio. We stopped at the end of the street as a gaggle of kids crossed in front of us.

"So how was school?" Mom asked me.

"It was fine," I said, slouching in my seat, hoping I wouldn't be seen.

"I was thinking of doing tuna casserole tonight," she said. "And *L.A. Law.*" My mother and I enjoyed this show, but I wasn't in the mood. For the first time, the fundamental syllogism of adolescence occurred to me: *Your mom loves you. Your mom is biologically obliged to love you, even if you're a total loser. Therefore her love means nothing, and you probably are a total loser.*

"That's great, Mom," I said. "That sounds great. Um, I need to talk to you about something."

She shifted instantly into concerned mode, which comes more naturally to my mom than any other mode. "What is it, sweetie?" she said.

"I don't want to ride home with you anymore," I said. I wasn't even looking at her, but everything suddenly felt different, and I knew I'd hurt her badly.

"I just...no one else rides home with their mom, you know?" I said. A long pause.

Finally she said, in a voice almost entirely devoid of inflection, "So how does everyone else get to school?"

"They get rides with other kids," I said. "Or they take the bus."

"I've always said you can get a ride with someone else's mom," she said. "That was the whole point. And if there was a bus for you to take, believe me, I'd be more than happy for you to take it." I didn't say anything. "Do you think I like spending an extra forty-five minutes every morning and forty-five minutes every evening in the car?"

I remained silent, partly because I had believed that she did enjoy it. She always seemed happy to see me, and happy to be driving along listening to the radio, just the two of us. I wasn't sure if she'd never liked it at all, or if she was pretending because I'd hurt her feelings. We drove the rest of the way in silence, except for the radio: "More Than Words," "Justify My Love," commercials for local mattress stores. Of course there was no way for me to get to school without her.

My mother parked on the street and I shadowed her into the house. She put her handbag heavily down on the kitchen counter and, still in her coat, began grabbing cans of food out of the cabinets. I skulked past her and into my room, where I took off my shoes and sat on my bed with my knees tucked under my chin. For a long time I played out the conversation we'd just had in different ways: sometimes I said, *Thanks for driving me to school, Mom, I really appreciate it;* other times she said, *Well, we'll just have to move somewhere closer to a bus line.* After running both versions half a dozen times without much satisfaction I gave up and reached for my backpack. I had a few new pieces of information to add to the notebook: Danielle Orr had said hi to me in the hallway, and Rebecca Castillo seemed to have dumped Steve Papp for Dave Breuer, a definite trade-up. I unzipped the bag and flipped through the items inside: my ring binder, my chemistry textbook, my paperback copy of *Stranger in a Strange Land.* I couldn't see the notebook at first, but this was not unusual because it was smaller and thinner than most of the books I carried to and from school. I went through the bag's contents again, more systematically, and felt an abyss of panic open beneath me. I pulled the books and folders out of the backpack one by one. I held each upside down by its spine to allow anything hidden between the pages to drop onto the bed. I reached my arms into the empty backpack and ran my fingers over the interior's nylon surface, peering inside and taking in the rubbery scent. I unzipped the small pocket on the front of the backpack, although the notebook wouldn't have fit inside, and removed my wallet, my calculator, the house keys I carried in case of an emergency, two black pens, a green marker, two Jolly Ranchers, a Jolly Rancher wrapper, and a dime. I stopped and looked at the pile of objects on the bed. None of them was the notebook. *It's probably in my locker at school,* I thought. *Or if it's not I can always kill myself.*

It wasn't in my locker. I unpacked the contents — textbooks, binders, two sweaters, returned homework — and scrutinized each item before setting it on the checkerboard linoleum in a pile that Ron Nathorp, at the locker next to mine, kicked over with the back of his heel. Kids packed the hallway, bumping and shouting, and I expected each one who passed to say something like, *So, Danielle really likes Guns N' Roses, huh?* or *Yeah, how about Vicki Gordon's tits?* or *You must be the lamest person in the world!*

I tried to recall every step I'd taken since the previous lunchtime, when, in the privacy of a third-floor toilet stall, I had added a datum about Karen Longnecker and Julia Mossman. (Many of the observations in the book, to my surprise, described the friendships between girls.) I thought I remembered replacing it in my backpack afterward, although in these situations it's impossible to know whether you're recalling a specific event or just appropriating memories of similar events from other occasions. I didn't believe the backpack could have come open by itself: it was sturdily built, and the zipper was made by YKK, which is the sign of a reliable zipper.

I walked into homeroom with something large and fleshy in my throat but, to my relief, no one paid me any attention. By third-period English I found I could go without thinking about the notebook for minutes at a time, although eventually my thoughts would land on Gwen Vries or Nancy Chang and I would experience the urge to write something in the notebook and once again I would be filled with the dull certainty of imminent disaster.

Class ended, and we all joined the flow down to the cafeteria.

Each stairway doubled back on itself at a landing; on a trip from the fourth floor to the cafeteria you changed direction seven times. Between classes this was chaos, since we didn't self-organize into a file going up and a file going down, so every little flight of fourteen steps between a floor and a landing resembled two medieval armies colliding on a steep hillside. Before lunch, though, it was a different kind of chaos: the entire student body hurtling downstairs, gathering reinforcements at every floor. You could get swept down the last couple flights without effort, as if your feet had been lifted off the ground. One or two kids struggled upstairs like climbers in an avalanche.

I attained the cafeteria and looked around for somewhere to sit. Instinctively I took note of the four or five girls who were at the center of my narrowing researches. Ginny Oyler was sitting with Leah Toomey's crowd, which was new. And there was unusual hilarity at Michelle and Tara's table. Michelle's back was to me; she seemed to be reading something to Tara and Louise and Becky Busch and Lisa Buonano. I wondered what the joke was. And then my eyes met Tara's and she stopped laughing and began to make frantic shushing motions to her companions, patting the air with her hands, and the cafeteria seemed very big and very noisy, and I was sure there had to be some way to reverse one of the steps that had led to this moment, but of course there wasn't. And Michelle turned around in her seat and scanned the room and finally gestured in my direction with the gentlest nod imaginable, and the entire table looked at me and broke into laughter, except for Tara, who stared down at her lunch with an expression that I was unable to read.

The bathroom in the school's basement got very little traffic, and its heavy air smelled of damp cement. Warmed by the giant boilers next door, I sat in a stall and tried to reconstruct from memory my observations of 39 ninth-grade girls—not to preserve the information, which was useless to me since Michelle Kessel's lunchtime reading yesterday, but to imagine it through the eyes of its subjects. What would Becky Busch think, for instance, when she learned that, next to her name, I had written *Never smiles* and *Insists that trees are not alive b/c they don't walk around*? Or Nancy Chang, whose entry, in its entirety, read *Smells good:* publicly she'd be repulsed, but would she also, secretly, be pleased? Counting out the thirty-nine girls on my fingers I reviewed my useless notes, meditating on each in turn, in the hope that I could wring the shame from them. I could distract myself for brief periods by examining the shapes where the paint had peeled off the cubicle's wooden wall: under the blue-gray was a coat of forest green. In sixteen minutes I was due in biology with Michelle and Louise and Tara. I had skipped it yesterday. I could skip it again today, become a truant, get expelled, start over at another school, but what I'd done would follow me there. When Carl Driesdale transferred to Wilson, everyone knew he'd been thrown out of his previous school for biting some kid on the dick. Was that even true? I tried to remember arriving at school yesterday, before I had ruined my life, and I wanted to weep from nostalgia. And then the bell rang, and by some autonomic reflex I got up and headed out of the bathroom into the treacherous world.

As I walked the five floors to the bio labs, pressed in by crowds, I kept my head down like a spy, glad for the first time not to be tall. I pushed the door open and everyone turned to see if Mr. McCallum had arrived. Michelle Kessel's caroling voice filled the lull with the words, "Hey Eric, it's great that you think I'm a user!"

There was general puzzlement—what possible connection could there be between Michelle and the quiet, doughy kid with the weird clothes? I took an empty seat at the back as though none of this was happening. Finally Angela Martin, who was nice but lacked subtlety of mind, asked Michelle what she was talking about, giving Michelle a chance to say, "Look!" and begin digging in her book bag. I stared at the chipped wooden surface of my desk, where compass points and Swiss Army knives had engraved forgotten initials, geometric doodles, the word *RUSH*.

"Check this out, you guys," she said. "This is Eric's secret notebook."

"Awww," said Angela, as though Michelle had taken out a dying bird. "You should give it back to him."

"Just wait," Michelle said. She began paging through the notebook. I knew what was coming, but it took her longer than I expected to find the entry. Where was McCallum? *"Angela Martin,"* Michelle read. *"Skinny. Vegetarian. Likes Matt McGahan."* Laughter, shouting. Angela put her hand over her mouth in astonishment. I'd never seen anyone do that except on TV. *"Plays flute in orchestra. Asked me how long until class. Seems like nice person. Member of Save the Environment Club."*

Abigail Slott said, "Oh my God, *no way!*" in a tone of pure joy.

"What is this?" Sean Lippard asked me.

"Wait, wait, wait," Michelle said. "There's more!" She looked around the classroom. "Oh, oh, Abigail's in. Wait." I tried to remember what I'd written about Abigail Slott. Michelle seemed to be flipping through the pages from the front, which meant she hadn't noticed the entries were alphabetized by last name.

"Here we go," she said. *"Abigail Slott: Pretty hair. Sarcastic. Plays volleyball. Visible bra straps. Often comments on smells. Mostly friends with guys—Sean L, Steve Olssen (boyfriend?). Can be scary. Ignores me."*

I started to disengage, reducing the classroom to a meaningless array of pure sensory data—light waves at different frequencies hitting my retinae, sonic vibrations in the air's molecules. *If Michelle Kessel humiliates you in the forest, does she make a sound?* It worked for a few seconds, until I became aware that the blur of red and yellow and tan to my left was Molly Clarke, who had never spoken to me before, and who was looking me up and down as though I were something incongruous and threatening, a leopard or a nudist. "What was this *for?*" she said.

"Oh, Molly, you want to hear yours?" asked Michelle.

"What did you write about me?" Molly asked me. I began to jiggle my leg rhythmically, counting the beats in groups of four and sets of sixteen.

"Yours is short," Michelle said. *"Molly Clarke: Quiet, shy. Went to Japan on vacation — interested in Japan."* I had thought it might be useful to know that, for some reason.

"Did he really call you a user?" asked Allison Ketcham, who had been omitted from the notebook for her strange pockmarked face and the frizzy hair that exploded from her scrunchie.

"Yeah, yeah, you wanna hear mine?" said Michelle. "OK: *Michelle Kessel — smart, pretty. Nice legs —*" and here she paused dramatically *"— or just short skirts?"* There was laughter, maybe more than she would have liked. *"Likes to be in charge. Doesn't laugh much. Lots of makeup. Popular. User."* She stepped on the last word hard, as though killing a bug. She skipped the next sentence: *Switches best friends a lot: Beth Gillman/Vicki Gordon/Liz Anderman/Louise Treadwell.* I caught her eye and realized that she wasn't just having fun — I'd made an enemy.

To Louise, in a stage whisper, she said, "Can I read yours?" There was no way the crowd would have let her skip Louise's entry once she'd announced its existence.

*"Louise Treadwell,"* Michelle read. *"Pretty, blond (dyed?), sexy clothes. Kind of dumb."* She enunciated this last very clearly, looking straight at me. *"Always turns in work late, says she left it at home. Mean."* She omitted *Always with Michelle.*

"I think that's all the people in this class," said Michelle. She had left out Tara's entry, in which I had recorded Michelle and

Louise's corruption of Tara's innocent love for her My Little Ponies. "You guys want to hear some of the others? You want to hear Vicki Gordon?"

It was in the middle of this speech that McCallum walked in. The room got quiet—McC. was not a teacher to fuck with—but Michelle was already looking through the pages. He hovered behind her for a moment, then reached down and snatched the notebook out of her hands.

Michelle was unflustered. "Sorry, Mr. McCallum," she said, sticking out her chin like a tiny prizefighter. "But that's not mine, the notebook, it's Eric Muller's." I admired the way she was careful to distinguish me from Eric Auerbach.

McCallum sighed—he hadn't even begun teaching and already he was faced with a distracting mess. He gestured with the book as though he was going to throw it at me, then opened it to a random page. After a few seconds he looked up at Abigail Slott and chuckled.

"Mr. McCallum," Michelle said, raising her hand perfunctorily, "there's some really disgusting stuff in there. Some of the girls think it's really inappropriate."

McCallum raised his eyebrows at me sardonically. Then he took the notebook's corner between two fingers, as though it were a kitten he was feeding to a tank of piranhas, and dropped it onto Michelle's desk.

"Put it away," he told her brusquely. "Now: photosynthesis."

As far as I could tell, Michelle never allowed the notebook into general circulation. (There were, after all, passages that she didn't want people to read.) Thus it became a collective fantasy object for the student body, more thrilling than the real artifact could ever have been. Besides the girl profiles, most of what I'd recorded was mundane—who talked to whom, who ate where, who whispered in class. In the school's dreamlife it was transformed into a deranged epic of perversion and lust. Over the next three weeks I was asked to confirm the following: that I had made a list of girls I wanted to have sex with; that I had spied on girls through their windows and taken photographs of them in the nude; that I intended to drug Angela Martin and force myself on her in the cafeteria; that I had collected and catalogued my masturbatory effluvia and planned to present every girl in the school with the relevant portion, in a Ziploc bag, on Valentine's Day. I denied each rumor with the kind of embarrassment that looks very much like guilt.

The ordeal was interrupted by a tedious, anxious vacation. I spent it in my room, working through a compendium of programming exercises and reading comic books about superpowered mutants, endowed with genetic gifts far beyond those of their parents, shunned by the fearful and the bigoted. We had Christmas dinner with my father, who announced over turkey cutlets and Stove Top stuffing that he was investing everything he had and everything he earned in the beverage company, divorce settlement be damned, and that the returns from this venture would soon enable him to fulfill his responsibilities to us in lavish style, and that my mother's failure to support him in his ambitions was the reason he'd left her in the first place, and that apparently even divorce couldn't free him of her carping and negativity. He finished this speech with the satisfied look of a man who has gotten something off his chest, then took a second helping of instant mashed potatoes. He stayed through dessert.

For New Year's my mom and I went to a party at the Oberfells': grown-ups standing around drinking, listening to Bruce Hornsby and the Range, talking about whatever grown-ups talk about. Bronwen was at a high school party, probably making out with somebody. "Stacey's going to ask Bronwen if you can go with her!" my mom had said that afternoon, but I quashed the idea, for obvious reasons. And so I wandered among the knots of chatting adults, drinking Pepsi, trying to avoid my mother and her sympathetic looks. Eventually I began hunting for a quiet place to reread *X-Men* issues 129 to 138, in which Marvel Girl, made omnipotent and insane by lust, destroys an entire planetary system.

Pete was in his room, identifiable by the stickers on the door: Garbage Pail Kids, skateboard companies, Ninja Turtles. He was kneeling on the floor with a curly-haired friend, surrounded by an elaborate arrangement of G.I. Joes. Pete was bigger than I remembered, and this made me feel like I was making insufficient progress, but I was glad to see him. Here was a person who might have some minimal respect for me, if only because I was older than him.

"What are you guys doing?" I said. I could imagine spending the evening playing G.I. Joe with a couple of ten-year-olds, justifying it to myself as a kind of charity work. He didn't answer.

"Cobra 3 to Squadron Leader," his friend said. "Preparing to execute Mission Danger Bomb."

"Hypersquadron activated," Pete said.

"OK, cool," I said, and ducked out into the hallway, where a tall man in a blue blazer was saying, "So the guy says because of the soil composition, just to *excavate* is gonna be twenty grand, and then it's another five to ten before anyone's swimming." Across the hall, unadorned, was another door: Bronwen's. It was impossible not to slip inside.

Because what happens in a girl's room, anyway? By what alchemy does this space incubate a child's body and generate breasts and ovaries and beauty? These rooms have a lot of work to do, and that's why they're so ornately decorated, as though with the ingredients for a spell. Bronwen's bed had a canopy of rough tulle, like a gauzy purple mist. Every inch of the opposite wall was covered with photographs: celebrities and models, friends in bathing suits or evening gowns. A collage compiled images of Bronwen and a skinny, dark-haired girl, accompanied by the legend Bronwen and Katie spelled in letters clipped from magazines ransom-note style, along with the slogans, extracted from ad pages or pull quotes, Why can't I have every-thing I want? and It's all about boys! I looked for actual boys, but apart from Tom Cruise and the Beatles they were few and far between.

On the surfaces of the dresser and the nightstand were jewelry boxes and nail polish and hand mirrors and lipstick, more than I could believe. In the small attached bathroom I peeked at the sham-poos and bath oils and skin creams, opened the cabinet to survey the contact lens solution and Q-Tips and Tampax. Everything smelled of fruit or flowers. Whenever I had thought about Bronwen over the past year, cringing embarrassment had burned away any other feel-ing, but here, surrounded by the paraphernalia of her self-invention, something tender began to stir. I felt as though I was backstage in the dressing room during a performance. In the bedroom closet I found the shoe tree, the nice dresses, the jackets. I tried the little top drawer of the dresser, and although I knew what was inside I was still startled by the profusion of underwear, a surprising amount of it in colors other than white. She had red underwear, gray, lots of pur-ple. Like the bed: purple was a theme, it meant something. There were only a couple of bras—she didn't really need bras. I listened for footsteps at the door, but I wasn't confident I'd hear them over the party. I pulled out underpants one pair at a time, inspected the cot-ton panels and the soft gussets, tried to infer Bronwen's body from their shape. I felt like the scholar-hero in the adventure movie, alone in the library at night, combing the leather-bound tomes for the clue he needs. The pair I was looking for wasn't in this drawer, it was with Bronwen as she laughed with her friends, took sips from an older girl's flask, positioned herself close to some boy at midnight, while I was stuck here with her underwear and her leggings and her sweet-smelling lotions, all the props she used to create the sublime fantasy of her girlhood. Though I was far from the performance, I was closer to the truth than I had ever been. And that's when Pete Oberfell opened the door and said, "What are you doing?"

"Nothing!" I said much too loudly. "Nothing. Just looking around." I tried to slip Bronwen's underwear into my pocket, but it got snagged and dangled halfway out.

He peered at me narrowly. Over his shoulder, his friend strained to see what was going on.

"Are you guys done playing G.I. Joe?" I said.

"We're in the middle," he said suspiciously.

"All right!" I said. "I just came in here to use the bathroom. Is this it over here?"

"Yeah," Pete said.

"Thanks," I said, and headed into the bathroom, leaving Bronwen's underwear drawer open behind me.

We left right after the ball dropped over Times Square. My mom had had a few drinks, and although she was a seasoned drinker she had a little trouble unlocking the car door. "So," she said as we pulled away from Stacey and Gary's house. "Did you have a good time?"

"Sure," I said.

"Eric," she said, making a left turn, "do you wish you had friends?"

I had imagined that my mother was somehow oblivious to my loneliness, that by splitting my time between school and her house and my dad's I gave the impression of a full and busy life. Of course, we lived together in a small bungalow where I'd just spent winter break teaching myself C and reading Chris Claremont's run on *X-Men* from the beginning.

"Yeah, sometimes," I said. "But, you know, I really like programming."

"I know," she said. "And that's great. But—" There were sirens, and she pulled over to let a cop car pass. The flashing lights turned her hands on the wheel red and blue. As she glanced over her shoulder and pulled out, she said, "You just don't seem very happy."

Graham Neale noticed me sitting at the back of the classroom and wandered over. "Hey Eric!" he said. "You have a good vacation, dude?" It was the first thing anyone had said to me since we'd arrived back at school that morning. He put a soft hand on my shoulder and squeezed. I knew this was a trap, but my heart reflexively opened a few degrees anyway.

"Pretty good," I said, looking up at him from my chair.

"Cool, cool," he said. "Something I wanted to ask you, OK?"

"OK," I said.

"What's it like to be such a loser?"

"Good one," I said, trying to pull my shoulder away. Graham held on.

"No, I asked you a question," he said, sounding offended. "What's it like?" He was going to watch me squirm on the point of this unanswerable presumptive question. I stared past him at the classroom door, the fire extinguisher, the map showing the emergency evacuation route, until Mrs. Blankenship came in with a stack of copies of *To Kill a Mockingbird*.

As soon as class was done I hurried out of the room and down to the basement, wanting only the warm, stale air of the bathroom. I would wait out the lunch period with the comics I had slipped into my backpack that morning: hundreds of pages of anti-mutant prejudice, terrifying possible futures, and psychic struggles against mind-controlling sadists, protected by Mylar bags and stiff sheets of cardboard. When I reached the bottom of the stairs, though, the door, with its ancient wooden Boys sign, was propped open by a yellow cone, and a heavy Mexican woman in a smock was pushing an industrial mop across the floor. From above I heard the throb of footsteps, the buzz of voices, the entire school heading toward the cafeteria over our heads. Farther down the scruffy hallway, past the huge room where cafeteria workers fed plates and trays into massive dishwashers, was the computer room. Keeping the promise I had made to myself at Wilson, I had never been inside. But things had changed, and a girlfriend was not on the horizon, and *computer nerd* was a more appealing identity than *kid who hangs out in the toilets in the basement,* barely.

I peered through the narrow window in the door. Guy Learmont, who was tiny and in my Spanish class, was watching a kid I didn't know play Toxic Ravine at a terminal on the far side of the room. In the months before I'd started at MLK I had imagined the inside of the building, the other students, the adult life I would finally achieve there. This fantasy, vague as to details but emotionally vivid and specific, had withdrawn from my consciousness the minute I stepped through the doors of the real place. But it had survived, undiminished, as though sealed in an airtight compartment in my brain, and now, in a gust of nostalgia for a world that would never exist, it returned. I mourned it for a second, and then I said goodbye and pushed open the door to the computer room.

"Fuck, it's Muller," Guy Learmont said as I walked in. Near the beginning of the year, Learmont had made the mistake of confiding in Jerry Osteen, and now the entire school knew he had only one testicle. Bill Fleig, typing rapidly at a terminal in the corner, didn't look up.

Brilliant white paint coated the walls, the pipes, the light fixtures, thick enough to give the room an alkaline scent. There were seven free computers, each with twelve times as much memory as the Packard Bell in my bedroom. Learmont's friend's machine emitted happy music and occasional shouts of "I'm hungry!" Thickets of code ran down Bill Fleig's screen.

"It's a test generator," Bill said, although I hadn't asked. "People were cheating in Gestetner's class, copying each other's homework and stuff, so he asked me to write a program that generates a different test for everybody. It just varies up the quantities and shuffles the order of the questions, and then it generates an answer key for each one."

"Gestetner couldn't do this himself?" I asked.

"No, he could," Bill said. "But he has to give me some kind of homework if I'm going to get AP credit for learning C++." Then he stopped typing and turned to look at me. "Is it true you were keeping a notebook on girls?" If the story had made it to Bill, who was earning extra credit constructing cheat-proof tests for a math teacher, everyone in the school had heard it.

"Fuck you," I said. Bill observed this display of emotion curiously. "OK, yes. Yeah, it's true. I was keeping a notebook."

"I was just wondering," Bill said. "I can see why you might do that."

Something hateful in my gut rose up against him: of course the only person in the school with any sympathy for me was Bill Fleig, he of the overbite and the giant calculator. "I'm really glad I've got your support," I said.

A muffled stampede shook the ceiling: lunch was over. Bill saved his program to a floppy disk, Learmont and his friend shut down their game, and I followed them out. In the first-floor hallway, on my way to world history, someone called my name and started to cheer. It spread, and soon dozens of kids had turned from their lockers and started to applaud, as though I was the hero at a parade. It wasn't about anything, just the crowd enjoying its capacity for spontaneous mass irony. I tried to play along, raising my hand to acknowledge the tribute, until someone behind me gave me a shove and I went down, stinging my palms on the linoleum.

I went back to the computer room the next day, and Bill showed me how the test generator worked. Then he announced that he'd started building a spreadsheet program. "Every few years a new one comes along and demolishes the old one," he said. "VisiCalc got creamed by Lotus 1-2-3, Lotus got eaten by Excel, now I'm going to beat Excel."

I looked at his designs: he had some clever ideas for macro functions that Excel wouldn't have for three or four years, but he hadn't thought much about user experience. I made some tentative suggestions, careful to show respect for the work he'd put in. Like most people who are confident of their genius, Bill accepts thoughtful criticism eagerly, and so I spent a few days thinking through the interface for him, mapping it out on paper in classes and at night. I could already tell it was the only area in which I might improve on Bill's work. Most software makes people struggle, and so when they notice it they see it as an enemy. But if the designer can anticipate not only the user's goals but the user's instincts and assumptions, users will feel that the software cares about them, pays attention to their needs— loves them. And they'll start to love the software back. All feelings of love toward technology are this kind of reciprocal love, I think.

I designed the user experience model and most of the front end for the spreadsheet program, and watched as Bill built it. That's how I learned how good Bill Fleig was. Faced with a troublesome bug, he didn't scroll through the program's text to follow a variable's path but stared blankly ahead, nodding, unspooling hundreds of lines of code in his mind, as though the only processor he needed was his own cerebral cortex. At the lowest point in my life I had found a friend to explore this new territory with, although it wasn't the friend or the territory I would have chosen.

(We finished the program eight months later. Bill sent demos to software publishers, all of whom said the spreadsheet market was oversaturated. I happen to know that a copy of the demo made it to Redmond about two years before features we'd designed showed up in Excel, with the interface completely botched.)

Outside the computer room things changed without getting better or worse. The applause thing became a daily occurrence, then gave way to a variant in which people I passed in the halls slapped me on the back. It was as though they were congratulating me, but painfully hard and with sarcastic intent. Everyone who attends high school has seen this kind of thing happen, but little in the adult world resembles it, and so for most adults the cruelty of adolescence is a half-remembered dream, a vague and tumultuous carnival with no associative triggers to connect it to present experience.

By that point my notebook wasn't mentioned much—the school-wide conversation had moved on. (There were exceptions: once, on the stairway, Barry Cushman said, "Hey Eric, is Monica in your notebook?" and Monica Hintz said, "Shut up, jerk!" and pushed Barry into the wall, but she was smiling while she said it, and I realized that this was how flirting worked.) But it was freshman year, and the class of 1996 needed a pariah, and I had stepped forward to volunteer.

I spent weekends in my room, hacking away on my computer, wishing I had more RAM or some friends. Around me people were starting to sleep together, and to talk about it, and I spent more and more time and energy imagining sex, guessing at what it might be like, wondering if I'd ever find out.

# 5

If I cut loose, I'll revert to the animal side o' my nature—so totally that I may never regain my humanity.

—Wolverine, *X-Men* 147

THE SECOND DATE WITH Maya is a daytime triumph in which we sit side by side in lawn chairs on the roof of my building, looking out at other people's roofs, passing a bottle of wine. The gravel crunches beneath our sneakers. In the thorny zone of potential disillusion that follows a first kiss, we effortlessly sustain our conversational momentum, right up until I ask what her parents do.

"Uh, my dad's an art dealer," she says, her hands tucked into the sleeves of her jacket. "My mom died when I was six."

The imperatives here are multiple and contradictory: I don't want to drag her into self-exposure, or spoil the afternoon with grief, but I can't allow myself to appear cowardly in the face of tragedy. "How did she die?"

"She had cancer," Maya says, nestling the wine bottle into the pebbles. "Two kinds of cancer at once. She was being treated for lung cancer when they found the stomach cancer."

"Do you remember her?"

"I have this strong sense of, like, *mom*. But when I think about what she looked like all I can see are photographs."

The smell of roasting coffee beans blows over us, a smell that bears no relation to the flavor of coffee itself. I take a risk. "Where were you when you found out she died?"

"I was in my room," she says. "I was playing with my Etch A Sketch, and my dad came in and told me she was dead. He wasn't crying, and I said, *Why aren't you crying?* and he said, *I've been crying, honey. I've been crying for half an hour.* He'd waited to tell me—he wanted to compose himself first. I was so furious. I'd been drawing on my Etch A Sketch like an idiot while my mom was dead. I kept screaming, *Why didn't you tell me?*"

After this there's a sense that we've navigated something tricky together. Soon we go downstairs, rubbing our cold hands, and fall kissing onto my bed. We pin each other by the wrists; we wrestle like kids; we grind like teenagers. And then I start to unbutton her shirt, and she resists with a quick shake of her head. We go back to kissing for a while, but we've lost focus, and soon we're lying on our backs looking up at the rafters.

"All right if we wait a while on the sex thing?" she says. It's not quite a question.

"Sure, yeah, no problem," I say. "Take it slow." She smiles, and we kiss some more. In a way it's worse but in a way it's better. I do want to have sex with her—for the obvious reasons, and to seal the deal. But more than that I want to avoid wrecking everything.

For the next few weeks we see each other almost every night, which makes me feel as though I've passed into another world with different laws. I start to discover how her ordinary life functions, although obviously you can never discount the impact of the observer on the phenomenon under observation. I quiz her on her history, which she presents as a series of phases passed through like railway stations. The binge-drinking phase started at fifteen and was over by the time she went to college. She characterizes it as a response to her difficult relationship with her father, about whom she says little. College saw the advent of the radical activism phase. Since moving to San Francisco she's become open to the possibility of ambition, although in her case the desideratum is not money but prestige, which is currency among journalists. For the past year she's been appearing on the local public radio station once a month. At the paper she pushes every deadline, and because she's a star she gets away with it. This inspires resentment in her coworkers, particularly the editor who has to stay late to wait for her copy. She's apologetic but not fearful, because as long as she brings in good stories, no one will fire her for making the editor work late. She comes to my house in the evenings, and we eat dinner and kiss and fall asleep together, and those two hours justify everything that has ever happened to me.

I was living in the same suburban bungalow where I'd grown up, working for a wire-transfer company in downtown Denver, when Bill Fleig convinced me to move to San Francisco and spend three years with him in a mildewy apartment in the Tenderloin, making what turned out to be $18.4 million but could have been nothing. His argument had two planks, one practical and one ethical: that his idea for a web-based microprofiling service could make me rich, and that lubricating the flow of information about individual consumer preferences would constitute a meaningful contribution to human happiness. He never sold me on the second one.

We worked on the program until we could navigate it more easily than the street outside our apartment. We worried about bugs in the code, about the strain on the servers, about whether the database queries would scale. We worried about competitors, about users, about funders. Worrying every second of every day was insufficient to exhaust the list of things that could destroy us, so we worried about not worrying enough. I retreated into a social universe bounded by Bill Fleig. I sometimes thought about girls, in an abstract way, as a problem to be solved, but I was saturated with problems already. The small sum Bill's father had invested was dwindling, and air was leaking out of the NASDAQ, and failure was stalking us, a hungry gleam in its eye.

And then, after two offers had fallen through and the IPO

market had collapsed and our rivals were dying around us like trees in a Dutch elm epidemic, Atrium Inc. offered us $18.4 million for the work of just less than three years. To my horror, Bill had rejected an earlier bid that valued us at $3 million. He vacillated about this one. He still thought of our service as an economy-changer, a vector for billions of consumer dollars, rather than what Atrium wanted to buy, which was an ad-targeting feature for a midsized media conglomerate. I threatened him with everything I had—walking out, selling my share—and his parents applied what little pressure they could, and finally, in a sunny conference room off the 101, in front of four men in shirtsleeves and ties, we each signed our name seven times. There was a round of handshakes and a strange physical sensation, a sad release. And then the code wasn't ours anymore and we missed it, although the previous day we couldn't bear to think about it for one more second.

Male friendship, like a wave, requires a medium to travel in, a project or a context, material on which to display solidarity or insight or wit. Ours was the mass of Perl and C++ and HTML known as Demographic of One, and now, less than a year later, we struggle to recapture the frantic, loyal mood of our collaboration.

We can't drink together because Bill doesn't drink, so today we're meeting at an Italian café in North Beach with round tables big enough to accommodate about one and a half people each. This is the only place Bill ever wants to meet: it's fifteen yards from his doorstep, and no one acknowledges him even though he comes in twice a week. Today he doesn't even order an espresso because he's planning to catch up on sleep. He hasn't had any Diet Coke since eleven this morning, and a crash is imminent. He stayed up last night fixing bugs on his new project; all he'll tell me is that it's something to do with multithreading. Instead we talk about the mess that Atrium has made of Demo1's interface in a misguided attempt to bring it in line with recent trends in e-commerce. Bill is unsurprised.

"That's what they paid for," he says. "They'd fuck up the back end too, if they could understand how it works." During the courtship phase, Atrium sent over a couple of technical managers to kick the tires, and Bill answered their questions with such naked contempt that I was sure they'd go back to their bosses and claim that our code was trivial and fragile, out of spite.

We pick at the bones of our one topic some more, while Bill nurses his mandarin-blossom tea and speaks more slowly than usual, leaving long pauses during which he seems to collapse on himself. Emerging from one of these pauses with a jerk, he says, "So I got a phone call from your father."

My shock flares up and dies. "He wanted to hire you, didn't he?" I say. Could my father possibly remember Bill from when I was in high school? No, he found Bill's name in the articles about Demo1.

Bill grins. "He said, *You know, Eric is exploring other opportunities right now, so we've got this big, this big opportunity open.*" The imitation of my dad's business manner is surprisingly accurate, and I bristle: I'm the only person who's allowed to do impressions of my parents. "He also said that you spoke highly of me, so thanks for that." Bill's sarcastic mode is so deadpan that many people don't recognize it.

Someone leaves the café, and as the door shuts it bellows a gust of cold air toward us. "You know I would never give my dad your phone number, right?"

"I didn't mind," he says. My dad is not the pit of guilt and confusion for Bill that he is for me. "I told him to call my agent."

"Your what?"

"I said, *All the top programmers are being handled by agents now.* I told him I was represented by the Creative Artists Agency in Los Angeles."

I can see how this has played out: my dad has called the Creative Artists Agency in Los Angeles and said he'd like to speak to the agent representing Bill Fleig, and the receptionist, a young actress with a phone-sex voice, told him they don't have a client by that name, and he said, *Sure you do, he's a computer programmer,* and she laughed her condescending Los Angeles laugh. I feel a little sorry for my dad.

Bill relates the rest of the conversation: Dad wouldn't reveal his plan over the phone, but Bill asked where Dad was getting funding, and Dad said, *We've got enough private money to get us to the point where the revenues kick in.* This sets a little bug of anxiety nibbling at my stomach lining. Bill asks me about the business plan, and I tell him I've signed an NDA. I wouldn't care—it's not like my dad is going to sue me—but Bill has made enough fun of my dad today, and I don't need his opinion of the online stereo market.

My espresso has cooled enough to drink. I drain the tiny cup and head to the counter for another, mostly to precipitate a break in the conversation. Café Florio is a one-man show, and the line backs up and snakes around the tables. I stand behind a family of tourists from England and two young women in office attire, one white, one Asian. The shiny devices behind the counter burble and hiss. What is my dad talking about when he says *private money*? I shouldn't care about my dad's money now that I have my own, but when I was growing up, my father's bank balance was central to my parents' abiding conflict—and, I was led to believe, to my survival—and I feel instinctively protective of it. The two office girls push past me with their drinks, and Florio takes my order.

When I finally rejoin Bill, he's on the brink of collapse: his arms are splayed out across the tabletop, and his head is cocked at an angle that exaggerates his long neck and makes him look like a stork. Recognizing that further attempts at conversation will be futile, I turn and watch the two girls leave with their lattes. The Asian one is chubby and kind of pretty, and I realize that I may never have to hit on anyone again.

\*     \*     \*

If not for Cynthia and her misplaced faith in me I would have ignored Bill's email, in which case I'd probably still be living with my mom and working for MoneyWire. They hired me to work on something they called Project Tyrannosaurus, presumably because it sounded cooler than Project Rewrite the Transactions Code from Scratch. It was a death march. The original system had been written almost twenty years earlier, and since then hundreds of new features had been added by dozens of successive programmers, like a medieval cathedral built by five generations of stonemasons. The resulting contraption worked, just about, thanks to patches and voodoo. (Every night we rebuilt the database, an operation that tied up the servers for twenty-five minutes. No one could explain why except to say that terrible things happened when we didn't.) There were layers written in obsolete dialects, subroutines that existed only to avoid problems with discontinued hardware, Y2K fixes that bottlenecked every operation. Everything we added broke something else, usually something in a completely different part of the code, and just identifying the point of collapse often took days. It seemed likely that we would work on Project Tyrannosaurus until we died, and our replacements would discover our contributions, our hacks and workarounds and abandoned attempts at efficiency, and curse our names as we cursed those who had come before us.

My third week at MoneyWire, while I was getting up to speed on the codebase, I found a bug that lowballed the company's commission on transactions into Hungarian forints by about 2 percent. I fixed it in ten minutes (the hard part with some bugs is finding them) and showed it to Kevin, the project manager. I had just saved the company approximately the cost of my salary and benefits in perpetuity.

"Holy shit," Kevin said, standing over my shoulder and squinting at the screen. "Don't mention this to anyone or they'll have a fucking cow."

"Kevin, I just fixed it," I said.

"Yeah," he said, "but they'll think it was our fault in the first place."

Kevin's management style involved the imposition of hopelessly ambitious, allegedly unbreakable deadlines for each stage of the project. The fact that we were always on a deadline, and had blown all the previous deadlines, enabled him to keep us on a permanent emergency footing. The night I received Bill Fleig's email, for instance, I didn't make it home until 10:38. On my way to my room I saw through Mom's open doorway that she'd fallen asleep sitting up in bed, her head lolling, the paperback in her hand flopped open. I crept in and set the book on the end table, then turned off the bedside lamp. "Mmm," she said, without changing position. In the morning she would complain about having slept in her contacts again.

In my room I checked my email, expecting nothing but nightly digests from mailing lists devoted to open-source projects. I almost didn't notice the message from wdfle@mit.edu among them.

Bill's message was brief. It didn't say how he'd gotten my email address, or ask how I'd been, or describe the idea that was motivating him to drop out of MIT to move to California and found a company, or explain why he was proposing to do so with someone who had rejected his friendship. Despite these lacunae, the email reopened certain possibilities, such as happiness and California, that I had given up on. I had worked hard to inure myself to their appeal, and for an email to dangle them in front of my face felt like a cruel and personal form of spam. Why did Bill Fleig always show up when you didn't need him? I selected the email and clicked the Delete button.

Bill's proposal would have vanished from my mind if Cynthia hadn't come home for spring break the following weekend. At her parents' kitchen table we talked about life at Wesleyan, her latest romance, the brutal organic-chemistry class that would keep her from applying to medical school. I hoped she wouldn't ask me anything about myself.

"So are you applying to CU?" she said.

That had been the plan. The brochures and forms had arrived in the mail but I couldn't bring myself to fill them out. I'd investigated scholarships at Stanford and elsewhere, but the development offices told me I wasn't eligible thanks to my father's financial state: a decent salary, not bankrupt, just a lot of debt. They wouldn't take into account the fact that he wasn't going to give me any money. They couldn't, or everybody's father would try it.

"I'm not really thinking about college right now," I said.

Against all the evidence Cynthia interpreted this optimistically, as proof that I had some brilliant and unconventional alternative in mind. "So what are you going to do?" she said.

"I might start an Internet company," I said. It was just something to say, splitting the difference between a joke and a sense of possibility. I didn't want to disappoint her.

"That's so great!" she said. "What's it going to do?"

So I had to continue. "You remember that kid Bill Fleig from MLK?" I said. "He wants me to work on something with him."

"You're going to start a dot-com!" she said. "I want to get in on the ground floor! You're going to make us all rich!"

"I don't know if I'm going to do it. I mean, it's so geeky, and most of these things flop."

"So what's the alternative?" she said, in all seriousness, and I realized I couldn't answer her.

Three and a half years and eighteen million dollars later, on the cold first sunny day of the year, Cynthia and I sit on the hillside at Dolores Park, looking out at the pastel houses and the towers and cantilevers of the Bay Bridge. Cynthia wore essentially the same thing every day since high school—blue jeans, T-shirts, hooded sweatshirts, sneakers—until she came out, at which point she switched to black jeans. She's having some trouble acclimating to her new sexual identity.

"I just feel dumb that it's taken me so long," she says. "What is this, the 1950s? Was I in the *closet?* That's so passé."

I, on the other hand, have acclimated quite successfully. Cynthia's not masculine—her gentle manner suggests some kind of woodland creature, a fawn or a hobbit. But there's something flirtless about her that makes our friendship possible. We have covered the basics: has she told her parents, is she maybe bisexual, is she ready to encounter a familiar set of genitals in a new context. "OK, I need to ask your advice," she says. Everybody likes being asked for their advice. "Should I be a butch or a femme?"

"Don't ask me," I tell her, swallowing the sweet flat last sip of my beer. "I'm not in your target demographic."

She tugs on my arm. "Help me with this," she says. "It's taken me too long to get here, and now I have all this catching up to do. I'm in the car with Sam the other day, and I'm driving, and she's telling me about her day, and I'm thinking, *This is what it feels like to be the guy.* But then other times I want her to be the guy."

"Do you have to lock yourself into one or the other?"

"You kind of do. Some women go for butch and some go for femme, and if you don't fit in either category, nobody goes for you."

"This is fascinating," I say. "I can already see that your burgeoning sexual identity will open a rich vein of sociological insight for me."

"Listen," Cynthia says. "How do you talk to girls? I try to talk to these girls, and it's great, they love me, I've got a dozen new best friends. But it doesn't feel *romantic.*"

"No one is born knowing how to talk to girls," I tell her. "It's like how no one's born knowing how to program in C++. When I first met you I was developing an approach to the problem that was compatible with my personality and affect and skill set." And this approach, properly refined, has been the basis of my technique ever since. You make yourself available, but you hold something back, too. If you don't have anything to hold back—because what do you have to offer, as a sixteen-year-old boy? You live with your parents, you're unaccustomed to the length of your limbs, you've spent the past four years building up an encyclopedic knowledge of X-Men continuity…So you fake it, you feint, you draw her attention to the empty space you're guarding to make her wonder what's there. Does this translate to girl-on-girl situations?

"It's like anything else," I say finally. "Try different approaches. Iterate. Pretend you're in a movie, and you're playing a character who's more charming and confident than you." The fact that I have nothing to offer but truisms should be a warning sign. Later I will see that we've chosen the wrong problem.

The sun disappears behind us, quick enough to notice. We walk back to Cynthia's, her hand on the handlebars of her bike. On the corner we initiate plans for a double date—she suggests dinner at her house before I can stop her—and say goodbye, and I continue down Guerrero Street, over the ridiculous hills, to Maya's. We are going to rent a movie and get takeout.

On her narrow street people sit on stoops drinking Mexican beer from cans. The sky is glutted with cables, as though the whole city's phone calls travel past her window. As I approach the building, the metal gate swings open and Maya's housemate Bradley emerges; he's a professional bicycle activist, and as far as I can tell his relationship with Maya consists exclusively of polite arguments about noise levels. He holds the gate open with a look that suggests my presence here is just one more way in which he is poorly treated.

"How's it going, Bradley!" I say, to annoy him. He grunts and lets the door clang shut behind me. At the foot of the stairs is a sheaf of mail bound with a rubber band; visible on the bundle's outside is a catalogue offering deals on professional broadcasting equipment. I scoop it up and bring it with me to assert my semi-resident status.

Maya meets me when I'm on the penultimate step. Our faces are at the same level, and we take advantage of this to kiss for a minute. From the living room I can hear CNN: *The United Nations' chief weapons inspector said today there's no evidence that Saddam Hussein possesses weapons of mass destruction . . .*

When she brings the kissing to a close, I hand her the mail and excuse myself. Bradley has decorated the bathroom with neo-Buddhist iconography, and a stick of incense sits half-ashed in a special wooden tray on the toilet tank. Reaching down to flush I feel the effect of the afternoon's beers for the first time, as though I had to divest myself of their fluid content before the compromising chemical remnant could make itself known.

Maya is in the kitchen, looking at the mail spread out on the table. Roused by my presence she grabs an envelope and pushes out of the room. The timbre of her footsteps changes as she descends the stairs, and then the front door opens. When she returns her hands are empty and flutter at her sides like birds. She goes straight to the sink and washes them and then says, "You ready to go?"

"What was that?" I say, but she just shakes her head and gets her coat.

She walks quickly, despite the twilight crowd, and I am almost dancing to keep up with her. I tell her about my father's pursuit of Bill Fleig, his stupid plan, his recent visit.

"I hadn't seen him in three years," I say. "Apparently he'd spent the whole time eating."

"Did he want money?" she asks.

"Uh—no," I say, trying not to trip over an abandoned VCR. I bet those non sequitur questions are unstoppable when she's interviewing someone. "Where did that come from?"

"That's what typically happens when somebody gets in touch with a relative who recently made eighteen million dollars," she says, dropping a small explosive device into the conversation. "At least according to *Behind the Music.*"

"Ah, so you know about that."

"I'm a reporter, Eric," she says. "I know how to use Google. Why do you think I agreed to go out with you in the first place?"

"He didn't want money," I say. "He wanted me to go work for his dot-com. He tried to start a soda company when I was in high school, I think I told you." In fact I remember exactly what I told her, but I'm trying to chart a course between repeating stories, like a narcissist, and revealing that I remember every word we've ever spoken to each other, like a psychopath. "But so now he's decided that this whole Internet thing is his big moment, although of course he didn't realize it until everyone else had packed up and gone home."

"Do you see yourself as a nervous person?"

"I see myself as a life-support system for feelings of anxiety," I say. "The anxiety is the organism and I'm the habitat."

"Nice point," she says. "I wonder what I'm a habitat for."

"You're a habitat for beauty and wisdom."

"Shut up," she says. "I'm a habitat for you and your bullshit."

"You're a very comfortable habitat."

In the video store we gravitate inexorably to New Releases, examining the cases of movies we'd skim straight past if they were alphabetized under Drama or Comedy. I do not point this out. Picking a movie is inherently a fraught process, necessitating compromise, pregnant with the possibility of resentment.

"Do you want to hear the plot of every party-people movie ever made?" she says, picking up an empty box and running a finger along the spine.

"Every what?"

"The party people are a bunch of people who like to party in a particular way—maybe in a raunchy wet-T-shirt way, or maybe in some culturally specific way like breakdancing or something. And they have a special place, the party place, where they like to party. But the party place is somehow threatened: some anti-party authority figure wants to shut it down, or else a real-estate developer wants to buy it and turn it into something very unparty like a golf course."

"I know this kind of movie."

"So the party people have a *big party* to raise money, and they end up raising enough money to save the party place! The end."

"You are perhaps the perfect woman," I say.

In the morning, when she gets up to dress for work, I test my privileges by staying in her bed. She selects an outfit—heavy wool trousers, frilly white shirt—according to some impenetrable algorithm, standing on tiptoes to get the sweater she wants from a high shelf. Her clothes are flattering to her thin, small body, but they seem to have been chosen to avoid notice: they're a kind of urban professional camouflage. The exception is her cat's-eye glasses, which are a trademark and hence perhaps a different kind of concealment, a distracting detail.

As she scans the room to check for anything she might have forgotten, her eyes land on me and she laughs inexplicably.

"Wanna have lunch at Ajax?" she says, and I have to hide the thrill I feel at being tossed a slice from the hours she owes her employer. We agree on 12:30 and I watch her walk out of the bedroom. *That's my girlfriend,* I think.

After she's gone I embark on a careful and unsatisfying survey of her things. The furniture is from Ikea. The plants are both thriving. No personal photographs are on display. On the bookshelves are canonical works of poststructuralism—*History of Sexuality, Gender Trouble, The Gulf War Did Not Take Place*—with yellow USED stickers on the spines and, in the margins, ballpointed notes that refer to a private set of associations. Everything in this room is part of a hermetic system, like a dictionary of an unfamiliar language: you can look up a word, but all you'll find are more words you don't know. I spot myself in the full-length mirror, standing in a girl's room in my undershorts, examining her copy of *Of Grammatology*, and the exercise suddenly seems ridiculous. I shower, uncertain which products are Maya's and which Bradley's, careful to replace everything properly, then dress and make coffee and sit in the tiny, tidy kitchen with wet hair, reading yesterday's *Chronicle*. This solitary domestic activity makes me feel possessive of the apartment, and when it's time to leave for our lunch date the click of the front door behind me is a small banishment.

In the middle of the café, unmissable, is the familiar mountain of my father, his haunches spilling over the sides of a wooden chair. Across from him is a younger man in rimless glasses, typing into his PowerBook as my dad talks. Maya is two tables over, reading a newspaper. The sight of Maya Marcom and Barry Muller in a single space detonates a little charge of incongruity, like those episodes of *Scooby-Doo* with guest appearances by Don Rickles or Batman.

There's no safe way to get Maya's attention without my dad noticing. To keep him from turning and seeing me I duck onto one of the couches. Peering through the gaps in the crowd I line up a view of Maya, then reach for my cell phone to call her. Her small hand darts into her purse. Watching someone you love when they don't know you're there is always briefly heartbreaking. She answers, and I hear her voice in stereo, digitally clear in my right ear, in my left faint but perceptible amid forty other conversations and the unpleasant background music.

"Don't look around," I tell her. "Meet me out front."

"Gotcha," she says, strangely unsurprised to be drafted into some secretive operation. She folds her paper and shrugs on her overcoat, glancing at the people around her. Then she strides past me and I follow her out into the cold sunshine.

"Sorry about that," I say on the sidewalk. "My dad was in there."

"I knew it!" she says.

"Uh, how?"

"He's hard to miss," she says. "His features kind of look like yours."

"I'm going to kill myself now."

"No, you're not fat, and your eyes are different. But there's a resemblance. God, now I've seen your dad!" She seems happy about this. "So what do you want to do?"

Introducing them is not an option. It's bad enough that she saw him: now she has this nightmare image of what I'm going to look like in twenty-five years, swollen with carbohydrates and self-regard. Meanwhile I will never see her mother and thus will be denied a glimpse through the spyhole that parents open into the past and the future, evidence of your childhood and a preview of your inevitable decline. I carry this unease with me as we head down the block to another restaurant, a frighteningly cheap taqueria. The decor suggests a school cafeteria, and the pervasive smell of disinfectant is paradoxically evocative of filth, but Maya assures me that the enchiladas are fine. Sitting at an uneven table by the big refrigerators, I take a tentative bite—they're good.

"So what if that had been your dad in there instead of mine?" I say.

She peers out from behind her glasses as though we're playing chess and I've overlooked something important: *Are you sure you want to do that?*

"He abused me, sexually," she says. "Starting when I was nine." She stares at me, eyes narrowed, challenging me to disappoint her with some failure of compassion.

This new information requires me to rearrange various ideas and assumptions in its light. I can see her through time, the terrified nine-year-old girl and the fierce, brilliant woman she called into existence to protect her. I had imagined meeting Donald Marcom over dinner, trying to persuade him that my intentions are honorable.

"So you were trapped with him for another nine years," I say. "And your mom wasn't there to protect you."

Her shoulders relax, and the confrontation goes out of her stare: I've passed a test.

"I blocked it out," she says. "I didn't even remember it until I was in college."

She calls her editor and tells him she's doing an interview, and we drive back to her house in silence. I hope I'll be able to do whatever it is I'm supposed to do now. She looks through the windshield and sits very still.

Back inside we hang our coats and take off our shoes. The faint thump of house music signifies that Bradley is at home, and we move carefully to avoid provoking him out into the common space. In her room she leaves the lights off, and the clouds outside the window make everything seem dim and insulated. We lie on her bed in our clothes and as it gets darker she tells me as much as she can.

After her mom dies it's just the two of them. At school she forgets for most of the day that her mother is dead, just as she used to forget that her mother was alive, until at 3:45 she sees her father standing stone-still outside the school gates, surrounded by women. They go home together and he tries to make the foods her mother made, but he does it wrong. As a family they are incomplete, a stool with two legs. He can only make conversation by quizzing her. She learns to speak articulately on any topic.

Her classmates' parents offer to help, and for the next few months Maya is taken to one of their houses most weeknights after school. Every family is different. Some watch TV during dinner and some don't watch until after dinner and the Lehrmans don't even have a TV. Later she will realize that her father was grieving, that while she was playing with Nina Barrick or Jenny Chen or Jenny Goldish he was lying on his bed curled into a ball or sitting on the couch watching TV with his hand in his pants. At the time she didn't think of him as having internal states; she thought of him as being somehow missing, even when he was driving her home or serving her dinner.

She learns that when you say *My mom is dead,* kids say things like *Did your dad kill her?* Grown-ups, on the other hand, usually give you whatever you want. As a teenager she will realize that she has learned to deploy her mother's death to her advantage. She has to train herself to stop.

Starting in the fourth grade, the texture of her memories is different, as though seen from a greater distance. She remembers her teachers, her best friend Christine Dunlap, a class trip to the La Brea Tar Pits, but not much that happened at home. She has a generic memory of her father sitting in the living room, reading a book and watching television at the same time. It's important that he be sufficiently entertained. Did he read with the TV on every night? Just once? Never? She spends a lot of time in her room, where she inhabits a vaguely sketched fantasy world in which she has a dog who speaks to her telepathically and accompanies her on adventures. As an adult she sometimes remembers the dog as though it were a real pet. She knows that she didn't just gradually outgrow the fantasy; it ended with some specific event. She can't think of this without a pang of guilt, and she suspects that she must have killed the dog.

Every morning before work her father goes outside and swims one hundred laps. Every evening he prepares dinner, which is eaten at eight. Alcohol is involved. At dinner he introduces topics for discussion: *What grounds are there for believing in God? Would it be ethical to genetically engineer children for high intelligence?* She'll improvise an answer, and he'll probe her to determine whether her thinking is sufficiently rigorous. She remembers being thirteen and wrestling with *What is art?* and realizing, with a burst of angry exhilaration, that he'll challenge her no matter how she answers.

Around that time he starts to ask her about boys—whether she has an interest in any of the boys in her class, whether she's acted on that interest. He asks in the same spirit of intense but clinical scrutiny with which he might ask *Should drugs be legalized?* It doesn't register as prurient. The discomfort she feels at this new line of questioning is continuous with the discomfort she feels when he's interrogating her in the usual way. Despite the discomfort she answers straightforwardly. There's not much to tell anyway. Soon, though, she begins dating, and there are things she doesn't want him to know, and she's in a difficult position: she has allowed a precedent to be established in which she answers his questions. She lies to him and confuses her desire for privacy with shame.

Once or twice a year Donald goes to New York to attend auctions, keep up with clients, comb the antique stores for pieces that might be misattributed or undervalued. After Maya turns sixteen and can drive herself to school, she stays by herself in the big ranch house up the canyon road. These weeks are accompanied by a relief so intense it's frightening. She occupies as many rooms as she can—lying on the living-room couch with a book until early in the morning, leaving her used dishes on the kitchen table. The time always passes in a rush, as though she were gulping it down.

Her first semester at Ward College, her father flies up to Concord after his New York trip to take Maya and her roommate Emily out to dinner. He's in a good mood, and she assumes that he's bought something from someone who didn't know what it was, or sold something for more than it's worth. They order in French, except for

Emily, and drink red wine, and when she and Emily get back to the dorm her head is dragging with exhaustion—from the wine, and from the effort of finding things to say that her father will deem interesting or clever or sufficiently justified. He might have been a trial lawyer: he's one of those men who think the truth of a proposition can be measured by the force of the arguments marshaled on its behalf. In the restaurant, in front of her roommate, she had tried to transmute the first heady months of freshman year into something her father might accept as dinner-table conversation, to turn her wild new discoveries—that she's still smarter than her peers, that she carries her anxiety with her no matter how far she gets from home—into something more than assertion and anecdote. Back in her dorm room she looks around at the institutional furniture and the anthropology textbooks and the other props and accessories of her life and feels as though she has betrayed them.

At dinner Emily had told a story about a party they had attended that was broken up by the police. Donald had listened and nodded and given every sign of enjoying the story, and Maya knew he was thinking, *Well, this girl is a worthless idiot.* After Emily finished, he had directed a conspiratorial smile at Maya, and she'd had no choice but to smile back. Lying on her bed afterward she remembers her father's look and her stomach wells up. She runs down the hall to the bathroom and vomits into the toilet, shaking. He has never punished her, as far as she can remember. Only rarely has he raised his voice. But she is scared of him.

She hurries back to her room, stepping over the hippies who have turned the hallway into their common space. Inside, she locks the door. Emily is studying with her headphones on. Maya sits on her bed and starts to sob. She knows that if Emily hears her crying she'll be in trouble, but she can't stop. Finally, in the gap between two songs, Emily hears. She takes the headphones off and asks Maya what's wrong. Maya can't tell her. She sits on her bed, shaking and sobbing, afraid that Emily is going to call Donald and tell him to come and take Maya away. She knows she's behaving strangely, but the experience feels self-explanatory.

Emily, whose parents write her long letters every week and frequently send baked goods or seasonally themed candy, doesn't know what to make of Maya's crying. Over their first two months at Ward they have affiliated themselves with different groups, but they still go to each other for sympathy. Now Emily is frightened by Maya's unresponsiveness. She goes down the hall to Joyce and Melanie's room, where she tells Melanie about the drama and asks her for counsel. They form an urgent little klatch, describing Maya's breakdown to visitors in tones of deep respect.

Maya lies on her bed. She's still afraid of her father, and she wonders why. He has never done anything to harm her. This is her story, as she has told it to herself since she became old enough to tell her own story: her mother died and left her with a father who was unable to meet her need for affection, and her personality has formed around the ambition to be smart and tough enough to win his love. But that doesn't explain the fear. Tonight he had told her he missed her, and charmed her the way he sometimes chose to, especially in front of other people, telling little jokes and asking gently skeptical questions and savoring her answers. For some reason she thinks of her mother's jewelry, which her father had given to her all at once on her sixteenth birthday. Most of it is back in Los Angeles; she brought only her favorite pieces to college. She wants to drop them down a storm drain.

Then a sudden flash of something terrible, something much worse than the fear. The feeling takes her over for a second, two, and then passes. This is what the fear has been pointing toward all this time. She lies on her bed. The feeling seems unconnected to anything in her mind. Except this: when her friends started talking about masturbation, she didn't admit it, but she knew she would never, ever do that.

And she's smart enough, she's read enough books, and she knows: this is what happens to people who've been abused. It seems incongruous, a category she's never imagined occupying, but she tries it on. *Abuse:* she turns the word over in her mind like a stone. *Does this belong to me?*

Every night she wakes in a panic — sweaty, heart pounding, the sheet clenched in her fist. In the daytime she feels as if she has to relearn every social tactic. She develops an odd mannerism: a little pause after someone directs a question or a remark to her, in which she calculates the appropriate response.

She has never seen a therapist; she was brought up to feel a mild contempt for people who did. Her father went to a Freudian analyst in the 1960s and came away from the experience eight thousand dollars poorer and more deeply embedded than ever in his own personality. "It's a trap," he says whenever the subject comes up. "Why would they want you to get better? They have a vested interest in uncovering more and more problems, so you'll keep coming back." This is the opinion of therapy that Maya has filed away as her own, until Lauren, in her capacity as WPC for Maya's floor, tells her about the psychotherapy and counseling services available free and in confidence from Student Health Services.

She fears that the therapist will work in an office decorated with sentimental kitsch — teddy bears, inspirational posters — and will try to hug her therapeutically. These concerns are put to rest the moment the therapist fetches her from the waiting room. A middle-aged woman with a severe black bob, a knee-length leather skirt, and high boots, she suggests a professional dominatrix more than a mother substitute. Maya has been steeling herself for their session since she made the appointment nine days ago. She hopes she'll be strong enough to recall and confront her past in its horrifying glory, to replace her nebulous feelings with clarity — where she was, how old she was, what he did. Abreaction, catharsis: if she can remember, she won't have to keep reliving the feelings. She has imagined the shrink urging her to force the memories into consciousness, like a physiotherapist exhorting a quadriplegic to push his atrophied muscles back into service.

It's not like that. The therapist asks why she's there, and Maya finds herself unable to answer. She sits in silence, staring at the shiny leather of the therapist's boots for three or four minutes, before she can find a way to speak.

She gets it out by telling it as a story rather than a fact: *We went out to dinner, and I came back and threw up, and this feeling came over me, and ever since I wake up in terror every night, and here's what I think it means.* The therapist doesn't encourage her to remember anything, just asks about her relationship with her father. Maya tells her, and things seem sinister that until now had only seemed sad. The therapist makes notes on a yellow legal pad that she holds on her knee in landscape orientation, writing across the lines. The end of the session comes more quickly than Maya had expected, at which point the therapist suggests that they meet once a week.

Over the next semester Maya and the therapist become friends. The therapist likes Maya and thinks she's clever: she laughs when Maya says something self-deprecating or amusingly honest, and she occasionally allows her own wit and warmth to break through her professional reserve. She doesn't push Maya to talk about anything in particular. They spend one early session talking about Maya's frustration with her history professor, a self-important fool, and as Maya walks out of the Health Services Annex toward the library she realizes that they didn't mention her father at all. Two weeks later, after a difficult night in which panic woke her twice, she finds herself describing her experience more vividly than she has managed before.

"It goes beyond emotions," she tells the therapist. "It's a physical feeling—not like someone touching you, nothing concrete, but...it's not in the senses, it's in the body. It's like—in high school they thought I had appendicitis and I had to get a CT scan. You know how before you get scanned they make you drink those chemicals to make your organs show up? And they say *strawberry flavor* or whatever, and you tell yourself it's a milkshake, but as soon as you taste it you know it's not a milkshake, it's not even food, it's something that *does not belong in your body.* You have to force yourself to drink it, not because it tastes bad, exactly, but because your body doesn't want it, and you have to overcome your body's deep, deep resistance to drinking it. God, I can taste it now, and it's been three years. Anyway: that's what this feeling is like, times a thousand. Like your body is stating as clearly as it possibly can that what's happening is not right."

The therapist has been sitting absolutely still, as though to avoid disturbing a grazing deer. She waits a few seconds more, to be sure Maya has finished talking, and then asks, "Are there any thoughts that accompany the feeling?"

"When it first happened, there weren't any thoughts," Maya says. "Except maybe *No, no, no.*" She and the therapist smile sadly at one another. "But now I usually think about my dad. Nothing specific, just thinking about him. I don't know if he's in my mind or if I'm, like, trying to think of him." The therapist nods.

At the following session, Maya tells the therapist about her sexual history, which now spans three years and seems to her a complex narrative with developments and reversals and surprises. She's clever and tough, and boys have always liked her. The boys she likes are the ones who don't have a clear place in the social hierarchy, not at the top and not in the middle striving for the top, but off to one side. She tends to break their hearts. She feels sorry for them when this happens, but there's something she likes about the naked emotion, the pleading and seriousness. It feels sad in a way she might call *realistic.* And she enjoys the power, the boy swept up in his passion for her while she vacillates and searches her feelings and remains unmoved. She also enjoys sex. From the beginning, or what seemed to her the beginning — sixteen years old, Jeff Keyhoe, in his room — she was adept at it, confident, confrontational. One thing bothers her: intermittently she'll find that she's not really present; the sex is going on and she's missing it. Once, with Jake Sohnfeld, an orgasm returned her to herself and she realized she had no memory of turning over onto her back.

The therapist refers to this as *dissociation*. "How often does this dissociation happen?" Not often, but more than Maya would like. "Is it frightening?" Not frightening so much as saddening, like she's being deprived of something. "Does it seem to you as though it's connected to the abuse?" It's the first time she has referred to *the abuse,* and it feels right, like snapping together the tongue and buckle of a seatbelt.

Maya arranges to stay with Emily's family in Boston over Christmas break. She presents it to her father as a fait accompli. He objects mildly.

In their second session after the vacation, the therapist gently asks Maya if any memories of the abuse are coming into focus. Maya is silent, examining the knotted strings at the edge of the rug on the floor of the therapist's office. Then she says that, yes, certain images and ideas have lately come into her mind, along with sensations more specifically located in her body. The therapist carefully asks her if she feels she can describe any of these memories, and Maya does so: the feeling of her father's large hand between her legs, and of his smooth chest pressed against her face. After this session she goes to the library to research a paper on Max Weber and bureaucracy, then returns to her dorm and cries.

As the summer break approaches, Maya makes arrangements to join a group of students on a volunteer trip to Gaza, where they build homes alongside a crew of Israelis and Palestinians. The trip keeps her away from Los Angeles for all but a week, during which she stays with a high school friend. She sees her father for a single lunch, at a restaurant. During the meal she describes things she saw in the Middle East, things that didn't matter to her; she offers sketches of her professors, making them sound pompous and stupid in a way she knows her father will appreciate. As she listens to herself speaking, a valedictory feeling comes over her, and she knows she will never see her father again. Back at school sophomore year, describing the conversation to her therapist, she realizes that she remembers almost nothing her father said.

New memories emerge, escalating in clarity as though titrated according to how much she can tolerate. She has replaced her life story with a new one: a tragic childhood, a long adolescence of denial, and now the first steps into maturity and self-knowledge. Eventually the therapist asks her if she has considered confronting her father with what she believes.

Five days after she mails the letter, her father calls. She sits on her bed with Emily, still her roommate, as they listen to his voice on the answering machine, alternately begging and commanding her to call him back. In his fifth message he threatens to fly out to Concord to get her away from whatever has brainwashed her. After that she sees him everywhere—outside her dorm at night, in the crowd at a lecture, at the other end of the cafeteria. She avoids walking alone.

Whenever she sees his handwriting on an envelope in her campus mailbox, she drops it unopened into the recycling with the catalogues and the varsity sports schedules. He sends one with a printed address, to trick her. Inside are two articles about "false memory syndrome." *My daughter was brainwashed by a feminist cult!* She starts checking the postmarks on her mail.

She wonders if he'll cut off her tuition. She almost wants him to: she can't bear that her existence here—her presence in classes, the food she eats at the refectory, the room she shares with Emily—is dependent on him. Her therapist offers to help her declare herself independent of her father so she can negotiate financial aid. She finishes college on scholarships, loans, and a work-study job manning a cash register at the college bookstore. She tells the bursar's office to tear up her father's checks, although she suspects that he keeps sending them and they keep cashing them.

The panic attacks diminish in frequency and intensity. For much of her junior year she takes every opportunity to talk about the abuse, and about the epidemic of child abuse in America, and the connection between the silence surrounding that epidemic and society's attitude toward women in general. It thrills her, for a while, to force her past into people's faces like a gun. But by graduation it has started to feel juvenile, and to remind her of the way she used to provoke people by mentioning her mother's death. She stops talking about it so much, so loudly, although she doesn't deny it. She particularly dislikes talking about it with boyfriends. She wants to keep her whole dark childhood as far as possible from her sunlit sex life; she finds that telling drains the simplicity from sex, which is a loss for her and a victory for the feelings she considers her enemy. She never gets comfortable with the word *survivor*, the term of art used in books and on message boards and by the Berkeley therapist she briefly sees after her move to San Francisco: it seems too obviously to have been chosen as a substitute for *victim*, as though you could absolve yourself of victimhood by refusing the word.

By now she hasn't spoken to her father in more than five years. From her aunt she has heard that he is remarried, to a younger woman.

I don't know much about the recovered-memory debate of the 1990s, and what little I have gleaned from magazines does not come to mind as we lie beneath her comforter in the afternoon light and talk, occasionally giving each other reassuring little strokes and squeezes. Much later I will read Susan L. Reviere's scrupulously evenhanded survey *Memory of Childhood Trauma: A Clinician's Guide to the Literature,* with its assertion that "no particular attributes of a given memory can be used to determine its veracity, and the ability of even professionals to make such distinctions is demonstrably poor." But I am in love with Maya, and her command over her autobiography is near total, and she evinces no doubts about what has happened to her, and neither do I.

We lie on her bed and kiss gently. She squirms against me in an unfamiliar way, and it's clear that things are different. The first time you have sex with someone it's all about mirroring. When she introduces a particular kind of tenderness or friendliness or roughness, you respond in kind. With enough calculations per second you can generate the impression of spontaneous compatibility, the way a grid of tiny pixels becomes a photograph. (If you pick up on certain types of passivity or submissiveness from her, obviously, you want to put an inverter in the signal path so that your response is complementary rather than imitative.) But this abuse thing changes the equation. Is it possible that by some defensive maneuver she transmutes her awful history into pleasure? If so, is that a triumph or a capitulation? It's a lot to factor in. Any sudden moves and the memories she's been blocking for so long could come rushing back. My hand is on her ass now, a great ass, everything I'd hoped it would be. I want to stop and ask her about the abuse thing and how I should be factoring it in, but she seems like she's doing fine. It would be weird for me to be the one to freak out. Plus she'd probably feel stigmatized. She's kissing the underside of my chin. She doesn't seem like a person who's about to have a breakdown. Maybe that's exactly the kind of person who's the closest to a breakdown. Maybe she's brittle. My hand is under the back of her shirt, and the natural thing would be to undo the clasp of her bra. Is that too rapist? Is there a way to manifest male desire that doesn't, in the wrong light, look like brutality? I move to stick my tongue in her ear; that can work wonders. Unless her dad used to wake her up that way or something. In which case I'll just have to apologize.

She's unbuttoning my shirt. This is a crucial bit of data. I start unbuttoning hers, and then her bra is off, and I run my hand over her breasts, which are small and pretty, and all I can see is her father doing the same thing, and he's so much bigger than her, and he probably loves her, but he loves her the wrong way. And she's kicking off her jeans with this gorgeous little writhe of her hips. She's beautiful. I want to keep her safe. Our chests are pressed up against each other and the contact feels strange and intense, the way it always does the first time and then never does again. She's reaching down and undoing my pants, and everything's starting to speed up, and now we're fucking, and in my head I am me and her dad and her nine-year-old self all at once. It's awful. Fortunately, she can't tell, and she seems to enjoy it.

I'm roused by the throbbing and rattling of my cell phone on the nightstand. Maya doesn't move, but I don't know if she's a deep sleeper or if she's strategically pretending. The phone's screen says MOM. The words *I love you, Mom* did not enter my head once last night. I answer the phone and slip out into the living room in my underwear. When I get there, my mom is already talking.

"Come home for my birthday, Eric," she says. "I need you here. I'm lonely, and it isn't working out with Wade." The sound carries in here, so my end of the conversation consists largely of murmured *Mmm*s and *Uh-huh*s. "It's not like my standards are so unrealistically high. I've given up on looks entirely at this point. I'll go on a date with the ones who don't put a photo up on the website, that's how ready I am to settle. But Wade—in his first email he said he runs his own business, doing digital photo printing or something. Turns out he makes fake IDs for the kids at the high school. A real prize, I'll tell you. It's going to take me forever to get my profile back up there again! You remember, we spent hours on that profile, making sure all the descriptions of me were good."

I do remember this project, as you'd remember a severe bout of food poisoning. "You didn't just deactivate it?" I say, leaping, as I so often do with my mom, to the single least important point. "You actually deleted it?"

"Eric, I'm forty-nine years old," she says. "I don't know the difference. And plus, yes, I deleted it. That was the arrangement Wade and I had, to take down our profiles. And now my birthday is coming up, and he's not going to be there, so it's going to be just Stacey and Victoria from work, and I told Stacey you were coming."

I do something that is either stalling or acquiescing and get off the phone. Maya, sprawled like a starfish across the center left of the bed, doesn't stir. I slide in next to her and lie awake for a long time, until eventually I find myself at a party whose guest list comprises me and two dozen naked women. The room is small, and we are dancing in close proximity, and while dancing the women rub against me and against one another.

We cut to a businessman in a limousine. The businessman is hungry: he requests some hamburgers, which appear on his lap in a McDonald's bag. A disembodied voice sings the McDonald's jingle, "You Deserve a Break Today." I am annoyed that the party has been interrupted by advertising, but even asleep I am aware that the dream's lavish production values—all those naked women!—have to be subsidized somehow.

# 6

What makes a good hack is the observation that you can do without something that everybody else thinks you need.

—Joel Spolsky, interview in *Founders at Work*

MR. NAYLOR HELD UP a test tube containing a vivid blue solution of copper sulfate. I leaned toward Danny Keach, sitting to my right, and in a low parody of Naylor's orotund Southern voice said, "I've filled this test tube with a sample of my urine." Halfway through the sentence I became terrified that Danny would think I meant that it was *my* urine. But he laughed hard enough to cause a small disturbance—he was an enthusiastic laugher—and I had my first experience of social triumph since Tara Pulowski confessed her woes to me two years earlier.

I wouldn't have had the courage to attempt such a joke until recently. By the middle of junior year a self-conscious maturity had begun to settle on the class of 1996, and my classmates had begun to treat me with neglect rather than contempt. We aspired to adulthood now, and outright cruelty usually sounded juvenile. My ninth-grade notebook was mentioned rarely, almost nostalgically, as though anything that had happened a full two years ago was the work of a younger self for whom I couldn't be held accountable. Who knows by what social contagion, what hormonal surge or slump, these transformations happen?

At the end of class I wandered alongside Danny as he met his friends Cindy and Paul at a water fountain on the second floor. As far as I could tell they hadn't expressly planned to meet, but their habits had grown entwined around one another's, and they tended to intersect at certain interstitial points in the day. We all continued down the hall to the student lounge, and I waited for one of them to say, *Uh, are you going somewhere, or are you just following us?* but it didn't happen. Cindy even interrupted a story about her English teacher's idiocy to fill in the background for me, an accommodation for which I was pathetically grateful.

The student lounge comprised some beat-up furniture in the stump of a hallway, as though someone had said, *Let's just dump it all there and call it the student lounge.* By custom it was reserved for juniors and seniors, but the seniors had off-campus privileges and hung out at Carl's Jr. Danny and Cindy and Paul took the couch, Cindy on Danny's lap. I was perched on one arm of the armchair, trying to look comfortable. The three of them were in the broad middle of MLK's social hierarchy, neither popular nor picked on, and the idea of spending a free period with them would not long ago have seemed as realistic as playing professional basketball.

"The platypus is the coolest animal in the world," Paul was saying. "Because it doesn't fit into all the, you know, the *categories.*" Paul had a long, narrow face on which he wore wire-rimmed glasses that made him look prematurely serious.

"What are you talking about?" Cindy asked him.

"You know, it's like, it's not a mammal—" Paul began.

"There's a million things that aren't mammals," Danny said. "Birds aren't mammals. You're not talking about how birds are so rad." I wasn't sure if Danny was being serious or if he just couldn't be bothered to sit through an explanation.

"I know what you mean," I said to Paul. Everyone ignored me.

"I'm not a mammal," Danny said. "Am I the coolest of all the animals?"

"Are too a mammal," said Cindy, reaching up to tweak his nipple through his T-shirt, making him cry out. Cindy was Danny's girl-friend. She was less pretty than he was — her smiley features seemed lost in her chubby face — but she wore jeans and sneakers every day, and she never wanted to do anything besides hang out with Danny and his best friend. I had noted these qualities abstractly: having a girlfriend of my own seemed a ludicrous ambition. You need friends to get a girlfriend, especially in high school, where everyone's social life is on display.

"Cindy loves to pinch my nipples," Danny said a bit too loudly, grabbing her wrists to prevent her from doing it again.

"Ow!" Cindy said happily. "Let me go!"

And then I heard a deep voice call my name, and Bill Fleig walked up to me — to us — and said, as if it were a point of general interest, "We're getting the Amiga that used to be in the principal's secretary's office."

I'd known he would wonder why I wasn't in the computer room, but I hadn't expected him to come looking for me, in violation of the implicit parameters of our relationship. But here he was, talking about the computer from the secretary's office, which was apparently going to be moved into the basement lab as the secretary upgraded. This was good news, but it could have waited.

"That's cool," I said, trying to sound polite rather than interested.

"It should be set up this week," Bill said, "if her new Deskpro arrives on time."

Danny and the others were watching blankly from the couch. I wanted to send Bill some kind of signal, something that would convey *Can we please not geek out in public?*, but Bill was deaf to signals. I considered saying *What's it like to be such a loser, Bill?* but that would have been counterproductive as well as cruel: being a jerk was out of fashion. What I needed was a tone of polite, dismissive condescension. It might be the only time in my life when I've consciously looked to my father as a role model.

"Hey, great!" I said vaguely, as though unsure what I was responding to. "That's real exciting for you, huh?"

Bill looked confused. "I told you it might be happening, remember?" he said.

"Sure!" I said. It was what my dad said to enact a general mood of agreement without actually agreeing to anything. "I'll have to come down and check it out."

Bill looked at me for a long time without any particular expression. Then he gave me a little nod that meant goodbye, turned, and walked away, and I felt seasick from the mixture of guilt and triumph.

I was filling out the Stanford application at my dad's kitchen table, wondering what I could list as extracurricular interests besides computer programming and getting a girlfriend. It was hard to concentrate with Dad yelling into the phone. "I don't give a crap about the controller chip!" he shouted. "You said the prototype would be done in March, and now it's practically June, and you're coming to me with this garbage about a controller chip!"

He put down the phone and looked over at me. "This guy told me he knew what he was doing," he said in his familiar wounded tone. Then his voice firmed up. "Sometimes you have to let people know who's boss, you know what I mean?"

"Sure, Dad," I said.

"It looks like we're going to have to postpone the launch," he said. It had already been pushed back twice. "There's some snags on the road, you come to expect that in business. Especially when you're doing something nobody's ever done before."

"Yeah," I said.

"It's really going to be something," he said. "The problem we're running into here is, well, it's the design of the machines. You've got to have six flavors in each machine, right, to give people the choice."

He counted them off on his fingers: "Cola, diet, lemon-lime, orange, root beer, and prune. That's like Dr Pepper, but ours is going to be called Mr. Popper. So you've got to put in a computer chip, where you push a button and tell it what flavor you want and the chip controls which flavor syrup gets pumped in. How about that? A computer in a soda machine!" I indicated that I had heard of such things. "So the guy who's building the machine, he said he could get it done in about six weeks. But now there's some kind of shortage of these chips, and he's telling me there's no way to get any more until the end of the summer, and so we're stuck with this great idea, and cases and cases of syrup and carbon, just sitting in this guy's warehouse, and there's no way to get the machines into the stores until the fall. This could be a very nice payday for everyone if these guys weren't so incompetent!"

"Yeah," I said. Spread out in front of me on the table were my mom's last few tax returns. She'd given them to me so that I could copy the figures onto the financial-disclosure form. Looking at the documents felt a bit too intimate, like seeing her undressed. I copied the numbers carefully with a fountain pen, and then moved on to the next section of the form.

"Dad, how much money did you make in fiscal '91–'92?" I said.

He craned his neck to see the forms. "What do they need to know that for?" he asked.

"They need to know, Dad," I said. "It's for, like, financial aid and whatever."

"See, the thing is," he said, "your income changes from year to year." He went over to the stove and began filling a pot with water. "That's how it is with entrepreneurialism—one year you might not make anything, and then the next year you're going to make a whole lot, to make up for it."

I said, "I have to send the forms in a couple weeks if I want to apply early decision."

"Why don't you call them?" he said, striking a match to turn on the burner. "Call the admissions office and say you don't think it's fair that your parents should have to disclose their whole financial lives. Start a consumer protest! If enough people complain, they'll have to change the policy."

"But no one is complaining, Dad," I said. "The only person who's complaining is you."

"Well, and I'm the one who's going to be footing the bills, aren't I?" he said, turning to face me. "Look, Eric, it's like this: Right now I don't have any money apart from my salary from the college. Of course, there's going to be a bunch of money soon, when we get the machines into the stores. But when you apply to these schools, they're going to think, *OK, teaches college, makes a good salary—let's touch him for everything he's got.* Look, it's not that I'm not willing to pay for your education—nothing's more important than education, I've always said that—but if they make me pay for it right now, there won't be enough left for the business." He lifted the lid off the pot, but the water wasn't boiling yet. "So just leave my name off entirely. Where they have a space for *father,* write *N/A.* That stands for *not applicable.* Just write that." He reached into the cabinet for the spaghetti.

Cindy was at home with a cold, and Paul was in class, and Danny was in an expansive mood. "Do you have a free period?" he said when I ran into him in the hall. I told him I did, although this was not true. "Because I want to get out of here," he said. "I can't deal with being cooped up in this place, you know?"

"Where can we go?" I asked. It was a freezing Thursday afternoon.

"Anywhere, dude," he said, sweeping his arm to take in the great world around us. "Let's hit the road!"

"Yeah, man!" he said as we left the school building. "We're out of there! Later, losers!" He was carefully looking straight ahead, and his breath was visible in the air. "We spend all our lives in these boxes, right? They want us to fuckin' stay in that box until we're eighteen so we can graduate and go straight into another box and spend the rest of our lives there!" He said this with no malice, only excitement at the break we'd made.

There was no one in Carl's Jr. except four senior girls who ignored us and an old guy with a cup of coffee and packets of sugar all over the table. We ordered combo meals and piled our puffy coats and wool hats next to us on the plastic seats.

"It's like, they're just training us for some stupid office job anyway," he said. He was the only one of us with even a slight claim to coolness, deriving from his wide, satisfied face and a voice that always gave the impression of minimal effort. "I mean, what do they teach us? They should be teaching us to be, like, *poets* or something. If the schools taught everyone to be a poet or a musician or something instead of, like, an *accountant,* the world would be a whole different place." I nodded dumbly. "But maybe not everyone's got it in them to be a poet," he said, retreating a little.

"Yeah," I said, "but they should at least have the opportunity."

"That's right!" Danny said, raising his Coke as if to toast me. "It should be like, *OK, it turns out you can't be a poet, you can't be a painter, you can't be a, a whatever—you're going to have to drop out and be an accountant.* And the poets should get paid ten times as much as the accountants, instead of the other way around."

I was getting it now. "And if your kid said he wanted to be an accountant, you'd say, *Where did your mother and I go wrong?*"

"Exactly!" Danny said, slamming his drink down on the table. "That's exactly right."

I met Hannah Pronovost two days before her father died, which was a huge stroke of luck. She and Cindy had been at school together until ninth grade, when Hannah had started at Danville Academy and Cindy had come to MLK. Now Hannah's father was fighting a hopeless battle with a vindictive tumor, and Cindy was going over to their house every night to keep Hannah company. She had started carrying herself with the special dignified glamour that teenagers acquire when they make contact with something important and grown-up. We didn't see her much outside of school anymore.

"This is so stupid," Danny said. We were sitting in his bedroom waiting for *Saturday Night Live*. "It's like, we could be in the country, communing with nature or whatever, or we could be in the city where there's things going on—but no, either of those are too dangerous, so we live in fucking Aurora." It was only he and Paul who lived in Aurora, but I wasn't going to point that out.

"But your kids can play outside because it's *safe*," Paul said contemptuously.

"Yeah, OK, but in exchange for safety you're stopping them from having any kind of real experience!" Danny said. "It's like, if you're really going to live, you can't just be safe every minute of your life."

"No, right, I know," Paul said, embarrassed that Danny had missed his sarcasm.

"I'd be happy if I could see my girlfriend occasionally," Danny said. "It sounds really bad over there."

"Bad like how?" I asked.

"Well, he's *dying*," Danny said. "I mean, imagine if, like, any time you saw your dad, that might be the last time you were ever going to talk to him."

"Wow," Paul said. He was sitting in a beanbag chair on the floor, and he tipped his head all the way back onto the carpet and looked up at the ceiling. "When you think about it, death is, like, the worst thing out there."

"Maybe I should call her," Danny said at last. Calling Cindy at Hannah's house was discouraged—it risked intruding on the family's grief. But he found the number in his wallet, then picked up the phone—he had his own line—and dialed. Paul and I heard the tiny ringing sound from the receiver's earpiece.

"Um, hi," he said. "Is Cindy Gerney there?" He sounded embarrassed. I had expected him to say something to acknowledge the situation, some kind of condolence, but I wasn't sure how you'd do that with people you didn't know.

When Cindy came on, Danny spoke gently, as though it was she who was sick. "Do you guys want, like, cheering up or whatever?" he said. "I thought we could come over, bring a movie or some KFC or something. To take her mind off it."

After a minute more he put down the phone and said, "So we're going over there," like a platoon commander announcing a dangerous sortie.

Paul had a driver's license and a Honda Civic that seemed too small for his long frame. The back seat was shallow and cramped, but I didn't mind. There are few ways to feel more fully included than getting into a car at night, bound for an unfamiliar destination, charged with purpose.

On the way we talked about how to respond if Hannah's mother answered the door. "Don't mention it," Danny advised. "Be serious and everything, don't be all joking around, but don't be like, *Oh, I'm sorry your husband is about to die.* Nobody wants to hear that."

"Fuck," said Paul with a thrilled shudder.

But it was Cindy and Hannah who let us in. Danny embraced Cindy, then adjusted his features into a somber expression and said, "Hi, Hannah," in a doleful voice.

"We've got to be quiet up here!" she said in a whisper. She was short and had buggy eyes and a ponytail.

The front hall was huge and unlit, although it wasn't even ten. The girls led us through the dark kitchen and down into the basement, which was bright and carpeted and which gave the impression of having once been a playroom for an adult male. There was a wet bar and a pool table and a big TV, plus cases on the wall that might have held rifles, but upon this manly foundation there had accumulated a decade's worth of aerobics videos and *Sweet Valley High* novels and Strawberry Shortcake paraphernalia, and now the room felt like an archaeological dig, with the stratified remains of multiple civilizations piled on top of one another.

"Sorry," said Hannah, shifting from foot to foot. She didn't have shoes on, just white tube socks. "We can't make too much noise upstairs."

"This is an awesome basement," I said.

She smiled nervously. "We've got a pinball machine," she said. She opened a door to reveal the laundry room, where a machine with a Flash Gordon theme stood alongside the washer and dryer.

"Does Danny still have the high score?" Cindy asked.

"I think my cousin beat it," Hannah said apologetically.

"That's going to change this evening," Danny said, making Hannah smile. I admired the way he could use his narcissism to reassure her.

Danny turned on MTV and cranked the volume until Cindy made him turn it down. Then Paul set up the balls on the pool table while Danny took the first turn on the pinball machine. In the fridge by the wet bar there was 7 Up and that Hansen's fruit soda that no one ever drinks. We wandered around the room picking things up and putting them down again, looking for subjects to distract us from the dying man upstairs.

"So is this where you guys used to play Princess Land?" Danny asked. Cindy laughed.

"What's this?" I said.

"Oh, it was this game we had when we were little," Hannah said. "We just—we made up this pretend world. It was really dumb."

"We were both princesses," said Cindy, who didn't seem

embarrassed. "I was Princess Gloriana and she was Princess Paladine, and we ruled over the whole kingdom."

"Wouldn't the king have ruled over it, if it was a kingdom?" I asked.

Cindy rolled her eyes. "We weren't going for realisticness," she said. "We were going for being princesses."

"I can't believe you told them about that," Hannah said.

"The other thing I used to pretend is, I wanted to be a mermaid," Cindy said. "I'd pray that God would turn me into a mermaid in the night. But I was always worried that he would, and then I wouldn't be able to breathe outside the water and I'd die."

Danny shook his head at her tenderly. "You're such a freak," he said.

The two of them went to play pinball, and without Danny to steer the conversation there was a lull. Paul suggested a game of pool, and something about the too-casual way he raised the possibility indicated that he was good at pool. "You guys play, I'll watch," Hannah said. "I don't play pool."

My own billiards skills were untested. I hoped that my first game would reveal a natural aptitude, but whatever advantage my understanding of geometry and physics conferred was outweighed by my clumsiness. When Paul sank something he gave a tight-lipped little grunt of satisfaction and glanced over at Hannah, who perched on the back of the couch, legs dangling.

How should one act when one is losing? As my first shots sped off at errant angles I said "Damn!" and "Eucchh," as though I was playing below my usual skill level. After ten minutes of consistent failure, though, it was hard to sustain the pretense of disappointment. When the red I was trying to sink caromed off the cushion and tipped Paul's green stripe into a corner pocket I said, "All right!" as though I'd just done something of great skill. Hannah smiled.

My assist meant Paul was down to the eight ball. He tapped the far pocket with his stick to call it. After he made the shot he said, "And *that's* how the game is played."

I turned to Hannah. "Here's what he doesn't realize," I said, nodding slyly at Paul. "That game was just the first step in an elaborate hustle."

"So does that mean you want to put down the big money now?" Paul said.

I gave Hannah a dramatic wink, as though this was all part of my plan, and as I did I understood that this was how to wink at a girl: you make a joke of it; it still counts. "Not money," I said. "We're going to play for something more valuable than money—honor!" I wasn't sure what I was talking about, but I was going to keep driving forward until I went off the road or hit a tree. "I'm going to hustle him out of his honor!" I said, and Hannah laughed, and an unfamiliar kind of power made my knees buckle.

Paul saw what was happening, I think, but there wasn't much he could do about it. He racked up the balls and broke again, and sank two on his first turn. I made an elaborate show of chalking my cue, then sent the cue ball off the blue into a side pocket. Leaning over the table I looked up at Hannah and said, "He has no idea what's coming."

Paul cleared the table as efficiently as he could. "So hand over your honor," he said, and I said, "Oh, foul dishonor!" and did a little tearing-at-my-breast routine.

Danny and Cindy had emerged from the laundry room and were examining the videotapes in the cabinet under the TV. "What's good in here?" Danny asked. The collection was heavy on westerns and war films, all home-recorded, with handwritten labels identifying the movie by title and year of release. I thought of her father dying and his movies sitting here unwatched.

Hannah made an apologetic face. "We've got *Splash*," she said.

The couch only fit four, and there was a little unspoken drama about seating arrangements. Cindy and Hannah went for the floor, in one of those self-sacrifice contests girls get into when there are boys around, and Cindy won by perching between Danny's legs. So Hannah and Paul and I had to arrange ourselves. After some wordless three-way strategizing Hannah wound up between us.

Ten minutes into the movie, Paul actually did the thing where you pretend to yawn and then lower your arm onto the couch behind the girl. I had seen people do this as a joke, and I was astonished that he would be so bold and ignorant as to try it for real. Hannah didn't flinch, but a minute later she leaned forward and cupped her chin in her hands, her elbows on her knees, leaving Paul's arm lying uselessly on the back of the couch. After a reasonable interval, he withdrew it.

Halfway through the movie we heard the door open at the top of the stairs, and a straggly-haired silhouette in a dressing gown appeared. I felt Hannah tense up. "Hannah, it's time for your friends to leave," her mother said.

"Oh, God, I'm really sorry," Hannah said to us. She walked us to the top of the stairs and hugged each of us in turn. I knew that something more was required, something that would cement whatever bond existed between us, and so I brushed my fingers against the side of her neck, and she gripped my forearm and squeezed.

And then the four of us were cramming into the car, Cindy and I in the back seat. I hated forcing everyone to make a detour, but it was past midnight and there was no other way for me to get to Sheridan. As a nondriver I could only calculate routes that took in familiar landmarks like school or my dad's apartment, so we spent forty-five minutes rolling through empty streets until we came to the body shops and strip-mall restaurants of my neighborhood. Driving through the darkness we nursed a mood of grown-up seriousness, breaking the silence occasionally to say things like "God" or "Poor Hannah!" while my heart thrummed with astonished joy.

\*    \*    \*

Cindy approached me at my locker on Monday morning, which she had never done before. "That was fun Saturday," she said, with a smile that advertised secret knowledge. "Hannah thought you were really cool." My heart and stomach began spinning in different directions along multiple axes.

"Oh yeah?" I said. It seemed important to convey indifference, in order to suggest that I found out girls thought I was cool every day. Fortunately Cindy would not be deterred.

"Don't you think she's totally pretty?" she said. I didn't realize at the time that this is a trick girls use to make you think other girls are pretty. It still works on me now.

"Yeah, definitely!" I said, and Cindy, seeing that I was in the bag, smiled. She leaned against the row of lockers and took a notebook and pen from her backpack. Danny was watching us from down the hall. Cindy wrote Hannah's name and phone number, from memory, on a corner of a page, tore it off, and handed it to me. We didn't say anything else about it.

At home that night I stared at the number and wondered what I could possibly do with it. Would a girl think about romance while her father was dying? I imagined him clinging to life, wanting only to see her graduate high school, unwittingly wrecking my one chance at love. Or he would die and Hannah would retreat from the world into a protracted period of mourning. I brought the phone from the kitchen into my room. Even with the cord stretched to its full extent I had to sit on the ground by the door. What could I say when she answered? I considered various opening lines and tried to imagine all the possible replies to each, so that I could construct a flowchart with responses to each of her responses, but the project quickly became unmanageable. I had no idea what boys and girls said to each other on the telephone, or indeed anywhere. I returned the phone to the kitchen.

The next day I found Cindy and Danny standing in the school hallway, his arm around her shoulder. She looked unslept and bedraggled. Cindy never wore visible makeup, but she must have had some kind of cosmetic regimen, because today it was evident by its absence.

She let Danny speak for her. "Hannah's dad died," he said quietly, like a messenger in a play delivering his only line.

I phoned that night. "Hannah, it's Eric," I said. There was no response. "I just—Cindy told me about your dad, and I just wanted to say I'm sorry."

"Oh—oh, *Eric!*" she said. "Oh, wow, thanks for calling!"

"Sure," I said. "Cindy told me about your dad, your father, today."

"Yes, it's really sad," she said. "But I have my whole family here, and everyone's been praying for him, and I know it's going to be OK."

I wasn't sure what to say to that. "Yeah. It *is* going to be OK."

"I mean, it's not up to me, it's up to God," she said. "It's going to be hard, not getting to see him. But it's not—it's not something I'm meant to understand."

"No, right," I said. Everything she was saying was alien to me— I didn't think about death that way—but I wasn't going to argue.

"I should go," she said easily, as though we'd been talking about school. "Everybody's downstairs."

"Oh, OK," I said. I had failed to get my balance, and now my time was up.

"Would you—would you call me tomorrow?" she said.

"Sure, yeah," I said. "Yeah, I'll call you tomorrow!"

"Great," she said, like a normal teenager. "Talk to you then, Eric." We said goodbye and hung up, and I sat there on the floor of my room, my back against the door, wondering what had just happened.

Hannah Pronovost was a virgin, as I was, but that didn't make the playing field level. She had investigated the gamut of non-penetrative options with Ryan from Christian Youth Fellowship, who played the acoustic guitar and had big soft eyes and no evident sense of humor. They had broken up, for complicated and melodramatic reasons, but the possibility of a reunion was an immovable feature of the landscape of our relationship. It would never have occurred to me not to tolerate this.

Astonishingly, less than a month after Hannah's father's funeral, with no negotiation or warning, we began to have sex. This could only have taken place within the atmosphere of neglect that overcame the Pronovost home in the wake of the patriarch's death. Judging from the photographic portraits that appeared like mushrooms on every surface in the house, Stan Pronovost, a man of unnaturally upright bearing, would never have allowed us so many hours behind the closed door of Hannah's bedroom, but his widow, sitting slouched and glassy-eyed at the kitchen table, scarcely noticed my presence. There was something unhinged, too, in Hannah herself. The guards had left their posts, and no one was left to check her loneliest impulses. With no basis for comparison, I didn't recognize that normal rules had been suspended; instead I came to assume that any girl, in the right mood, could be seized by the white wildness that appeared in Hannah Pronovost's eyes.

As an unspoken condition of the sex I went with her to Friday night teen services. Hannah squeezed my forearm encouragingly whenever I joined the singing or said *amen*. I hated the obvious techniques by which my feelings were manipulated: the rousing songs, the energetic junior pastor, the gentle aerobic lift of all that standing and sitting and standing again. (Who could respect a God who would trick his followers in such mechanical ways?) But we learned how to have sex, and we said *I love you,* and from then on the barriers to entry—the improbability of that strange moment when two people start kissing for the first time—no longer seemed insurmountable. For a while Hannah Pronovost needed someone, and I made myself into the person that she needed, and while it wouldn't scale it was at least a proof of concept.

# 7

I saw the Iraqi soldiers come into the hospital with guns. They
took the babies out of the incubators, took the incubators, and
left the children to die on the cold floor.

—Nayirah al-Sabah, testimony before the
Congressional Human Rights Caucus,
October 10, 1990

IN ACCORDANCE WITH MY mother's request, I buy a ticket to
Denver for three weeks from now. It will be my first visit since she
moved into her new house, and I'm hopeful that a certain amount of
hometown-boy-made-good triumph will accrue. I fantasize about
taking my mom out to an expensive restaurant and being waited on
by Graham Neale, although the fantasy loses some luster when I
realize that in it I am twenty-four years old and still having dinner
with my mom.

During the interim between the purchase of the ticket and the
flight, Maya and I entrench certain small routines that gently downgrade
the time we spend together from Event status to Normal status. We
figure out all the basic stage-two stuff—minor arguments, watching television—until being with her starts to feel almost easy, apart
from when we're having sex. When she straddles me in the darkness,
her diminutive silhouette transforms from that of an adult woman to
that of a child and back again. I conceal her behind looped mental
footage of anonymous copulation. My performance, assessed on
metrics both intrinsic (stamina, turnaround time) and extrinsic

(partner satisfaction), is more than adequate, perhaps a personal best. Afterward she becomes giggly and playful, and I try to join in the fun. The wave of guilt that threatens to suffocate me usually dissipates after about forty-five minutes.

Until, huddled under her blankets one freezing night, we fall into the spoon position, which maximizes body contact and preserves our pocket of warm air. I slide my hand under her T-shirt, brush it against her nipples.

"How does that feel?" I say. She murmurs something soft. "Is that OK? Can I touch you there?"

"Yes, you can," she says. She doesn't sound surprised that I'm asking permission to do something I've been doing for weeks.

I ask again and slide my hand between her legs. "Yes," she says again. This ritualized exchange—permission requested and granted, requested and granted—overrides my internal monologue. I remember something Lauren said: "I'm so scared I make it like I'm not even there at all." Speaking to each other keeps us conscious, and this consciousness rescues me from Maya's father's lingering presence. "Can I fuck you?" I ask her, when the moment seems right, and she says, "Yes, fuck me," and it's everything her first forced couplings were not: mature, consensual, mutual. At the end I'm filled with all three of nature's greatest satisfactions—love, orgasm, and the discovery of a solution to a difficult problem.

"You know the guy who drives the snowplow to clear the roads?" she says a minute later. "How does he get to work?"

"Nice point," I say. I have picked up some of her locutions. Then I wrap my arms around her shoulders and squeeze her so hard I'm afraid she might break.

Maya drives through the early evening traffic with the controlled aggression of an adept video gamer. The Golden Gate Bridge— more famous and less useful than the Bay Bridge—is inside a raincloud, and the lanes are narrow and poorly marked, and she's driving a little closer to the pickup truck in front than I would. Aunt Veal offered to take us out to dinner in the city, but Maya wanted to drive up to her house in Corte Madera; she described the forty-five-minute journey as a road trip. But the spirit of adventure seems to have left her, and the CDs she chose sit unplayed in the glove compartment. Aunt Veal is the only relative with whom Maya is still in contact, and so dinner tonight carries a burden of unfulfillable wishes. Tomorrow I fly to Denver for my mother's birthday.

Off the freeway, Maya winds her way up a series of complicated hillside roads, past houses that become increasingly eccentric the higher we go. Corrugated-metal shacks and solar-paneled ecotopias nestle next to cliff-hanging glass-fronted dream homes. She pulls up in front of a miniature ranch house with something provisional about its construction, as though it were a sketch for a house to be built elsewhere.

Maya has described Aunt Veal as a hippie, which led me to expect a bosomy earth mother. But the woman who stands in the doorframe holding the screen open is skinny and angular, all nose and elbows. She wears clunky metal jewelry and a complicated black garment with a low neckline that displays the broad gulf of her cleavage. Her real name is Gail; the nickname derives from a speech she once made in a restaurant describing to five-year-old Maya how her mother's osso buco had been raised and slaughtered, a speech to which Maya responded with fascination rather than outrage.

"C'mon in, you guys," she says, as though we lived up the road and came for dinner once a week. The front door leads oddly into the kitchen, which opens to an underfurnished living room with a view of dirt and cedars. The house smells of creosote and dog. "So you're the computer geek, huh?" she says, to see if I'll take offense.

"Actually, we prefer the term *socially maladjusted technology adept*," I say.

She smiles marginally. "I used to date a guy who worked in the computer lab at Stanford," she says, the college's name provoking in me, as always, a burst of regret. "Nowadays computers are a business thing, or a toy gun, but originally they were a way to expand your mind."

"Sure," I say, because what else can you say when someone tells you something you already know?

We sit in canvas chairs on a deck overlooking the shallow canyon and eat stir-fried vegetables. Aunt Veal rests her feet on a large, senile golden retriever. The hot tub, mercifully, remains covered. We talk about my company, and about what I'm planning to do with all the money I've made. Aunt Veal suggests I start a foundation, one that would form the basis of "a real antiwar movement."

"Hey, I'm not Bill Gates," I say. "I could barely pay the overhead on a foundation."

This doesn't satisfy Aunt Veal, who seems to be imagining herself as director of her own foundation. "It's up to you to keep him honest, hon," she says to Maya.

"Oh, I do," Maya says, getting up to use the bathroom.

It's not clear how much privacy Maya's absence affords us, since the bathroom shares a wall with the deck, but Aunt Veal nevertheless shifts into a confidential tone. "So," she says, "you're serious about my niece?"

"I'm just trying not to scare her off."

"Because she's been through some rough stuff."

"I know," I say. "I think she's incredibly brave." This is one of those true things that come out sounding insincere. The exchange is cut off by the toilet flushing, and we wait in silence for Maya to return.

When our plates are empty and resting on the deck next to our chairs, Aunt Veal produces a tin from which she withdraws a pipe, a lighter, and a little pouch full of marijuana. Maya's smile is familiar and mildly exasperated. Aunt Veal prepares the bowl and takes a couple of long, profligate tokes that suggest a big stash and a secure connection. When she has exhaled for the third time, she offers me the pipe.

My chief experiences with marijuana, as with most drugs, came via Danny Keach, who during his first year at CU-Boulder brought various narcotics back to Denver every few weeks. I think he felt inexperienced at college and liked having me to initiate. Under his auspices I took mushrooms, which were interesting, and Ecstasy, which seemed to solve some deep flaw in my character, but I never saw the point of marijuana: I have no desire to focus more deeply on my involuted thoughts. But I'm a guest in Aunt Veal's house, and the offer of a pipe is an archetypically friendly gesture, so I take a small hit and let it out quickly. I don't even feel it. I extend the pipe to Maya, but she just wrinkles her nose. Aunt Veal takes it instead and says to Maya, "Shouldn't even break it out around you."

When she passes the pipe back I take another little hit, mostly air, to demonstrate that I'm not just imitating Maya, and then return it. "That's enough for me," I say, and my sudden awareness of the complex buccal manipulations required to pronounce the words makes me realize that it is in fact too much.

Maya asks Aunt Veal about her jewelry business, and Aunt Veal says she gets all the custom she can handle from her website. She gives me a significant look, and I'm not sure if it's because she wants me to be impressed that she has a website or because I embody the spirit of the Internet in a more general way. "I can totally help you with that if you have any problems," I say, a remark that wasn't quite justified by the conversation leading up to it. The others let it go. Already, I'm the stoned person everyone indulges and ignores, like a child at the grownups' table. I wish there were some antidote to marijuana. I look at the view, almost as shrubby and desolate as the landscape around Denver. As the sun hits the far side of the canyon I'm reminded of the way it used to drop behind the Rockies, too quickly, and something bleak occurs inside me. I realize I haven't been following the conversation for some indeterminate span and hope this hasn't been perceived as rude. Aunt Veal is in the middle of a monologue. "He was all the way up there, you know, and it worked for a while," she says, perhaps referring to an IT person she had hired to fix her website. I almost say *I can totally help with your website* but stop myself and run a quick test: Are you certain that your proposed remark will fit naturally into the conversation? If not, say nothing. "Yeah, that's too bad," I say instead, and they both look at me for a second and carry on talking. The air feels very still, as though we're at the bottom of a grave. Aunt Veal says, "You guys are just starting out, you haven't had to deal with this stuff yet," and I wonder what stuff there can possibly be that I haven't had to deal with already. And Maya—what hasn't she dealt with, much too early? As she adjusts her sunglasses against the glare I see the phantom hands of her father on her shoulders, and I wonder whether my fixation on his abuse of her reflects something perverse about male sexuality in general, or about me in particular. I should start paying attention to the conversation. Aunt Veal says, "Yeah, you're like your mother in that way," and Maya says, "Yeah, you've said that before."

"How is she like her mother?" I say, exposing my wavering attention. I have a constant fear that because I will never meet her mother I will never really understand Maya herself.

Maya and her aunt wordlessly agree to make this conversational detour. "Daphne was a pretty cool customer," Aunt Veal says. I've never heard Maya's mother's first name and am pleased that it's Daphne, which makes me think of mythical water nymphs and the pretty redhead from *Scooby-Doo*. "She didn't let her feelings show. That's why men fell over themselves for her." I do recognize this in Maya, the way she squints at the world, as though saving her responses for a critique to be published later. "She was kind of a mother to me more than a sister, what with our mother being basically out to lunch all the time." She's using the phrase metaphorically, rather than suggesting that Maya's grandmother had a lot of lunch engagements. "That was how I made it through high school, was thanks to your mom."

The light is pale by now, and Maya, in a sweatshirt, rubs her arms to warm herself. Aunt Veal got Maya's mom, and who did Maya get? No one. "I just wish she'd been around to take care of you," I say to Maya. Something feels odd, and I realize it's the first time I've referred to Maya's traumatic history in front of a third party.

"Yeah, I wish that too," she says. No one knows where to go from there.

Finally Aunt Veal says, "She would have done it. You should have seen her when you were born, she was so in love with you, she would have done anything to keep you safe." After the long silence this comes out sounding sentimental. I begin to wonder about the validity of the counterfactual: Who knows if Daphne would have taken care of Maya or not? Mothers often turn a blind eye to their children's abuse. Perhaps she would have been complicit. Perhaps she would have participated. Why am I thinking these things?

We get up to leave soon afterward. I try to stage a meaningful goodbye, complete with expressions of gratitude and affection, but Aunt Veal stays on the deck instead of seeing us to the door. Maya doesn't seem discomfited by this. By the time we're in the car it's officially dark. On the drive down the narrow unlighted roads I grip the door handle and watch the broken yellow lines pass underneath us like a filmstrip. Maya watches the road and communicates nothing; her facial muscles shift only in response to subcutaneous reflexes. This removal of ordinary social animation is something you rarely see on people who are awake, and it seems to suggest that I do not exist. We roll over the bridge, windows up, and through the empty streets of San Francisco, stopping at red lights for ghost traffic. Did I ruin things by bringing up her childhood? Is there a way to apologize without repeating the original mistake?

At least I can reassure her of my benevolence. Back in my bed I resume the strategy of gentle and sympathetic questioning that I initiated last night. The call-and-response once again seems to lull us into a state of trust. "Is this OK?" I ask before I enter her, and she says *yes,* a beautiful full-voiced *yes* that infuses my chest with warmth.

Lying atop her, my hips pronated to generate clitoral friction, I prop my upper body on my forearms and gaze down at her. Her eyes are three-quarters shut, and she's emitting delicate little grunts, and to all indications she's in the early throes of sexual transport. And then, in a normal speaking voice, she says, "You can be rougher if you want."

I am practiced at fighting down the malevolent creatures that come swimming through my gut at such moments, with their waving tendrils and spiky fronds. There's no time for panic. But how to respond? How much aggression is called for? I could ask for more information, but evidently she's tired of respectful communication. This is a situation that demands instinct and spontaneity and getting everything right without planning a strategy or weighing the available evidence. I clutch at a hank of her hair and pull gently, but now my balance is precarious. Plus am I acting out the incestuous rape of a ten-year-old? I can't do this. I finish much as I had begun, but with more vigor and less eye contact, and then I say something about having to pack in the morning and we go to sleep.

The flight to Denver takes three and a half hours. I'm in a window seat, in business class, watching the flight attendants. One is a bony blonde, close to forty, with a powerful smile and an amiable demeanor that allows her to dispense with the *honey*s and *sweetie*s that most flight attendants her age begin to introduce into their repertoire to compensate for the fading of their physical allure. The other, a brunette with a soft face, watches her senior colleague and tries to mimic her charisma. I'm not sure it's learnable but I respect the attempt, especially since she could still coast on her gorgeous pink skin and lazy Southern diphthongs. I spend the flight looking back and forth between the western United States below us and these women walking purposefully up and down the aisle. I'm trying not to think about last night.

The guy next to me is good-looking in a way that seems to project the adjective *good-looking*. After stowing his overhead luggage he sat down and smiled politely, to indicate that he wouldn't try to talk to me, then turned his attention to the Sharper Image catalogue. Now, during the lull before the final beverage service, he starts chatting to the younger stewardess, complaining humorously about the ratio of cheese to crackers on the snack trays. The blonde, on her way back from the cockpit, stops to see what the hilarity is about, and soon he's entertaining both women with elaborations on this unpromising theme. He starts doing emphatic little gestures with the cheese; he goes to slam it down on his tray table in mock frustration, but he can't really slam it or the table would whack him in the knees, so he does this restrained little fake slam. The flight attendants laugh anyway, leaning against nearby seat backs in on-a-break postures. I pretend to read the in-flight magazine. He's ridiculous, this guy— everyone looks ridiculous when you watch them flirting. But there's a chance that he's about to sleep with two stewardesses, so who's ridiculous now? Plus you have to admire the way he's making use of the materials at hand—he's done a good six or seven minutes on the cheese and crackers. (It helps that the thrust of his argument is sound: you really do need another cracker.) Now the blonde asks him what he's doing in Denver, and I can't tell if she's making conversation or opening the logistical negotiations that will culminate with these three in a hotel room together. If it's the latter, would that be the zenith of his traveling career, or is this what the world is like for men with quarterback arms and geometric chins? The lives of others are a perpetual mystery.

I wanted to rent a car at the airport, in case I need to get out of the house at some point, but my mom insisted on picking me up. The last time I came she met me at the gate, but now you can't get through security without a boarding pass. Irrationally I look for my name on the hand-lettered signs held by the limo drivers, but no, there's my mother, standing off to the side and waving shyly. She looks older than she did when I was twelve, a development that still surprises me. I bend down to hug her and she throws her arms around my neck.

"Well!" she says. "How was your flight? Are you thirsty? Did you drink water on the plane?" (The dehydration that results from air travel is one of my mom's preoccupations.) She is impressed that all my stuff fits into a carry-on, although I'm only here for two nights.

She leads me through the parking lot to her SUV. I offered to buy her a car, but she refused; the house was enough, and not having to make mortgage payments enabled her to trade her hatchback for this hideous Nissan. "I'm so glad you could come!" she says once we've pulled onto the freeway. "You must be so busy these days!" The fact that I have millions of dollars and no job makes my mom uncomfortable: she doesn't know what I do all day. Nor do I, really.

"I'm just sorry I missed your real birthday," I say. (It happened three days ago; tomorrow's the party.) The dull clouds emit biblical shafts of light, reminding me how much I hate Denver's melodramatic weather.

"How are things with Maya?" she says. I've only told her a little, but apparently she can tell it's serious.

"Everything's great," I tell her. It's true, if you filter out all the stuff I don't want to think about right now and couldn't tell my mom even if I did. But I have the urge to say something more, to tell everyone how important Maya is. The newspapers are printing the wrong headlines, focusing on the inconclusive reports of weapons inspectors and intelligence agencies when they should be describing her sense of humor and beautiful little breasts. "I'm kind of totally in love with her," I say, because it's also true.

Mom glances at me nervously before her eyes flicker back to the highway. "You will make sure she signs something, right?" she says.

"I don't know what you mean," I say, although I can feel understanding blooming like a rain cloud.

"Oh, I shouldn't say anything," she says. "And I'm sure if you've picked her she must be a wonderful girl. It's really wonderful, Eric— I'm so happy for you! I just mean, well, you've worked so hard, and it would be terrible to lose all that. I know something about how women can be."

To the west the mountains look tapped out, as though the last minerals have been extracted and there's nothing left but piles of dust. I calculate the number of hours until I get back to San Francisco and see Maya again, away from my mother and her anxiety: forty-three. No, it's an hour later here: forty-four.

"Mom, I've been seeing her for six weeks," I say. "We're not getting married for a while."

Mom turns off the highway and heads toward the subdivision in which she chose her new home, a freestanding manse surrounded by identical siblings, all painted the same lilac with purple trim, out in the windy grassless plains to the south of the city. I haven't been here since the closing, when my mom wept and one thin strand of my life's accumulated fear and guilt was severed. I asked her if she wouldn't prefer something closer to town, something cozier, something that's not identical to every other visible structure. She talked about the absence of noise and crime and dirt, but I suspect the property's true appeal was less tangible. My mother fears hotel beds and used clothes and public swimming pools, objects with a history of occupancy by strangers. Moving into a *new-construction home*, as the developer's literature put it, was like an exorcism.

I follow her inside and swing the surprisingly light front door shut behind me. The hall, with its elevated ceiling and pretentiously sweeping staircase, looks almost exactly as it did when we came here with the talkative woman from the sales office. My mother spent her life in houses that were too small, and the idea that she might finally have enough room made her giddy and scattered.

She heads straight into the kitchen without offering me a tour, and, unprompted, begins to make grilled cheese sandwiches and tomato soup, a meal I have always loved. I want to sit at the kitchen table, from which I have watched her cook thousands of meals, but there isn't one: the table is in the dining room now. Does she usually eat there, or does she take her food into the living room and watch TV? The stainless steel refrigerator is decorated with magnets in the shape of pumpkins, but there's nothing for the magnets to pin up. As she greases and flips the sandwiches, we talk about her work, about that jerk Wade, about the party tomorrow. Neither of us wants to talk about Maya anymore, which means there's not much to say about my life.

When she's made two grilled cheeses for me and a half sandwich for herself, we carry the plates and soup bowls into the dining room. I return for paper towels and silverware and we sit down on opposite sides of the table, smiling at the familiar situation and the unfamiliar setting. She blows on a spoonful of soup and says, "Well, your dad called."

"You talked to him?" As far as I know, my parents hadn't spoken in seven years. "How was that?"

"Honestly, it was hard," she says. She sets the spoon back in her bowl without tasting the soup. "He had his friendly manner, and he asked how I was doing, and I didn't know what to tell him. And then he asked if I'd been in touch with you! As though you were a friend from school or something like that."

"Did he say anything about having dinner with me?"

"He said that he had offered you this job—*pitched you,* was the way he said it—and that you had turned it down, and that you were making a big mistake and I should talk to you about it. He said here was your big opportunity for lightning to strike twice, and you were about to miss it."

"Did you tell him to go fuck himself?"

Mom frowns at the language. "No, I didn't," she says. "But I told him you were smarter than both of your parents combined and you could make your own decisions."

I make a noise that attempts to thank her without endorsing the insult to her own intelligence. "If he bothers you again, tell him to call me," I say. "There's no reason you should get dragged into this crap."

"I'll be fine," she says. "I'm not scared of your dad."

After dinner I check out the rest of the house—too many surfaces, not enough objects to rest or hang on them—and retire to the guest bedroom. I'm almost certain I'm the first person to stay in this room. On the verge of sleep, my mind snags on Mom's frightened admonition about a prenuptial agreement. I know she's trying to prevent my life from being sabotaged the way hers was. But I have to believe it won't be that way when Maya and I divorce. We will be reasonable, sympathetic, adult. I wish I could be certain. Will we be trapped by bitterness and regret? Will we be able to find one another through the thicket of hostility, to reach out and clasp hands and say, *Here I am, I loved you once?*

Victoria, who works with my mom, is the first to arrive. She brings her son Carlos, aged ten months, fleshy and grumpy. We sit in the living room in front of the big picture window, and my mom fetches a bag of Tostitos and a bowl of salsa. (I worry that Victoria will feel patronized by the quasi-Mexican snack, but she dips happily.) When the doorbell rings again, my mom is bouncing Carlos on her lap, so I volunteer to answer it.

Stacey Oberfell is standing in the doorway. "Look at you!" she says. "The prodigal son returns!" The adjective seems uncalled for. "So let me see you," she says, stepping inside and appraising the effects of eight years on my physiognomy. "Well, you're looking more and more like your dad."

In the living room, Mom and Stacey embrace, and Stacey meets Victoria, and we all sit down on the big matching couches and armchairs. "Here we are," Stacey says. "The house that Eric built. Or bought, anyway."

"Oh, I wouldn't know how to build it," I say. "So how are things, Stacey? How's the family?"

"Everyone's great. Bronwen and Pete were so jealous when I told them I was going to see you. Bronwen's training to be a nurse, we're all real proud of her." I would like to learn whether she has a boyfriend and if she ever mentions me, but I don't ask. "Pete graduated college last year, and now he's in officer candidate school, if you can believe that."

The thought of fearful nine-year-old Pete in uniform is hard to accept, especially with troops massing in Kuwait. "And what about Gary?" I say, as if Gary and I were peers or buddies. A sudden worry: Have they divorced? Did I hear about it and forget?

"Oh, he's great," she says. "His practice is doing real well, and we moved to a place in Aurora Hills, a real nice place. Not as nice as this place, obviously"—she gestures at the huge empty space above our heads—"but still real nice."

I had thought that membership in a twelve-step program guaranteed a crowd at your birthday party, but there is no sign of a sponsor or any fellow addicts-in-recovery. I imagine my mom at a meeting, sitting alone at the back of the room, next to a big urn of coffee. It's strange to be the only man here, a feeling compounded by the fact that Victoria is probably a few years younger than me. I am aware of some subtle pressure of expectations, as though I'm supposed to produce something. The conversation seems lost in the massive house—or maybe it's the disconnectedness of the guests: Victoria from work, Stacey from long ago, me from biology.

Carlos begins to cry, and Mom passes him back to Victoria with a flustered look, as though she must have done something wrong. Victoria casually takes out her breast and attaches Carlos to it while I stare at the floor. "So tell me about your life," Stacey says. "Any more million-dollar companies? You've got to tell us about the next one so we can invest!"

"Uh, no, I'm not really working on anything commercial right now," I say. "I'm still doing some programming, but it's mostly open source."

Stacey smiles and nods to convey that she has no idea what I mean and doesn't want me to explain. "Well, we're all real proud of you," she says. "I said to my kids, *See, I told you you should be learning computers.*"

"It sounds like they're doing good, though," I say. "I mean, there's a big nursing shortage, right?"

"Oh, sure," Stacey says, bored. "So Margo—how does it feel to be the big five-oh?"

"Well, I feel…," my mom says, and then takes a pause that stretches out like the blank terrain visible through the window. Then she remembers her lines: "I'm just so grateful to be here. There have been so many hard things, and now," smiling at me, "I'm here in this beautiful house, and I'm back at work, and I haven't taken a drink or a pill in one year, four months, and six days, and thanks to you guys and God I'm on the right path." By the end of this litany she sounds cheerful.

"We can all celebrate *that*, right?" Stacey says, as though distinguishing it from something else. The moment seems to call for a toast, but only Victoria and I have glasses, both of them filled with Diet Coke.

"So is it time for the presents?" says Victoria. "And is there maybe some kind of cake?" She gives me a twinkly smile, and I realize too late that I'm here as a host rather than a guest, responsible for the apparatus of the festivities.

"Uh, no, I, uh, I didn't get a cake," I say. Stacey's face takes on a look of private hopes borne out. I can't look at my mom.

"We've got presents, anyway," says Victoria. Long ago it was decided that my mother liked pumpkins, and that gifts for her should involve pumpkin iconography: her kitchen clock is in the shape of a pumpkin, and her apron is decorated with pumpkins. I suspect that, for my mom, the pumpkin theme's chief function is to minimize the amount of time other people spend thinking about what she might enjoy. Victoria has brought a ceramic jack-o'-lantern whose black eyes and mouth are cute rather than scary. As a child I felt strongly that jack-o'-lanterns were a corruption of the pumpkin idea, belonging to Halloween rather than to my mother's birthday, but I don't remember Mom expressing any feelings on the issue. She is more affected by Victoria's card, which bears a printed poem titled "To a Woman I Admire."

Stacey's gift is a framed print, a painting of children making sand castles, that calls attention to the house's acres of barren wall. Every minute or so I reexamine the knot of bad feeling at the back of my head and remember the cake thing. My hope is that my gift will redeem me, at least in part: a gold and topaz brooch, more expensive than anything else my mom wears but not so ostentatious as to be out of place. She extracts it from the little square box. "Oh, Eric," she says. "Oh, it's so pretty!" She affixes it to her sweater carefully, squeezing the pin between threads. "It's the most beautiful thing I own." She is trying to make me feel better about the cake, and I appreciate the attempt, although it only makes my failure more vivid.

Nothing has been planned for the rest of the afternoon. Was this my responsibility too? Drinks at some nearby Applebee's is out. If I could leave for half an hour I could get a cake at the supermarket and then stop at Blockbuster and pick up a movie about four middle-aged women who learn to build fulfilling lives without men. Everyone works to find neutral subjects and eats chips and salsa until all the chips large enough to convey salsa are gone.

"So your mom's been telling us all about your new girlfriend," Victoria says, giving me a look that is like flirting but with everything sexual or romantic stripped out. Young mothers do this sometimes, mechanically recapitulating the forms of a ritual they've outgrown.

"Nothing too personal, I hope," I say.

"Oh, she just says you're *madly in love*," Victoria says, drawing out the last three words wickedly. I dodge the topic with an embarrassed shrug, out of fear that my filial affection will seem inadequate by comparison. If it were Maya's birthday I'd have made sure there was a cake.

After another hour the shadows of the hills outside begin to spread, and the guests take this as permission to leave. On her way out, Stacey says, "I'll get your email from your mom and give it to the kids. I'm sure they'd love to know what you're up to." Finally Mom and I are alone.

"So that was nice," she says.

"I'm sorry I didn't plan better," I say.

"Oh no, well, no, don't worry about it," she says. "I don't think anyone really likes birthday cake anyway, do they? And this," touching the brooch, "is really special."

Soon the central heating shudders on, and we order Domino's and watch the news: two kids are dead in a house fire in Colorado

Springs, and someone forged the evidence that Saddam Hussein tried to buy uranium from Niger. I try to come up with things to say about the stories, but I keep thinking about my mother sitting here alone, with a frozen dinner instead of a pizza. Tomorrow she will drive me to the airport. I had imagined some kind of dull social calendar revolving around book group and NA meetings, but there is no evidence that any such events have been skipped or rescheduled on account of my visit. The house: I thought it was the right thing but it's too big, too empty, a consolation prize. Mom watches TV while I stare out at the last traces of light, barely enough to distinguish the hills from the sky.

Maya comes downstairs in her jacket. I am carrying plastic bags containing a six-pack of beer, a loaf of French bread, and two different kinds of cheese. When she appears in the doorway I quash the impulse to pick her up and spin her around because many small people dislike being picked up, even affectionately, and this probably goes double for small people who have been sexually abused. I've advised her to snack, since Cynthia has a weird metabolism and no sense of ordinary physical appetites; she once served six people a dinner consisting of nothing but roasted yams. As we walk over there I try to tell Maya about my mom's birthday party. It's a delicate task, because I don't want to pierce the bubble of sadness that's been sitting on my chest ever since. The cake debacle I omit entirely.

"It's as if she's on the moon out there," I say. "A hundred identical houses, just far enough apart that you never see another human being."

She stops to push a piece of sidewalk jetsam to the curb with her foot, with a care that seems protective of both the trash and the foot. "That's not how I think of the moon," she says.

Cynthia and Maya were introduced at the party, but this is their first meeting with me in common. As they greet each other at the door, they project the knowingness one uses with friends of friends, to announce *I've heard good things about you.* Cynthia leads us up the stairs and into the kitchen, where Sam is sitting at the table, slouched low in her chair. She doesn't stand when we come in. I recognize her as the sartorially butch/physically femme half of that couple at the party: slight and pretty, with a thin, unformed face and tight black curls. She could almost pass as a boy but for her creamy skin and the platinum stud like a mole in her upper lip. The trend among San Francisco lesbians is to stake out a position on the border between butchdom and transgenderhood, where pronoun choices are fraught and unpredictable. (Cynthia has explained this to me with the earnest pedantry of someone displaying recently acquired knowledge.) For a straight man, lesbianism is like communism: utopian in theory, disappointing in practice. Maya and I sit down and open beers as Cynthia pushes some kale around on the stove.

"So how did you guys meet?" Maya asks Sam.

"Mutual friends," says Sam with a self-deprecating roll of the eyes, as though this were universally agreed to be the dullest and least promising way to meet.

"And you guys met here!" Cynthia says. "I'm so proud!" She turns and holds out her beer for us to clink. I would toast more enthusiastically were it not for the botched nature of that meeting. It was here that I was introduced to her, fixed her a cocktail, failed to speak to her. This is where the whole thing started, and now it's where the end is about to begin.

When Cynthia sets down the plates of kale and green beans, I try to catch Maya's eye so we can share a humorous look, but she's too polite for that. We start to eat, and there's a little pause in which we savor our food and wonder what we're going to talk about. Maya, who is professionally skilled at meeting people, begins questioning Cynthia, starting with her job but probing backward into her childhood and forward into her ambitions. I remember having that intense, benevolent scrutiny trained on me, and I miss being the object of her curiosity. Maya's skill at interrogation gets results, as usual: I didn't know Cynthia was thinking about training to be a nurse practitioner, or that she sometimes considers moving back to Denver. In anticipation of this evening I've nurtured a fantasy in which Maya and Cynthia become friends and the three of us form a group with me at the center. In reality, though, their obvious amity threatens to unstop and blend separate vats of emotion in me, a disconcerting prospect. I tear off some French bread and spread a dollop of soft cheese over it.

As she fetches a second round of beers, Cynthia announces that armed National Guard troops are posted at either end of the Bay Bridge again. They come and go according to geopolitical weather patterns indecipherable to civilians.

"So now we're going to invade Iraq," Sam says. Her tone is jaded, almost bored. At some point an invasion has become inevitable.

"I keep thinking I missed something," says Cynthia. "Like, didn't some other people just attack us? And so now we're going to invade a completely different country, just because they've got nuclear weapons? I mean, Canada's got nuclear weapons, right? Are we going to invade Canada?"

"Yeah, but they don't have oil," Sam says. Her arm rests on the back of Cynthia's chair, and she strokes the back of Cynthia's neck while she talks.

Maya is knowledgeable and eloquent on the subject of the looming war, and Cynthia and Sam are soon reduced to echoes. I'm the least politically astute person at the table: I've just spent two and a half years preoccupied with the challenges of personalized online marketing. I didn't vote in the 2000 election—Bill and I were too busy to register, and California was a lock anyway, and neither of the candidates seemed especially inspiring or scary. What interested me most was that the election was essentially a tie, and that the balance was tipped by poor interface design. Bill and I laughed about it for thirty seconds and then went back to work. As the conversation becomes an exercise in emphatic agreement—the invasion is a done deal, an oil grab, a sop to the energy services companies, a fuck-you to international opinion, a narcissistic projection of imperial power, an Oedipal acting-out—I find myself missing Demographic of One. For thirty-five months Bill and I made two dozen decisions every day: which protocols to use, which features to build, what to do first, what to skip. (Bill usually deferred to me on design and won the technical arguments on the merits. I changed his mind exactly twice, and in fifty years I'll still remember how.) A discussion like this one, that gets its strength from the fact that everyone shares a position, would have been an unthinkable waste of resources. All I wanted during that time was a girlfriend, and now, in a striking proof of the ineradicability of human loneliness, I've got this great girlfriend and I miss working sixteen hours a day with Bill Fleig.

"And it's really *convenient* for them that 9/11 happens right after Bush becomes president," Sam is saying, with the half-ironic smile of the conspiracy theorist.

"So what about the WMDs?" I say. Sam gives a derisive little snort. I don't think I've ever used the phrase *WMDs* before tonight, and it sounds phony and stupid. "Obviously the president is an idiot. But that doesn't change the fact that maybe they've got these weapons."

Maya is unruffled. "That's what UN inspections are for," she says. "Look, this is the same thing the government has always done. They create these villains to scare us, and then they exploit that fear."

I don't want to challenge her, but the prevailing and totally unearned confidence sets me on edge. There's too much we don't know, and even if we had access to all the classified intelligence, the situation involves too many interdependent variables to allow anyone to predict outcomes with any confidence. "I'm not saying we should invade," I say. Cynthia and Sam are shuttling their eyes back and forth. "I just think we need to be wary of getting into a little festival of certainty. Can't we admit that we don't really know?"

Maya sets down her knife and fork. "You can reserve judgment as long as you like," she says. "And, you know, congratulations, you've won the gold medal for scrupulous empiricism or whatever. But meanwhile you're abandoning the battlefield to the other side."

I give a little nod of concession and get up, shaking with disloyalty, to clear the plates and fetch the ice cream. There's a silence while the air clears. Political disagreement is rare in San Francisco in 2003: the areas of consensus are just so vast.

"Do you write about this stuff for the paper?" Cynthia asks Maya, bringing the subject into a personal register and thus defusing it.

Maya shifts gears easily. "No, I do local-government stuff," she says. "Sometimes it feels a little irrelevant, especially these days."

Standing at the counter I force the scoop into the overfrozen ice cream. Sam mentions an acquaintance who writes a nightlife column for Maya's paper, and they compare notes. Sam appears to treat the world as a set of interconnected play structures to which she has total access: gender, fashion, clubland. The recovery movement and its therapists and sweaters and self-help workbooks must seem passé to her. A historical shift has taken place while I wasn't watching, and among young radical women the emphasis has shifted from personal oppression to self-definition. A few years ago, sexual abuse was the only thing on daytime TV. Now it's anthrax attacks and shoe bombs and chemical weapons. So what happened to the sexual abuse? Maya's talking now about her editor, her assignments, things I've heard before, and I imagine her as a helpless child, her father creeping down the hall to her room. I picture him as the Hooded Claw from the *Perils of Penelope Pitstop* cartoons. I have trouble envisioning the abusive act itself. Although of course it happens. And she's never said he was actually inside her. Her memories aren't clear. This line of thought is about to destroy everything. There are weapons, hidden out in the desert, or else there aren't. The babies ripped from their incubators a decade ago in Kuwait, left on the cold floor to die, were a fabrication. These blurry sense-memories that vanish and then return, like lost sailors to their families' doorsteps: him pressing up against her in the night, his hands on her body, his breath on her face. How sure can she be?

# 8

There are known unknowns; that is to say we know there are some things we do not know. But there are also unknown unknowns—the ones we don't know we don't know.

—Donald Rumsfeld, February 12, 2002

WHEN I WAS SEVEN, Nicky's mom dropped me off at home and I knew that my parents had been waiting for me, although I'm not sure how I knew this. My mom said, "We're getting what's called a divorce." I knew the word—it had happened to Dennis Yoder's parents, and everyone was really quiet around him for a few weeks—but I wasn't sure what it meant in practical terms. My father was teaching evening classes and often came home after I was asleep. I don't know that I was sure who he was or why he lived with us.

It was explained that Dad was going to move into an apartment in the neighborhood, and I was going to visit him there sometimes. I didn't understand why I would be visiting him. Would it be like when we visited grown-ups who didn't have any kids and there weren't any toys there? I asked about that, and my dad said he'd get some toys. He sounded tired when he said it, and I thought that the toy store must be really far away from his apartment.

And then my mom said, "This doesn't mean we don't love you anymore. You understand that, right?"

It hadn't occurred to me that what they were saying had anything to do with their love for me. They didn't want to be married to each other, and having been around their marriage I didn't blame them. But the idea that they didn't love me anymore got stuck in my back teeth and I couldn't get it out with my tongue.

The most painful ideas are the hardest to dislodge.

When we get home from Cynthia's I pretend to be drunker than I am, gulping down a big glass of water, tossing my jacket onto the couch. I say I'm tired too many times, and then we go to bed and I lie awake for seven hours.

Maya can wake herself at the time of her choice. At six minutes to seven she slips out of bed, fully alert, like someone moving from one scheduled activity to the next. As she dresses I lie still and imitate the even breaths of refreshing stage-four sleep. Her ablutions seem to take an inordinately long time. Finally the apartment door swings shut and I roll onto my back and look up at the ceiling and with no enthusiasm begin to masturbate. I used to masturbate with a dry hand, and then I discovered the advantage gained by lubricating your palm with saliva, and now I can't remember how I used to do it without chafing. Perhaps I began with delicate little strokes, and for ten years I've been incrementally increasing the pressure in the interest of a more stimulating masturbatory experience, and now I flail at myself with vigorous pumps that would have frightened and overwhelmed me a decade ago. When this feeble attempt at self-soothing is finished I shower, make coffee, sit down on the couch, turn on the TV, and look back and forth between CNN and the gray view outside until at last I pick up the laptop from the coffee table.

If you were to make a map of the web pages that turn up when you Google the term *recovered memory*, you'd see two clusters. One represents the recovery movement, which advocates for people who believe they've been abused. The other represents the false memory movement, which defends people who claim they've been wrongly accused. There are lots of connections within the clusters, but very few between them. Both sides have tragic stories to tell: traumatized children molested by trusted adults, innocent parents caught up in witch hunts. Some recovered memories have been corroborated; some have been disproved or recanted. Most of the websites are made by amateurs, and their clumsy designs make both sides seem crankish and untrustworthy.

I'm left with this: Maya believes her father did terrible things to her. In the past few years she's begun to remember him doing them. But what does *remember* mean? The images appear on her mental screen, or the feelings of terror and violation arise in her body, and they're tagged as memories, as traces of things she once experienced. But how did they get tagged that way? The brain is complicated. There's an experiment: You take two brothers. The older brother says, *Hey, remember the time we were at the mall and you got lost?* The younger brother says, *Huh, I don't remember that.* And then the next day he says, *Oh yeah, I kind of remember.* And then the day after that he says, *I was looking at the Transformers in the toy store and I turned around and everyone was gone.* None of it ever happened.

There is a temptation to discount stories of abuse merely because they're horrible. It would be reassuring to turn every case of child abuse into a delusion, but they're not all delusions. A college professor, on vacation with his wife, finds himself thinking about a former camp counselor, a man he last saw twenty-five years ago. For the first time, he remembers that this man sexually abused him. He investigates and finds three other campers who were abused by the same counselor. Camp employees recall finding the man in bed with a fifth boy. (This boy, now an adult, has no memory of the incident.) The counselor went on to abuse boys at a church in California, a school in Oregon, another in Texas.

For a while, celebrities told their recovered memory stories on television every afternoon. Memoirs of abuse crowded the bestseller lists. And then sometime around 1998, it stopped. Was it a fad? Or did we bump up against a question we couldn't answer and agree to change the subject?

Is there a way to talk to her about it? *Doesn't it behoove you to strive for a realistic sense of what you do and don't know about yourself?* I should probably skip the part about what it behooves her to do. *Isn't it a kind of intellectual dishonesty not to acknowledge the ambiguity of the data?* That's even worse. Am I atop some high horse, proclaiming, *I cannot love someone whose self-examination is insufficiently rigorous?* Or is it that, to love something, you have to know what you're loving—otherwise you're not loving the thing itself, you're loving some construct of your own?

Of course I can't say any of this to her. What if everything she believes is true? Absence of evidence is not evidence of absence. Her mother dies and leaves her alone with her abusive father. She endures torture, grows up a stranger to herself. She struggles to know the truth, to put aside her defenses and live honestly in the face of the unbearable. And her lover demands proof? Accuses her of fabricating her memories? Monstrous.

I keep imagining that I'm about to stumble on her father's secret diary or her therapist's case notes, whereupon the truth will come out. This will not happen. Nor will some profound and obviously authentic instinct well up in Maya and make itself available for consultation. Maya has no special access to the truth, and nor do I. The only person who does is Donald Marcom, and his word is the least credible of all.

His gallery's website displays only photographs of European bronzes and bas-reliefs. Subsequent search results include abstracts of articles in academic journals and deal reports in the trade press. What would happen if I were to ask him? Would I be able to tell, from something desperate and honest in his eyes, if he was lying?

Maya's investigation of the towing company will run in this week's paper. She has uncovered a predictable but still newsworthy pattern of infractions: improper towing, overbilling, low-level graft. Today she called the company's owner and presented him with the list of charges.

"He just kept saying, *It's bullshit, it's all bullshit,* over and over," she says. "I said, *Can you be more specific?* and he was like, *Yeah, specifically, your story is bullshit,* and then he hung up the phone."

I'm visiting her at the paper, which looks disappointingly like the office of any other midsized business. It's past nine and the newsroom itself is deserted, but copy editors and layout artists huddle in peripheral warrens. Maya filed her story half an hour ago, and now we're sitting at her cubicle eating takeout pasta from foil containers. Her editor is in his office with the sliding glass door shut, his feet on his desk, the printout in his hand, a ballpoint pen sticking out of his mouth. At any moment he may pull Maya away to clarify a sentence, resolve an inconsistency in the spelling of a name, draft an explanatory sidebar.

"How are you going to feel tomorrow, when it comes out?" I ask.

"A little edgy," she says. "Not about the story—the story's good. I'm just afraid he's going to call and yell at me." She tears a bread roll in half and swirls it around in my leftover vodka sauce.

"So what if he does call you?" I say. "You can't just hang up?"

"I could," she says. "The thing is, when people get upset they let stuff slip out. You're meant to start taking notes, ask questions. One time I heard Angela on the phone with some guy who was yelling so loud I could hear his voice over the receiver. He goes, *This is off the record, bitch,* and starts laying into her. And she goes, *Sorry, I'm not going to talk to you off the record. Anything you say I'm going to quote you.* He just lit into her, out of control, and she was grinning like crazy while she was typing it up. I can't do that. I get too freaked out when people yell at me. For obvious reasons."

At this last turn toward self-analysis she seems to switch modes, from casual chat to something more substantive. If her memories of abuse are correct, the moment calls for a swift, smooth expression of understanding and sympathy, nothing dramatic or intrusive. But what if they're not correct? Does she then, on some level, perceive sympathy as gullibility, or does that presume some nonexistent stratum of accurate knowledge? As I wrestle with this problem I'm staring blankly at my empty pasta container, which surely seems callous whether her autobiographical narrative is genuine or fantastic. Acting like I believe her is probably the lower-risk strategy and the one to adopt in perpetuity. But in addition to possibly looking like a dupe I'd likely be niggled by doubt, which would be a drag on my performance and could on any occasion erupt into an incident of poor judgment. Maya is looking at me in a way that makes me worry about my facial expression. I have been silent for almost half a minute, which makes it too late to respond without justifying the caesura. I could change the subject, which would be a gross conversational foul but would move us to safer ground, if I could construct a coherent sentence on any topic other than the one I'm thinking about.

"Are you OK?" she asks.

"Fine!" I say. "Tired. Up late last night. Sorry. That's too bad. About getting freaked out when people yell at you. That must be hard. Because of—it must be really hard." She's peering at me now with frank curiosity, as though I'm a species of animal she's never seen before.

A shout from the editor breaks the silence. "Get some rest," Maya says, squeezing me on the arm.

I walk home, past unfinished lofts stunted by the crash, and distract myself by thinking about Bill's new project. I half wish he'd ask for my help, but if there's no user-facing design I wouldn't have much to contribute: multithreading is a notoriously difficult field in which I have no real experience.

Inside my apartment I lie awake again, wondering whether Donald Marcom sleeps and what it means if he does. Then I give up. I am searching for flights to Los Angeles when I realize what I'm doing. I take my hands from the keyboard and press on my eyelids. This can solve nothing. Pedophilia isn't visible on the skin like a rash. But the point is not to interrogate or diagnose him; the point is to fill in the empty space in Maya's story. I have to address this, and I can't address it alone, and I can't raise it with her. And Donald Marcom, of Donald Marcom Fine Arts, 20977 Wilshire Boulevard, Los Angeles, is the only other person here.

Transmuting the problem into the world of practicalities, of web searches and plane tickets and my credit card's three-digit security code, brings on a surge of exhaustion. I barely reach my bed and manage to remain there for nine hours, gorging on unconsciousness, emerging every few hours and plunging back down again.

When I'm finally awake things feel different. Sitting at the kitchen island drinking coffee it's possible to believe that any problem can be solved by a man of action with adequate resources. I can get from my apartment to Donald Marcom's gallery in an hour and a half. I will go to Los Angeles in two days, learn what can be learned, for whatever that's worth. The sun streams in over Potrero Hill and turns the dust motes in the air into tiny stars.

The gallery is in a glorified strip mall—a fancy white minicomplex with valet parking and a sushi restaurant and a dental practice— behind frosted windows on which DONALD MARCOM FINE ARTS has been stenciled in a discreet sans-serif face. This physical evidence of the man's existence in the world is jarring. It would be easy to turn around, reclaim my rental car, drive straight back to the airport, call his secretary to tell her I've been waylaid. We spoke when I made the appointment yesterday: she had the voice of an older woman, hired for her skill and competence rather than her client appeal. I told her I was going to be in Los Angeles on short notice and was keen to see the collection. She started asking questions, being chatty; I actually thought, *Wow, she's friendly,* before I realized she was trying to figure out whether I was worth her boss's time. Invoking Silicon Valley freed up an hour in his schedule. I remember this successful bit of self-impersonation as I press the buzzer, then step back and wait for her to open the door, tall and canary-blond and professional, to admit me into the presence of the unknown.

Instead, it's him. It takes me a second to recognize him, because rather than the faceless villain of my imagination he is a specific human being in a herringbone suit. Maya didn't inherit his coloring—his skin is ruddy and his hair, now gray, was probably once red—but she got his features, and this proof of their genetic connection stirs something queasy in me. Why is he so tall? Maya isn't tall.

"Thank you for coming down," he says, stepping back to let me in. The gallery is a wide room crowded with densely wrought objects: bronzes and marbles and terra-cotta reliefs, busts and figures and little mythological scenes, each on a white podium or mounted on the walls. The ceiling is high and the blond wood floor and white walls are deliberately neutral, but there still seem to be too many sculptures; they compete with one another. "I'm so pleased that you're interested in this stuff," he says. "Why don't you sit down. Can I get you some water, or coffee?" His enunciation is nimble, almost British.

At the far end of the gallery are two chairs, with a coffee table between them on which catalogues have been laid perfectly square with the corners. A bit farther are two desks, one grand and wooden, the other small and practical and made of glass. The larger one is covered with books and journals and legal pads, piled and spread-eagled, with Post-It flags marking pages. The other holds only a flat-panel iMac. Donald apparently leaves everything computer-related to his secretary. She said, "So we'll see you tomorrow at two," but she's nowhere in evidence, and it is Donald himself who fetches the coffee. The chair is the kind that sinks your hips down below your knees and settles you into a semireclining posture that will require effort to climb out of. After some business with the coffee that takes place outside my field of vision, he sets it down and sits opposite me.

"Why don't you start by telling me how it is that you're here and not in the studio of some San Francisco wunderkind," he says. His pronunciation of *wunderkind* is unapologetically German. He crosses his legs and folds his hands on his knee. He reminds me of a psychoanalyst, someone who will listen to your dreams and point you toward what you really love.

I am prepared for this. "I've read a bit about Renaissance Italy," I tell him. "I recognize it. It was like the sixteenth-century version of Silicon Valley." He smiles. "I don't just mean all the money floating around, I mean the innovation, the new ideas."

"When they rediscovered the art of antiquity, a whole new world opened up," he says.

"It was like the solution to every problem they'd ever faced was lying there waiting for them to find it and put their name on it and make a ton of money," I say. He seems to like this.

"Now I know you work in technology," he says. "I'm going to seem very ignorant to you, because I am. Do you think you could explain what it is that you do?"

Apparently Donald prides himself on acquiring a deep understanding of his clients' tastes and desires. "I write computer programs," I say. He nods. "I started a company that made a particular program, and a little while ago we sold the program to a much bigger company, and now I'm out of a job."

He steeples his fingers. "And no one had made this kind of program before?"

"No one had made one that worked as well as ours did." Among men in offices, this kind of boasting passes for hard-nosed realism, and Donald responds with a little moue of tribute.

"You must be clever, of course, but I don't know enough about your field to know what sort of cleverness it requires," he says. "Is there a lot of mathematics?"

"There's some math," I say. "There's more design than math. Where it overlaps with math is that it's satisfying for people who like closed systems."

"Tell me about the design," he says. "I assume you don't mean design in the visual sense."

This gentle interrogation is reducing me to a pleasant state of passivity, the kind children experience when a benevolent adult asks them questions to which they know the answers. "It's like architecture, a little," I say. "You're working with all these constraints—the limits of the environment and the hardware and the language—just like an architect has to worry about gravity and wheelchair ramps and where to put the plumbing. But you're building something for people to use, and you want them to be happy when they're using it."

"I understand," he says, making it sound like a compliment to my explanatory skills. "And your ability to do this has made you quite a lot of money." The quasi-British inflection makes it unclear whether he's using the word *quite* to intensify or to qualify the amount of money I've made. "It can be very disruptive, money," he says. "A lot of my clients made their money all at once, in a big lump, like you. There's a strange thing that happens: the fulfillment of a dream always brings with it some larger disappointment about the dream itself. Have you found that?" It's impossible not to see Maya in him.

"Something like that," I say. "It was different because I wasn't trying to get rich." I was trying to get out of Colorado, and to distract myself from my loneliness.

"Yes, that would help," he says, and he seems glad about it. "Well, I'd be happy to show you what's here and talk you through it. If you'd rather be alone with the work, I can step into the other room. But there's something in particular I think you might be interested in."

We haul ourselves out of our seats and he leads me to a podium on which a bronze Mercury, in winged helmet and sandals, extends his left arm upward. The original Flash had a helmet like that. It makes me think of the famous cover of *Flash* issue 123, "Flash of Two Worlds," in which the streamlined Flash of the modern era crosses into a parallel universe and meets his helmeted Golden Age counterpart.

"Giambologna," Marcom says. "The link between Michelangelo and Bernini." He clears his throat. "There's a story about Giambologna in Vasari. He was a young Turk, very impressed with himself and his abilities. He'd just arrived in Rome, and he made a wax model and finished it with exquisite care and delicacy, and he took it to the studio of the great Michelangelo." He uses the Italian pronunciation. "And Michelangelo took the model out of Giambologna's hands, this young upstart who had, you know, dared to cross his threshold, and he began to remodel it. He destroyed Giambologna's model, reshaped it into something completely different. And he handed it back to Giambologna and said, *Now go away and learn to model before you learn to finish.*"

He's not smiling anymore.

"Now, would you mind telling me why you're here?"

I've had it all wrong.

"Have you come to do some kind of violence to me?" he says.

"Jesus," I say. "No. That's not it."

"You came to see what a monster looks like?"

"I just wanted to find out the truth."

He takes a deep breath, and as he lets it out his features soften. "Then I'm very glad you're here," he says. "There are certain accusations, even today, that still compel belief merely by being issued. Are you in love with her?"

"Yes, I am," I say, taken aback by the question but also suffused with the kind of pride we reserve for unambivalent feelings.

"I'm glad," he says. "I hope she always has someone to love her, especially someone like yourself." The word *love* sounds strange in his precise diction, the way it does in old movies. "You couldn't have gotten to where you are if you weren't a rational person. And so I'm going to implore you: Look at the evidence. Look at the science, the pseudoscience, that these people use to justify themselves. Just look—skeptically, rationally look—and make up your own mind."

"I've read the literature," I say. "It doesn't resolve anything. That's why I had to talk to you."

"Imagine my position," he says. "I'm charged with proving a negative. I'm sure I made mistakes with her. I had to bring her up alone, and I was out of my depth. But I did not once touch her in a sexual way. My God, to have to make that statement!"

This kind of impassioned denial, true or false, always has the aspect of a performance. "Maya told me about how she remembered it, what it felt like," I say. "I don't know how to say this, but…it fit with other things about her childhood, things she remembered all along."

He stiffens, and I can see how she would have been scared of him. "Those things are post hoc!" he says. He shuts his eyes for a moment in a barely visible effort of self-mastery. "Are there things I would change? Of course there are. Show me a parent who would say otherwise. But this stuff about molestation, about abuse—this is pure revisionism! Her childhood wasn't always easy, but it was entirely innocent of *that!*" After everything I've felt for him over the past half hour—the way he spoke to me about technology, about art, about money; the way he showed me his despair—I don't like disappointing him.

"How did you know who I was?" I say.

"Daphne's sister Gail," he says. Everything is always more

complicated than it seems. We face each other in silence among the bronze and marble.

"Tell me what it was like," I say. "When she was a kid."

He looks at me gratefully, and I realize I've made a terrible mistake: I will have Donald's image of his daughter superimposed on my eyes every time I look at her.

Watching Maya grow up was a daily heartbreak for Donald, because what she was growing up into was her mother: the same small features, the same fine dark hair and slender shoulders, the same intelligence and self-possession. The toughness that I thought had been cultivated to protect her from his depredations was present, apparently, in the twenty-year-old Barnard junior with whom Donald fell overwhelmingly in love as a graduate student at Columbia. Their marriage wasn't always easy—"I'm not an easy man to be married to," he says—but he'd wanted an intellectual equal for a wife, and he'd found one. "You must be the same way," he says.

Maya's birth forced him to reevaluate his ideas about himself. "My parents were not loving people," he says. "I don't think I had a template for parental affection. And then the moment she was born I was swallowed up by this child, by this astonishing surge of love I felt for her. I didn't understand what was happening."

Four years later he'd almost found his balance when everything collapsed. They were trying for another child, and Daphne had failed to conceive after a year and a half. The CT scan found something growing inside her, not a baby but a tumor. For a year the cancer and the chemotherapy fought like hyenas over her body, and at the end there was nothing left of Donald's wife but the wisp of a corpse and the six-year-old who seemed to have stepped out of photographs from her mother's childhood. For weeks Donald couldn't look at his daughter without crying.

When he began to emerge from his mourning he promised

himself that Maya wouldn't be starved for attention. He left his job at the Getty and went into business as a dealer so he could set his own schedule, collect her from school, attend plays and soccer games (although Maya turned out to be uninterested in organized events; she preferred forming secret clubs with her friends). He worried about losing his salary, but Daphne's parents helped, and then he turned out to have a knack for buying and selling that might have gone undiscovered had he remained at the museum spending other people's money. So he picked her up from school every afternoon, and they ate dinner together every night, and he helped her with her schoolwork in the evenings. When she turned thirteen and began reading real books in English class, he would read them too and discuss them with her at dinner. Every summer they went to Europe; by the time she was sixteen she'd seen the Uffizi, the Musée d'Orsay, and the Sagrada Familia, and how many of her classmates could say that?

Between Daphne's death and Maya's desertion he had only one real relationship with a woman. He couldn't tolerate dates; sooner or later he always developed a passionate loathing for the anxious divorcee sitting opposite him in the restaurant. They fell into two categories: the ones who tried to be what they imagined he was looking for, who treated every question as a test with a correct answer, and the ones who made a show of being themselves, who got boozy and loud and, when he declined their invitation to come inside for a nightcap, mean. He gave one of them a try, for Maya's sake mostly. Donald and Valerie were together for almost two years, and the three of them went away for the weekend a few times, and to Italy once. Valerie and Maya got along fine, but in her presence Maya became polite: cheerful and courteous and well hidden. Remarkable that she knew how to do that at thirteen.

She decided to go to college back east. Donald made a pro forma case for UCLA but he was proud that she wanted to go off on her own, to make good on the independence that had been forced on her twelve years earlier. He tended to look down on the intellectual culture of his adopted state. They'd moved there for him to take the Getty job, a good job for a young man, and to be closer to Daphne's parents in Pasadena. He imagined Maya would stay on the east coast, in Boston or New York, and eventually he'd move back as well, relocate the gallery or accept a position at the MFA or the Frick. He'd take her to the theater or the '21' Club, treats she couldn't afford for herself, and he'd give a toast at her wedding and make her cry.

The first weeks of her freshman year they talked every Sunday and often more. She described her classes, her professors, her friends. There was already a new reserve about her, but he understood that she was surrounded by excitement of all kinds, intellectual and political and social—he remembered it from his own college days—and keeping her father in the loop wasn't a priority. He planned a trip to New York, although it wasn't wholly necessary, so that he could come up to Concord and take her out to dinner and get a look at the daughter who had somehow reached adulthood with no parent but him.

The dinner was awkward. He asked about her classes, and she answered in that maddening polite way he'd seen her use on Valerie, as though everything he was asking was beside the point. She became animated only when discussing trivial things, parties and friends and the details of communal living. She threatened to major in something called cultural studies. He didn't recognize this blithe girl, so unserious about herself. The roommate, a real bimbo, didn't help. Back in his hotel room afterward he worried that Ward was the wrong choice, that he should have pushed her to go somewhere more rigorous. He reminded himself that she had never acted out during her adolescence. He had allowed her to set her own hours, to stay at friends' houses as she pleased, to keep her social life largely hidden from him, and she had repaid him by graduating near the top of her class. Here, finally, was her teenage rebellion, a few years late but appropriate, even necessary. He chose to interpret it as an act of generosity that she had waited until she was out of the house before it began.

They didn't talk much for the rest of the semester. He tried to take it in stride. He allowed her to spend Christmas vacation with her friend in Boston, summer in the Middle East. She was, after all, an adult.

And then the letter arrived.

On his first reading he didn't understand what she was saying. The language she used was foreign and distracting, full of the jargon of political correctness. (He'd worried about that when she'd chosen Ward, and here it was, flowering up from his daughter's hand.) She made vague allusions to events that he couldn't identify: "what you did to me all those nights." He reached the end mystified as to what she was accusing him of. What had he done to her, all those nights? When she was a girl he had tucked her into bed, read a chapter of *Great Expectations* or *Oliver Twist*, and turned out the light. At some point this had ended, and she began putting herself to bed. And then, with a heave of revulsion, he got her meaning.

He was dimly familiar with the idea of repressed memory. He understood repression in the Freudian sense, feelings pushed out of conscious awareness. But the contemporary notion that shocking, dramatic events can somehow go unrecalled for years, only to emerge, intact, on the therapist's couch...he hadn't noticed when this piece of sophistry had entered the popular wisdom. And now his daughter believed that her childhood, the decade he'd spent battling for her happiness in the face of her mother's death, was a pretext, a cover story for awful crimes against her. He's no longer the loving father, he's the pervert, the twisted man who can satisfy himself only by turning on his own child. Every tender thing between them, every wound dressed, every wish assuaged—all vanished.

The dinner-table seminars, the bedtime readings from Dickens, the bike-riding lessons and trips to Paris and Rome, the years he put up with Valerie so that Maya would have someone to talk to when she began menstruating—these were no more than the most elaborate cover story ever devised. And his marriage, the passion between him and Daphne—do pedophiles have such feelings, or was this false too, a scheme to generate what he really wanted, a prepubescent? Donald's voice has gotten louder and his hand smacks the armrest of his chair. The moment he opened that letter, this became his story: the accusation, the defense.

He phoned and phoned, left message after message, until the roommate, that awful Emily, picked up and asked him to stop calling. He contacted the university and got passed around the phone network until he reached someone at Campus Affairs, an ignorant feminist, who said something about student privacy and made it very clear that, as far as she was concerned, anyone accused of molesting a child was guilty until proven innocent. He called organizations that dealt with child abuse, but none of them had anything to say about false accusations, and one asked for his name and address in a way he found sinister. He wanted to call his lawyer, but by then he had realized that he should watch his mouth, even with his attorney of fourteen years, whose son's wedding he had attended six months earlier. His life had become a Kafka novel, or one of the stories you used to hear from the USSR: an innocent man is caught up in the omnipotent machinery of persecution. And so he found himself in the public library, intellectual home to every conspiracy's victim, where he used the Internet for the first time. That's how he learned about the False Memory Syndrome Foundation. Donald spoke by telephone to a volunteer there, who reassured him that he was not alone and who sent him a packet of newsletters and clippings describing the epidemic that had swept his daughter away.

"It's the therapists," he says. "It is criminal, absolutely criminal, what these people are doing." His voice becomes firmer and more rehearsed. "You walk into their office and say, *I've been feeling a bit down lately.* Perhaps you're having difficulties in your life, perhaps you're feeling anxious or depressed, and you go looking for help. And they say, *I can tell just from looking at you that you were abused as a child.* They go down a checklist and say, *Which of these fit you?* and they read you a list of statements that could apply to anyone: *I feel different from other people, I feel uncomfortable about sex.* And when you say, *No, I was never abused,* they say, *Ah! The abuse was so awful that you've blocked it out.* They say, *It must have been someone you were very close to.* Sometimes they hypnotize you; they tell you hypnosis can bring these 'repressed' memories to the surface, when all it does is make you suggestible, so you produce whatever 'memories' they're looking for. Other times they say you won't get better until you can recover your memories, and they insist that you imagine being abused, write stories about being abused, until you start dreaming about being abused, and then they say, *Aha, the memories are coming back!*

"If you'd asked me before all this began, I would have told you that Maya was too smart and confident to fall for that kind of thing. But she was away from home for the first time, and vulnerable, and they took advantage of that. This therapist, she worked for the school, do you believe it? Ward College, to which I sent twenty thousand dollars a year, employs therapists who tear children away from their parents, who plant delusions in their minds, who warp their reality until they can't trust anyone."

Donald has had no direct contact with Maya since the letter. The registrar's office stopped sending him her grades. For want of other ideas, he hired a New Hampshire private investigator named Lucas Moore, a skinny man with a ponytail who could blend in on a college campus. Lucas shadowed Maya twelve hours a day for a week, watched her go to class, to the library, to parties, to cafés, back to her dorm. It was clear that daily observation wasn't going to reveal anything, so Donald and Lucas switched to a long-term arrangement in which, once a month, Lucas sent a photograph of Maya in some public location, along with the date, time, and place the photo was taken. Lucas watched Maya graduate and sent one last picture before she left Concord: in cap and gown, surrounded by friends.

Donald decided not to hire an investigator in San Francisco. He was remarried eighteen months ago, to a woman who supports him and believes him and has encouraged him to think of the period when he had a daughter as something that's over.

"You keep sending the letters, though," I say.

"I will keep sending them until I die," he says. "I still send her a gift on her birthday, too. I send her a check every year. She never cashes it. I started increasing the amount. I wanted to see if there was anything she'd consent to take from me. By last year it was up to fifteen thousand dollars."

"I don't think she wants your money."

"Apparently not," he says. He looks down at his hands, folded across his stomach, and gives a little grunt, some kind of communication with himself. "Thank you for listening to all that," he says. "I've had to give up my daughter to this madness. But this awful image of me that she plants—it's not something I can tolerate. There are people who hear my name and think, *Yes, that's the man who molested his little girl.* I want to go up to each one, to explain, to clear my name. Honestly, you have no idea what your name *is,* what it *means,* until something like this happens."

I would like to be able to say what he wants to hear, which is *You couldn't possibly be a child molester—you're a civilized man!* But how can I say that?

"I'm sorry," I say, pushing myself up from the chair.

When he stands I remember how tall he is. He wears a terrifying expression of disappointment, a look I'm sure Maya has seen plenty of. "Will you tell her I love her," he says. He knows I can't; he's just handing me a shard of his pain to carry around.

The outside world is bathed in sunshine. I start to drive back to the airport, but when I reach the freeway I follow the signs for north, toward home. California's interior is vacant and demoralized, and keeping my foot on the accelerator takes an effort of will. I drive for hours without stopping, until my throat is dry from the air conditioning and the fuel indicator dips into the red. Fuel indicators are calibrated so that actual emptiness is somewhere below the $E$ mark. Everyone knows this and calculates accordingly, and so the real function of the interface is to ensure that you can't tell exactly how much fuel is left. There is some value to this. I keep driving.

# 9

Success is also easy to handle: You've solved the wrong problem.
—Alan J. Perlis, "Epigrams on Programming"

I WAKE THE NEXT morning with the aura of something bodily amiss that foretells a cold. The chaos in my head seems more urgent. For three hours I stifle it by playing Metroid Prime. I am frozen on the couch, my thumbs animated like dancing insects, when the phone starts jumping with what seems like unusual force. I am in that state of meditative bliss and frustration that characterizes progress up a video game's learning curve: useful new gestures and strategies are moving from my conscious mind into my repertoire of automatic reflexes, freeing up the forebrain to tackle the next set of challenges. It's a hypnotic process, and hard to withdraw from. I pause the game and answer the phone with a feeling of distracted hyperreality. I am in my apartment, I am on Tallon IV, I am in phonespace with my father.

"Eric, I need to ask you for something," he says in a voice that I've never heard him use before. "I know you're not interested in my business. It would have been great to have you on board, but that's OK. But we've run into a little trouble, and we could really use your help. Not a job, I'm not trying to offer you a job again. I'm just—I'm in a tough situation, and I need your help, OK?"

Maya's past is a mystery, but mine calls me on the phone to ask for things. "What kind of trouble?" I ask. Metroid Prime, with its elaborately playable 3D environment and its carefully modeled physics, seems realer than this conversation.

GABRIEL ROTH

"Thanks, Eric," he says. "It's all the venture firms' fault. I did everything right: I had a real good idea, a real winner, and I put together a great team, with tech people and office people and everything you'd need. And I wrote this business plan, which really went into a ton of detail, with charts and everything, showing exactly what we were going to do. You know what a business plan is, right?"

"So what happened with the VCs?" I say.

"They wouldn't give us any money!" he says. "Most of them wouldn't even meet with us, wouldn't even hear our pitch. I don't know how these guys make a living, honestly, if they're not going to hear people's ideas. The whole thing's rigged. There's no way for the startup, the small business, to compete." For my dad to lose his faith in the marketplace is tantamount to a religious crisis.

"Wow, I'm sorry," I say, although in fact I feel vindicated. "So what are you going to do?"

"Well, I'm all out of options!" he says, his voice ascending the scale of indignation. "I mean, I've got this lease on the offices, and the server space—you have no idea how much it costs to rent this server space! And meanwhile there's the staff people waiting to get paid, and the contractors who designed the site, and we had to pay out the ass for the domain name."

"Oh Jesus, Dad," I say. "You staffed up before you had any funding?"

"I couldn't exactly go into Kleiner Perkins and tell them they should be funding us if we're not even a real company, could I?" he says, as though losing patience with a slow student. "You've got to spend money to make money. That's how it works."

"What money did you spend?"

"My money, Eric, money that I made. Plus I borrowed some from your grandfather. And I took out a second mortgage."

Oh my God. "And now what have you got left?"

"I'm all out, aren't I? I'm dry. And if I shut the whole operation

182

down now, number one I'll never get any of it back, and number two I've got all these debts that there's no way for me to repay. I'm looking at Chapter Seven here. I know you didn't want to come on board, and that's fine, you've got other irons in the fire, I can understand that. But you don't want to see the whole enterprise fold, do you?"

I am tired of this old man. "So what are you asking for?" I say.

There is a long pause, which I suspect is his attempt to convey how difficult this is for him, and then, in a rush, he says, "I need one point two million dollars." The word *million* comes out *miyon.* "That's what it'll take to get this off the ground. We can't count on a bunch of suits to give us the opportunity, I can see that now. We're going to have to take it ourselves."

After the events of this week, it's a relief to feel unambivalent about something. "I'm not going to fund your business, Dad," I tell him. "It's not a good business. That's why the VCs aren't going to give you money either." A blue bolt of pleasure travels up my spine. Does telling difficult truths always feel this good?

There is another silence, less deliberate this time. When he speaks again, his voice is quiet and somehow younger.

"That's all right," he says. "I wasn't expecting you to say yes, I was just trying everything I could think of. Let me ask you something else. I'll give up on the company, I'll shut it down. The staff will be disappointed, but it's OK. But I want to pay off these debts. The back pay for the employees, and the contractors' bills, and the rest of the month's rent. If I can pay that stuff off, then I won't have to declare bankruptcy. And the mortgage, a couple months, just until I can pick up some teaching work again."

"How much are we talking about now?"

"I can do it for two hundred thousand dollars," he says. He'd worked out the figure before calling.

"I don't know, Dad," I say. "I'll think about it." Something strange is happening, some reversal of the natural order, in which the inheritance passes from the son to the father, and resources flow upward through the generations. I hang up the phone and return to the game, but my eyes keep slipping down to the clock on the cable box where the hours and minutes are piling up. Maya is leaving the office in her overcoat, walking the seven blocks to my house, past the yard with the pit bull and the empty lot where the mysterious planks of wood stand like soldiers in the earth. I should put down the controller, shower, hide the evidence of the wasted day, prepare myself to deceive her about where I've been. But when she lets herself in I am under attack by a swarm of birdlike ghosts. She comes up behind me and musses the back of my hair, then goes into the bedroom, where the console's shots and explosions are muffled. Of course, her departure makes me anxious and I sacrifice the game and go to her.

We sit at the kitchen counter and eat Indian food. Not telling her that I met her father yesterday is surprisingly easy; I can see how people have affairs. I don't tell her about my dad's phone call either— maybe because, the first time he called, she asked me if he wanted money, and I'm not happy she turned out to be right. Other than deal with our fathers, all I've done since I saw her last is play GameCube.

"I think I'm pretty close to the end," I say. "Finishing a game always gives me a weird fake-accomplishment feeling. It's a lot like disappointment." She's bored: she doesn't play with her fingernails or say *uh-huh* in a distracted way, but the spark of her interest is gone. Bored, she's not magic anymore. For some reason I remember the imaginary dog she might have killed.

We finish eating and move to the bedroom in a state that combines vacant lust and a disinclination to keep talking. As I start to go down on her, I remember that I began that way last time; tonight I should have taken a more concupiscent approach, to demonstrate creativity and to flatter her with the suggestion of passionate desire. Ten minutes later, engaged in coitus a posteriori, I find myself watching as if from the side of the room. The perspective is cold and arousing, and I am handling the physiomechanics of the act with unusual confidence, until she says, "I need it rougher."

So what is this? An artifact of childhood trauma? A vestigial need to revisit that dark nexus of sex and coercion, to touch some wound inside herself? Or is it the other way around: the memories of abuse at her father's hands are masochistic fantasies, an ordinary kink misunderstood? I am not watching from the side anymore. I put my hand on the back of her head and push her face down. She makes an enthusiastic sound, or perhaps just a reflexive grunt. I am Donald now, and I give it to her, punish her for betraying me, for lying, for pretending to be a victim when she's just a slut. And then I ejaculate, much too soon. She wants to kiss afterward, which is almost more than I can stand.

Cynthia is one of those children who, lacking some gene for adolescence, have not once worried or disappointed their parents. Her grades were never less than adequate, her demeanor never hostile, her behavior never self-destructive. Every friend was presented to Doug and Rose Gerney over the family dinner table. (They adored Danny Keach, who recognized that charming them was a station on the path into Cynthia's heart and jeans.) She graduated college in four years and proceeded to obtain a skilled job. She flies home for major holidays and helps with the cooking. So it was a new experience for the Gerney family when Cynthia told her parents she'd decided that men just weren't her thing.

She calls to give me the news. "I need to tell you about it," she says. "Can I come after work?"

I make preliminary noises of regret: I'm speaking at this conference tomorrow and I'd like to go over some notes, take a bath, get an early night. But there's an uncharacteristic insistence in Cynthia's tone that makes me relent.

Sitting on my couch she describes the phone call, with her parents on separate extensions. Here's what I'm afraid of: she called and said, *Get Dad on the line, I need to tell you guys something,* and her mother leapt willfully to the conclusion that Cynthia was getting married.

"So how did they react?" I say. Doug is a bearish, mustachioed man who writes nonfiction books on manly topics: gambling, the rural life, the history of tobacco. I picture him standing in the bedroom of their house in Denver, holding the receiver to his ear, until I remember that they've moved into a smaller house, one I've never seen. Did he take Cynthia's homosexuality as a personal rejection? A lapse in his daughter's love? What the hell is fatherhood about, anyway?

They didn't disown her. Doug kept saying, *It's just such a surprise.* Rose said, *But don't you want children?* Cynthia explained that lesbianism doesn't preclude children, but Rose wasn't satisfied and Doug went to the kitchen to hold her while she sobbed into the phone.

I murmur sympathetically, but Cynthia sweeps my condolences away with the back of her hand.

"She just couldn't get over the grandchildren thing," she says. "I told her I could go to a sperm bank or something, and that didn't help." She blows the steam off her tea. "So I said you'd probably give me some if I asked." I can't think of anything to say to this except *Ha!* "And the thing is, she totally stopped crying. She made me promise to ask you about it."

"I'm flattered that your mom holds my DNA in such high esteem."

"No, she always liked you. And she was really impressed when you sold the company." This remark triggers a wave of disgust, but I can't tell where it's directed. To feel disgusted is to feel implicated.

"It'll never happen, obviously," Cynthia says. "I just wanted you to be prepared if she ever says anything weird about it."

"Color me prepared," I say, getting up from the couch to fetch some snacks and relieve the interpersonal intensity. "No, it's fine. Tell her whatever." In one of the infinite possible futures that branch from every instant, Cynthia is raising twins, a boy and a girl, with her chubby face and my inability to relate to people. On the way to the pantry I pass my laptop, which is sitting on the kitchen island, and of course I glance at the screen in case Maya has emailed to say how much she loves me. Instead there's a message from Donald Marcom with the subject *Checking in.*

I return to the couch with a box of chocolate marshmallow Pinwheels, but Cynthia knows something's not right.

"What just happened?" she says.

So I have to explain everything, even though I understand so little. Cynthia has heard me say that Maya was abused, and it never occurred to her to treat that statement as anything other than a fact. She wants to see Donald's email, so I fetch the computer from the island and set it down on the table in front of us. It reads:

Eric,

Your disinterested pursuit of the truth does you credit. Thanks to you I find myself more hopeful than at any time since this ordeal began. I hope you will keep me informed about your discussions with Maya—both for my own information and to allow me to respond to any further distortions.

DBM

This is one of those times when you have managed to be true to yourself, have obeyed unusually clear impulses, and then find yourself at the bottom of a pit, unable to explain how you got there. How did Donald Marcom and I wind up on the same side?

"He thinks you're working for him?" Cynthia says. I shrug.

"He's irrelevant," I say. "But...I need to figure this out."

"No, you don't," she says. She gestures at the computer as though Donald were a mischievous goblin living inside. "If he's an innocent guy and he lost his daughter, that's very sad and everything, but why is that your problem? You're her boyfriend. Just be her boyfriend."

By some unlikely chance, Maya Marcom is prepared to spend time with me. This astonishing person will be here at my apartment, of her own volition, in one hour. When she was picking her outfit earlier today, she might have momentarily wondered what I'd find attractive. And I'm going to get stuck on whether this story she believes is accurate?

"You're right," I say. I lean forward to the laptop and delete Donald's email, a gesture that gives me a little kick of satisfaction.

"There you go," Cynthia says.

"I feel good about this," I say. I stand up and look around the apartment. I feel a sudden urge to tidy the place up, although it's not messy.

"Jeez, you went all the way to LA," Cynthia says.

"Yeah, that's really weird," I say. "I can never tell her about that, right?" Cynthia frowns—she has a native distaste for secrecy. "I went to see him, behind her back."

"Right," she says. "Yeah, don't tell her." She smiles nervously, as though we're in a children's conspiracy, and once again I feel thankful that she's on my side. We order Thai food and eat it in front of the TV.

Maya and I ride to the Digital Future Conference in a cab. I don't usually take cabs with her because I have the idea that she'd rather not date a guy who takes cabs everywhere. I tried to dissuade her from coming—I don't know that I want her to see me in this context—but she insisted.

"Are you nervous?" Maya asks me.

"Nah," I say reflexively. "Not really. A little."

She smiles. "Is it all going to be super technical? Like, give me an estimate of how much I'm going to understand." This self-deprecating reminder of my expertise is reassuring, as she intends it to be.

"Oh, no, it'll be general-audience stuff," I say. "Whether you find it interesting or not is a different question."

She rolls her eyes — *This again* — but affectionately, which is the best I can hope for.

My goal with the cab was for us to arrive within five minutes of the 10 a.m. start time of my first panel, "Privacy in the Internet Age." I don't want Maya to see too many hallway interactions — men in pleated khakis pitching me on their startup or framework. Construction on Folsom Street slows the cab down, and then we have to collect our badges (mine has my name in big letters; Maya's just says GUEST), so we end up rushing through the hallway, past the programmers and MBAs in separate clusters.

We hurry into room 1F at eight minutes after ten to find the seats mostly full and three men milling around next to the big table on the dais: the moderator, the director of a consumer-rights non-profit, and the maker of an anonymizer application. The moderator, a columnist for *IT Security*, hurries over. "Oh good, good, you're here," he says, with a funny mixture of deference and irritation. "We're all ready to go!" Maya squeezes my arm and slips away to take a seat.

I take my spot behind a microphone and a pitcher of water as the moderator begins his introductions. I survey the crowd — *hey, that's kind of a lot of people* — and locate Maya, near the back, grinning up at me, proud, maybe?

In response to the first question, Jack Schell from the Center for Digital Privacy makes an appeal to fear: your secrets are a commodity; your personal information is bought and sold; a stranger is using your credit card and your social security number.

The moderator, whose name I've forgotten, looks to me for the rebuttal. I'm here to represent the bad guys.

I give the stump speech I used to give journalists who asked about Demo1's Big Brotherly implications. Sharing your information entails benefits and risks; decisions should be left to the individual. Demo1 presented its terms of use in clear English, required user opt-in, provided for admirably fine-grained preference-setting. We're in the early stages of a new mass medium. Remember the controversy around cookies circa 1998? Some people found it nefarious that the Internet could know who you are; it was as if your TV was watching you. But that's why the Internet's going to destroy TV: it's a mass medium that knows who you are. Whether you find that exciting or frightening is up to you. The subtext of the discussion, which I do not exhume, is *Will everyone find out I look at pornography?*, to which the answer is *Probably not, but you never know*.

Jack Schell says, "You founded Demographic of One in 1999. Last year you sold it to Atrium." His lips twitch as he represses a smile; he's prepping a haymaker. "All the data you collected on users was included in the sale—it's what Atrium paid for. Do you trust them to use it properly?"

Actually, that information wasn't worth much; we didn't have enough users. What Atrium paid for was our technology, the thousands of hours of concentrated thought that Bill and I put into the codebase. But what would Jack Schell know about that? I say, "The terms of use still apply."

"But you don't have any control over whether they stick to them, do you?" he says. "That's what happens when people's personal information becomes a commodity."

The crowd's silence has a special attentive quality: no one was expecting actual conflict. "Eric Muller, care to respond to that?" says the moderator, clearly imagining himself on TV. The other panelist, whose app is pretty good, hasn't said a word.

"You know what that information is?" I say. "It's what brand of dog food you buy. It's whether you wear a medium or a large. It's all stuff that the girl who rings up your purchase at the supermarket already knows."

"We're in the middle of a sea change that very few people are aware of," Schell says. He's drawn himself up in his chair to indicate that he's about to intensify his rhetoric. "The government is granting itself ever greater powers to track people's private information. The Internet is being used by corporations to gather data on customers. And the individual's right to control information about him- or herself is falling by the wayside. The point is not the intrinsic privacy value of any particular piece of data; the point is our right to a private self." A few spectators nod their heads vigorously.

I can't match Schell's oratorical style, so I opt for brisk dismissiveness: *There's no need for all that speechifying.* "The information we gathered exists on a level at which the individual is meaningless," I say. I look straight at Schell and smile. "The facts about what you eat or drink or wear or buy have no value. It's only when those facts are bundled with everyone else's facts, when you're subsumed in a mass of data, that you mean anything at all to Atrium or to any other company with six hundred million dollars in revenues last year. This whole discussion is predicated on a kind of paranoid egotism: *Everyone wants to look at me, everyone's interested in what I'm doing, the CIA is bugging my phone, Pfizer wants to steal my urine.* There's no need to worry about this stuff, because none of us is that important."

I've gotten kind of worked up, and by the end I'm sitting upright and projecting just as forcefully as Jack Schell. People laugh, although they're not sure if they're laughing with me or at me. Schell smiles at me, an all-in-good-fun smile—the professional privacy advocate, after all, is a parasite on privacy-encroachers like me—and then the moderator, out of pity, invites the man from SecreSoft to explain where his product fits into the debate.

When time is called the applause goes beyond the perfunctory, and there's a sense that the crowd has been given its money's worth. I make eye contact with Maya as she utters a celebratory whoop. She looks relieved, and I realize that she was nervous for me.

The audience for the next panel has begun to trickle in and hover at the back of the room, so we hurry off the stage. The moderator thanks us fervently, and Jack Schell begins following up on a point he didn't get to complete. Maya comes and stands close to me while he's talking. I wait for Schell to wind down before giving him a little excuse-me nod and turning to her. "You were so great!" she says, slipping her arm around my waist. Schell registers this, and I feel myself puffing up. Masculine dominance has an unfamiliar, hormonal tang. "You were great too," she says to Schell, perfectly.

As the group breaks up, someone at my elbow says, "Mr. Muller?"

A chunky guy in a T-shirt, with a beauty mark tragically reminiscent of Marilyn Monroe's. Of course, he has an idea that he wants me to fund, something about "social marketing."

"We've got to run," I tell him. "Send me an email about it." I lean in and murmur my address confidentially, although he could find it in ten seconds if he typed my name into Google. And then I take Maya's arm and head off toward the main entrance.

She has to get to her office. We hold hands as I walk her to the bus stop.

"He didn't have a good idea, that guy?" she says.

"Who knows?" I say. "Ideas are worthless. If it's a good idea, two thousand people are working on it right now. The only way to make money on it would be to figure out which of them's the smartest."

We make plans to go out tonight to eat and drink, and I put her on a bus and head back to the convention center. I'm not due at "Surviving the Crash" for an hour and a half, so I ride the escalator and find a bench on the unoccupied third floor. The walls are tinted glass, and the metal grid between the panes casts rhomboid shadows. There is something soothing and luxurious about all this expensive real estate sitting empty. As the hum of professional activity wafts up from the floors below, I feel saturated with contentment. I know everything I need to know right now. A janitor pushes a vacuum along the floor and I follow his path in the slant of the sunlit carpet fibers.

The second panel goes just as well as the first, or perhaps better. I make one remark that gets a full-on laugh from the audience, which makes me think I should have been a comedian — *This is the best feeling in the world; you're bringing joy to people, plus they worship you like a god.* I wish Maya had been here to see it. If she could see only one of the two panels, which would be preferable: the earlier one, in which I vanquished an opponent in verbal combat, or this one, in which I made a successful joke? This thought exercise is interrupted by a question from the moderator about raising venture capital.

My line on "Surviving the Crash" is *Just build the best thing you can and if it's good enough someone will pay you money for it.* That's true as far as it goes, but it leaves out the one million accidents that are necessary ingredients in any success story. For instance, this incredible girl who seems to like me. We might never have met, or she could have had a boyfriend or been a lesbian. But let's not discount the role played by my own perspicacity and adroitness. I used my native wit to track her down and my carefully honed charm to beguile her. I triumphed over every obstacle, and if most of those obstacles were self-generated, that only underscores the difficulty of the triumph. And this last hurdle, this level boss, this mental loop that I was almost trapped in ... No, I *was* trapped in it, and I jolted myself out and made it home. And now I just have to answer a few more questions from these aspiring entrepreneurs, all of whom want to be where I am, young and rich and basking in new love, and then I can go buy some new clothes and take Maya somewhere expensive, with fancy cocktails in specialized glasses. The panel ends, and there's clapping, and I hustle out quickly, avoiding eye contact with the scrum of would-be founders.

It's already dark when my cab pulls up outside Maya's building. The streetlights are high and weak and the block has a ghostly feel. I tell the driver to wait, let myself in, and call up the stairs to warn her of my arrival. She steps out of her room applying a final coat of lip gloss, and when it's done she looks at me with a smile that's some-how both calculated and innocent—it recognizes and enjoys its own devastating effect.

Her final steps down the hall toward me might almost be cho-reographed: as she moves she slides on a heavy coat, grabs her purse from a hook, slips the lip gloss into it. I'm on the second stair from the top—our spot—and when she reaches me she leans in and kisses me just enough to let me know she means it without messing up her lips.

In the cab we talk about what we're doing, the occasion.

"So this is Fancy Eric," she says, giving me the once-over. "I like it."

"These shoes are made from opossums," I say.

"Sustainably harvested opossums, I'm assuming."

"You could harvest these opossums for a thousand years, you'd end up with more opossums than you had at the beginning."

"Mine are vegetarian," she says. "They're made from kale."

My hand is on her thigh. "A special kind of high-tech kale."

"A kind of kale that's tanned and dyed to look like black leather."

"How does it taste?"

"You have *no idea*."

In front of the restaurant I climb out and extend a hand for

Maya. Presumably somewhere there are people who can perform the man-helps-woman-out-of-cab bit with no ironic flourishes on either side, but we have never met those people.

We are half an hour early because we want to wait in the bar, where we sit in a booth whose back rises above our heads and makes us feel cocooned in velveteen. A gentleman in his forties, who knows as much about liquor as I do about Unix, hands us lists of specialty cocktails that cost sixteen dollars and contain at least five ingredients. Maya chooses something involving gin and muddled blueberries; I order the second-oldest whiskey, which is a more masculine approach to spending a lot of money on alcohol.

"So!" she says after we clink glasses. "You were such a rock star today! I had no idea you were good at stuff like that."

"I'm not, really," I say. "You know how sometimes when you're feeling good you can do things you wouldn't normally be able to do." I am trying to say that she gives me special powers without quite saying it, although by the end of this whiskey I'll probably just be saying it.

"With me it's totally an either/or thing," she says. "When I go on the radio, I can tell from the first minute how it's going to go. Like with that school budget story—I knew it was going to be hard to sum up, and then I started talking and two minutes later I'm still trying to explain it. Two minutes is *forever.*"

"It wasn't that bad," I say. I don't think I told her I was listening.

"The thing is—and thanks, you're sweet—but the thing is, even if it was fine, it threw me off for the rest of the show. I couldn't give simple answers to any of the questions. And then when we started getting calls—did you hear the whole thing? There was this one terrible guy, this racist guy…"

"I don't think I heard that far," I say. Of course I heard the whole thing.

"So this guy calls in, and he was like, *The problem is they're spending all this money on trying to equalize the test scores, because the blacks always score lower than the whites, and we're going to spend all this money trying to make sure all the groups score the same.* And usually I know how to handle these guys, but—"

"I totally heard this," I say, because why the hell not? "You got a bit more heated, there was a little more fire in your voice, but you were still totally articulate and convincing. You said, *You invest in the underserved areas because that's where the need is greatest, but it's also where the returns are highest.* And the way you said it, it was like, *Good morning, sir—I'm going to be totally courteous and professional while I carve you into pieces.*"

She's a bit taken aback—she wasn't expecting a direct quotation from a radio appearance she made more than three weeks ago—but I think in a positive way. "Well, thanks," she says. "That's kind of what happened to you with that privacy guy."

"I guess so," I say. "I mean, he's not actually harmful like a racist, he's just irritating."

"Yeah, but you got some mileage from that irritation," she says. "And you were the underdog. If some racist nutjob wants to pick a fight with me, literally everybody listening to public radio in the Bay Area is on my side. You were there representing big scary corporations."

"I know—it's weird," I say. "I started this thing that was basically a supermarket loyalty-card program, and now somehow I'm the guy inside your computer watching you undress."

"Well, you did great," she says.

"Thanks. How's the drink?"

"It's the best thing I've ever tasted in my life. How's yours?"

"It's just like normal whiskey only without the part where it burns your throat."

"I didn't realize you were such a connoisseur!"

"That was actually a quote from my forthcoming review in *Whiskey* magazine."

And then she does this amazing thing: she scoots around the booth to me and leans into my side, tipping her head onto my shoulder. We sit like that for a minute as the whiskey reaches my fingertips and everything is perfect.

"So we're getting serious about this, huh?" she says.

"Yeah, we totally are," I say. "I mean, I am. I'm serious."

"OK then," she says, sitting up and looking me square in the eye. "I'm serious too."

At some point maybe this will feel like simple contentment rather than giddy euphoria, but that's hard to imagine.

"It's weird, right?" I say, as though we're just two people having a conversation about some normal thing. "You meet someone, you fall for them, you do stuff together and it's great and everything, and they're still basically a stranger." She's nodding and grinning. She's with me on this. "And at some point you have to decide, *OK, I'm not just on the outside of this trying to figure it out, I'm on the inside now.*"

"I was wondering when you were going to decide that."

"Really? You saw me being on the outside?"

"Yeah. I mean, I'm not a mind reader, but it seemed like at first you wanted to put me under an X-ray machine, and then that got really intense and hard to deal with, and then it kind of peaked and you got it out of your system."

"You know you are in fact kind of a mind reader, right?"

She laughs. "Nah, you're just not that great at hiding what's going on with you." Unbelievable. "So what was it? Just normal fear-of-commitment stuff?"

"Yeah, basically," I say. I get a weird metallic taste in my mouth at my impulse to dissemble at this of all moments. It's a bad taste and I'm sick of it. "No, actually, not just that. It was to do with the stuff from your past, with your father, the abuse."

She looks sympathetic. "What were you feeling about that?" she asks.

"Well, I didn't know if it was true or not," I say. "I mean, really, that's the thing about it, is that there's no way to know. So I got all wrapped up in this idea that I had to figure it out, I had to find the truth. I went and talked to your dad about it, is how worked up I was about it!"

That was probably a mistake. "What the fuck," she says.

"That's what I'm saying!" I say helplessly. "I was so wrapped up in this stupid way of thinking, having to figure out the, you know, the *facts* instead of concentrating on what's important, which is how you feel about it. And so I did this dumb thing and I…"

*"You called my dad?"*

"No, I, uh, I went to see him. In LA."

She just sits there looking at me. A certain amount of astonished bafflement appears on her face alongside the anger. I don't know how long it lasts, us sitting there with her visibly adjusting her feelings about me in light of this new information. Maybe a long time. Minutes.

"So what happened?" she says, working to minimize the emotion in her voice.

I'm not sure if the specifics make me come out looking better or worse. Probably a wash. Not that it matters. "I made an appointment to see his gallery, and I flew down there. I—"

"When was this?"

"Last week. Friday." She nods. "I just asked him what happened, and he told me his version."

"Which is what?"

"He talked for a long time. He really wanted to persuade me that you were wrong, that you'd been brainwashed or confused or something."

"And what did you think when he said that?"

"I thought I didn't know, and there was no way to know, and I was looking for some kind of certainty that didn't exist and I should forget about it and concentrate on, you know, you and me, and being in love, and the stuff that's important!"

The hostess is hovering just behind my right shoulder, which means our table is ready. Maya is ignoring her. Obviously we're not about to head into the dining room, look over the menus, order the pork shoulder, which is only available for two people and which seems to stand for everything I have just lost.

"How long did you sit there and listen to him?" she says.

"I'm not sure."

"More than an hour?"

"Probably."

Those are actual tears coming to her eyes. I've never seen her do that before: *welling up*. She doesn't want to break down and sob, but the tears won't stop coming. Also the look of hatred and betrayal. Never seen that either.

The hostess leans in and says, "We're ready for you in the dining room." She's smiling—she's been standing there long enough to read our mood and has chosen to ignore it. Probably I should tell her that we won't be needing our table after all, but what if Maya's about to start laughing, shake her head at my stupidity, and then tell me it's all part of why she loves me, and are we getting the pork shoulder?

I look over at Maya. "Do you want to..." She looks back witheringly.

I stand and tell the hostess, "I'm afraid we're not going to be able to have dinner." She walks off in silence. Maya hasn't moved, so I have to sit down and let this go on.

"So he told you about the false memory bullshit. You got the whole line."

"Yeah."

"That must have been right up your alley."

I don't know what to say to this.

"I told you about him, Eric. I told you about the interrogations, and the constant discussion of my sex life, and all the bullshit of living with him." Her hands are on the table, and she keeps squeezing them into fists. "So now you've decided that what happened isn't the *point?* You're just going to shake your head at the ineffable mystery of my childhood? Believe me, I know how little I know. I have a hole in my memory and I have to live with that every day, but at least I can own what I've got. Do I know for sure that my father raped me in my bed when I was eleven? No, I don't know that for sure, because I wasn't taking notes at the time. I think he did and that's enough to stop me talking to him. But I know he hurt me, and I know he hurt me sexually, and I can guess how old I was when it happened, because I know what I was like before and I know what I was like afterward."

The bar waiter chooses this moment to set down the bill in a thickly padded leather booklet. The room has filled up since we sat down.

She takes a breath. "I have to get out of here," she says. "It's important that you don't call me." She's speaking with exaggerated calm, trying to say what she needs to say before she breaks down.

"Look, I understand you're upset," I say. "Can we just talk about this?"

"I'm going to have to be alone right now," she says.

"That's fine," I say. "But can we just say we're going to talk? It could be tomorrow, or whenever, but let's just make a plan to talk when we're not both worked up." Everything rides on whether I can convince her of this.

"Play out that conversation right now," she says. "You think it doesn't matter if you believe me or not. But it matters to me. Am I going to decide it doesn't matter to me? Or are you going to start believing me by force of will? This is your thing, Eric, figuring this stuff out. Is there a solution to this?" She's no longer at risk of crying; the effort she put into summing up the logic of her position has steadied her. She gives me a few seconds to exhaust the possibilities, and then she gets up and leaves.

The only thing to do now is to contain the panic and despair for a few more hours, which is why, twenty minutes later, I find myself exiting a cab across the street from the I-Hole. It's a solution that presents itself fully formed, but if I had to show the working it would look something like, *What can possibly stop me from thinking about what just happened? Pretty girls taking their clothes off. Where can I find them?*

I get cash from the ATM in the lobby, despite the usurious five-dollar fee, because when I feel this bad I am allowed to waste money. Twenty-five dollars gets my hand stamped with a special ink that only shows up under black light. I give the cashier two more twenties, which he exchanges for singles to be passed around the club's microeconomy. There's a board above the cashier's desk with WHO'S DANCING Now printed at the top and, beneath it, nameplates engraved with the stage names of the dancers: Princess, Midori, Porsche, Tiffany, Asia, Mykel, plus New Dancer 1 and New Dancer 2, representing girls who haven't been there long enough to get a nameplate made. These nameless girls more than any others seem to hold out the possibility of happiness: perhaps their names are Jen or Heather; perhaps they are nice, normal women who happen to be incredibly hot strippers and who would like to hang out later. As I pass through the heavy velour curtain into the club itself the music has the viscosity of an element somewhere between air and water. The room is a big cuboid, dressed up with velveteen drapes but beneath them unmistakably cinderblock industrial. Everywhere around this rough-edged theater are women in sex costume: tiny shorts, skirts too short to serve a skirt's purpose, bikini tops and minuscule T-shirts and huge heels. It is a rich and thrilling set of possibilities, and the prospect of choosing from among these women makes me hopeful. I walk down the aisle toward the stage, making eye contact with the women without acknowledging the men at all. Men here have to extend privacy to one another, as in a restroom. We've brought our lust and sadness to this place to have them tended to by professionals.

The rows of theater seats, red and beginning their decay, run parallel to the long catwalk. I choose a seat midway along the front row and turn my attention to the dancer, a tiny Asian with a stretchy blue skirt hiked up all the way around her waist. She smiles with a distant mania as she shakes her breasts vigorously back and forth, a movement more athletic than erotic. She's too skinny, too crazy, but I lay two bills on the lip of the stage anyway, to establish my bona fides. I shift back in my seat and relax into the arousal and the music, feeling my concerns narrow to a pinprick.

The song ends and the dancer picks up her clothes, gathers the dollar bills scattered over the stage, and hurries off, no longer a performer, now just a naked girl stuffing things into her purse. Over the PA, the DJ instructs us to give a big welcome to Alannah, and a blonde emerges in a little white skirt, black shirt tied tight across her breasts. She's not small, and she seems to be overspilling her clothes. And then she selects me from the six other tippers in the front row, looks me straight in the eye, and unleashes a smile that generates in my brain the exact chemical correlative of *This girl and I are in love*. The male nervous system's response to a smile from a pretty girl—the sudden infusion of joy and fear—is no less powerful when you're paying for it.

Alannah begins to dance. Intermittently she shuts her eyes and resembles a girl dancing alone in her bedroom, imagining being watched. It's possible that she's enjoying herself. She's either an exhibitionist or a skilled pretender; there's no way to tell which. She makes her way to the end of the catwalk and back, smiling at each spectator in a nice-to-meet-you way, until she reaches me and, once again, it's as though we have some private arrangement. She holds my eye for almost half a minute, far longer than she gives anyone else. I sink into my seat, a luxurious erotic charge circulating through my body as sweet as any feeling in the world, and on the worst night of my life it's available for nothing but money.

As her final song goes into repeat-to-fade the DJ exhorts us to applaud and Alannah gathers up her take. On her way off the stage she grins at me, and then she's gone and I'm reeling.

There follows one of the mysteriously long pauses that sometimes interrupt the entertainment's flow at the I-Hole. The dancers fan out to proposition us; they're not allowed to solicit while another girl is performing. A thin woman with olive skin leans over the armrest to offer me a lap dance, and I decline quickly. I sit buzzing in my cushioned seat, trying not to look at the door from which Alannah will soon emerge. The DJ plays generic techno music and says over the PA, "Mystique to the back, Mystique to the back," like a paging desk at an airport. And then I feel a hand on my shoulder and Alannah is at my side, wearing her minimal outfit again, bending in close and saying, "So c'mon back with me." She takes my hand and we walk together, like a couple, away from the stage.

My visit is in danger of being brought to an end too soon. Alannah and I are about to go into a room lined with small curtained booths. Inside a booth, we are going to conduct a quick negotiation— I will not haggle; I don't want to corrode the excitement by getting stingy and realistic—and then Alannah is going to take off her clothes and rub her elegant body up against me. At some point I'm going to ejaculate in my underwear—there is a tissue dispenser mounted on the wall of each booth in anticipation—at which point the ability of the I-Hole and its subcontractors to excite and distract me will be tapped out, and knowledge of certain realities will flood back in to fill the void.

She exchanges a quick greeting with the beefy black security guard and leads me to a booth. Inside she says, "So it's eighty for a private," and I give it to her, and the awkward part is over. I fish my keys out of my pants pocket so they won't get in the way, hang my jacket on a hook. And then she puts her hands on my shoulders, sits me down on the banquette, and, grinning, turns around and prettily lowers her skirt. Her white thong is the smallest imaginable. She slides down onto my lap, then throws her head backwards onto my shoulder, while in the mirror I watch her undo the knot on her shirt for the second time. The perfume on her neck is sweet and fruity. She starts to writhe, and her skin is absurdly soft, and light seems to emanate from her pores. For some reason I am not hard. Alannah continues to move against and before me, demonstrating her deep and thorough grasp of the physical language of male sexual fantasy. The bikini top comes off, and then the G-string. Her breasts are swept across my face; her cunt and her asshole are offered for scrutiny; her eyes suggest an unstoppable sexual hunger. Why is something always wrong? Alannah is straddling me now, her back to me again — there are only so many positions for her to take — and in the mirror she wears a look of intense concentration. Her grinding on my lap suddenly feels incongruous. This isn't what I need. It seems important not to let her know. Once the song is over — is this the second or the third? — I will get out of this noisy windowless place. I see my own face in the mirror and think *Maya's gone,* and I watch my features crumple as tears stream down my cheeks and land, hotly, on Alannah's shoulder.

She jumps up, startled.

"Sorry," I say.

"What was that?" she says.

"Uh, I just — I've had a really hard day," I say, and this admission starts the tears flowing again.

She understands, now, what she felt trickle down her back, but she doesn't seem relieved. She stands in front of me, naked but for her huge shoes, and grabs her purse from the little shelf, a gesture that is somehow the opposite of pornographic. "So, what," she says. "Are we done?"

"Yeah," I say. "I guess we're done."

I have a mode for retreat, practiced during those long hours in my childhood bedroom. My job now is to soothe myself, and I dedicate myself to it. I ignore a series of increasingly urgent voicemail messages from my father. I spend days reading collected editions of old comics and watching TV shows on DVD. For boys of my generation, the dream was not to be an explorer or an Air Force pilot but to own every comic book and every video game ever made, and I am keeping faith with my childhood self. Perhaps girls were a distraction all along, a fool's gold, and the toys and hobbies they replaced were the true path. In my dreams, Cyclops and Wolverine fight each other to a stalemate over Maya's corpse.

Right now Maya is going to work, filing stories, complaining about me to a friend. Although I can't identify anyone she might confide in. I've been wearing the same T-shirt for three days. What if she turns up on my doorstep? I could change the T-shirt in anticipation of her arrival, but that would be self-defeating. I compromise by leaving a clean T-shirt on top of my dresser so I can pull it on when the doorbell rings. Months from now, when I've resumed changing my clothes and leaving the house, the T-shirt I'm wearing now will remind me of this period and I will try to smile but fail. I spend minutes at a stretch trying unsuccessfully to remember how she smelled. Maybe I should buy some of her citrus shower gel and become a pathetic old man who stands fully clothed in the bathtub sniffing at a bottle of shower gel. I've known her only a couple months, but I'd been waiting to meet her ever since I noticed Bronwen Oberfell's profile while watching television, and so my mind took her in: things shifted into position around her and wedged themselves securely in place. The problem of loving her is a bug, a big one, a showstopper, and I chew on it endlessly, nagged by the feeling that I'm missing something. There must be some way to love her that can coexist with ignorance. Maya's past is unknowable, but what part of anyone is knowable? We can only know each other the way we know distant stars: by observing years-old light, gathering outdated information, running calculations and making inferences.

Cynthia, worried about me, calls in the evenings. I try to present with the precise emotional blend that suggests psychological health for someone in my position: a mixture of grief and regret and wry sad humor and self-awareness, not repressing or wallowing but authentically experiencing and processing and healing. Cynthia is pretty acute when it comes to feelings, and delivering so complex a performance to the necessary standard of verisimilitude leaves me exhausted.

I consider hiring a prostitute, which I've never done, but I'm afraid it would provoke a repeat of the crying-on-a-stripper incident. I wonder if there are prostitutes who will let you cry on them, who will even make noises of consolation for a small surcharge.

The guiding idea, inasmuch as there is one, is to make myself comfortable while time works its anodyne ways on my heart. My dad's phone calls are sand in the gears. When I see his name on the phone's screen I erase the message unheard, but this makes me feel guilty, and my job at the moment is to minimize bad feelings, and after two messages a tipping point is reached. When he calls for the third time I find myself picking up the receiver and putting it to my ear.

"Eric, hi," he says with a mixture of surprise and wheedling. "Listen, I've got a —"

"What's your bank account number?" I say.

He makes some hemming noises and then begins to recite the digits, which I write on the margin of a newspaper. "And the routing code?" As he speaks I hold the phone two inches from my ear, so the voice saying the numbers sounds very small and far away. "This isn't going to happen again," I say before hanging up. I fax my signature to my financial manager to authorize the transfer. Five minutes later his assistant calls to let me know it's gone through. She has the pragmatic good cheer of a nurse, someone who knows private things about people. I won't speak to my father again until after the stroke, almost ten years from now.

That evening, the United States launches missiles at Dora Farms in southeast Baghdad, on the basis of reports that Saddam Hussein is visiting his children there. Fifteen civilians are killed. The reports turn out to be mistaken. Ten days later Pete Oberfell will parachute into Iraqi Kurdistan with the 173rd Airborne. Kirkuk falls quickly, and Pete's division misses almost all of the fighting, to the relief of Pete's family. The 173rd stays to provide security after the collapse of the Iraqi government.

Three years later, at Stacey Oberfell's request, my mother and I will visit him at his parents' house on Christmas Eve. The snow is unusually heavy, even for Colorado. On our way, my mother tells me that Pete's fiancée broke off the engagement a few weeks after he got home.

Pete is still pale but now he towers over me, with big adult-sized arms and legs. As we shake hands, he takes in my presence like I'm neither a good thing nor a bad thing but a fact to be aware of.

"You showed me that computer game that one time," he says, sitting down in a high-backed chair. "That was cool. I was going to learn computers right after I got back. I started taking a course."

"How'd that go?"

"It wasn't for me," he says. "I couldn't concentrate. I have a hard time paying attention to stuff like that."

Stacey comes in with mugs of coffee on a tray. Pete takes the first one.

"So are you glad to be back in the country?" my mom asks.

"Honestly, no," he says. "I hated every second when I was over there, but this is worse." The tone in which he reports these feelings is factual and uncomplaining.

"How can this be worse than *Iraq?*" my mother asks.

Pete's level gaze never flickers. "What do you know about it?" he asks.

"Pete," his mother says. Pete stands without saying a word and leaves the room. We don't see him again. Back in San Francisco I make a donation, in Pete's name, to a charity that helps veterans with posttraumatic stress disorder, and I wonder if Maya's name should be attached as well.

I will see her once more, while I'm out with someone else. I quit girls for a long time after Maya. Even after I could reliably get out of bed, even after I had started working on a JavaScript graphics library and buying a car and leaving the apartment, the idea of *meeting a girl* and *getting to know her* was too much to contemplate. And then, about a year ago, time and boredom and loneliness wore me down and I signed up with an online dating site.

From the moment I clicked CREATE YOUR PROFILE the whole endeavor felt exhausting. I didn't want a new set of protocols to optimize: what to write in the profile fields, what to say in an initial message, when to escalate from email to brunch — all the crap I'd wasted my life on, only now I was doing it alongside millions of extroverted and apparently well-adjusted people.

And then I had to go on these dates, dozens of them, one after another, all formally identical, struggling each time to remember that I was seated across from an entire human being with a unique consciousness and a full set of private associations, each of us iterating on our questions and answers like algorithms trying to mate. I was at the point of giving up when I met Annabelle. I liked her photo, with her overstyled clothes and wide-open face, and I liked the earnest way she actually answered the generic questions in the profile form instead of taking a meta approach like everyone else.

We went to a sushi restaurant where I'd been with half a dozen other girls, but I found myself saying different things to her. She was shy and unostentatiously perceptive, and I began cultivating a crush on her. It's going OK.

That was just over a month ago. Tonight I'm meeting her at a bar around the corner from her apartment, where she'll introduce me to some of her college friends. They're at a table in the back, five or six in all, more than I was expecting. You can tell they're younger than me. Annabelle sees me and waves, and they start to shuffle around to make room. And between here and there, Maya is sitting in a booth looking unsurprised to see me.

Her hair is different. In my absence she has continued living her life, setting and achieving goals, making decisions about her hair. Other than that, I'm not sure whether her features have grown sharper or the memory I'm comparing her to has blurred around the edges. She's with two women and a man, a friendly group. The jukebox is turned up loud, and I suddenly become aware that everyone in the bar is shouting.

Annabelle and Maya have each seen me acknowledge the other, so the calculations are multithreaded. My only option is to signal *one second* to Annabelle with an apologetic index finger, then say hello to Maya as if I were not in the process of crumbling into pieces all over the sticky floor of the bar. And so our final encounter is conducted with me acting as though I had something more important to get to, while she sees through me yet again.

She feels like a celebrity now, like someone with whom you have an intimate relationship in your mind. She smiles from the other side of a chasm.

What do we do now? Do we have a conversation? *I no longer imagine that you're about to call. I've almost stopped comparing other people to you. Sometimes I wonder what picture of me exists in your mind, and I have no idea.*

"So you're here on a date," she says as I crouch next to her seat.

"How did you know that?"

"The way she's looking at me right now," she says. I can't turn to look at Annabelle, so we're in a conspiracy again, which is impossibly sweet and painful. "You'd better go."

*You are the only person I will ever love,* I say, but only in my head, where it can't do any harm to anyone but me. "Hey, it's good to see you." As I stand up I touch her amicably on the shoulder, then wish I hadn't, and then head to the back of the bar to begin apologizing.

# Acknowledgments

Special thanks to Heather Abel, Nick Garland, Andrew Kidd, Anna Stein, and Laura Tisdel.

Thanks also to Reagan Arthur, Michael Pietsch, Marlena Bittner, Amanda Heller, Michael Noon, and everyone else at Little, Brown; Clare Alexander, Imogen Pelham, and Sally Riley at Aitken Alexander; Kate Harvey at Picador; Philip Hoy at the Waywiser Press; Michael Heyward at Text Publishing; and to Francie Barnard, Cynthia Barton, Wendy Brandchaft, Maxine Chernoff, Cassi Feldman, Alex Garland, Jake Kasdan, Alice LaPlante, Jim Nelson, Kate Nitze, John O'Brien, Peter Orner, Brian L. Perkins, Chuck Plotkin, Priscilla Roth, Zachary Roth, Kevin Shay, Wesley Stace, Jean Strouse, Annie Wedekind, Bob Woodward, and the Brooklyn Writers Space.

Maximum thanks to my wife, Tali Woodward, who makes everything possible.

# About the Author

GABRIEL ROTH has worked as a journalist and a web developer. He lives with his family in Brooklyn, New York.

BACK BAY · READERS' PICK

Reading Group Guide

# The
# Unknowns

A Novel

by

Gabriel Roth

# A conversation with Gabriel Roth

*What brought you to the point where you started to write your first novel? Are you the kind of person who's always had a novel bubbling up in them somewhere?*

It wasn't like that for me. I always enjoyed writing, and felt relatively competent at it, but I was never able to write fiction that was at all satisfying to me. I found myself working in San Francisco as a journalist, and I sort of realized it wasn't something I was especially good at. There were important skills for a journalist that I just didn't have. It seemed like writing a novel might work better for me than figuring out how to be a really good journalist. So I left the paper, did some work on my own, did an MFA at San Francisco State University, and tried to figure out how fiction works.

*The narrator of the novel, Eric, is a programmer who's living in San Francisco, just after the Dot-com crash and 9/11 and around the time of the U.S. invasion of Iraq. What parts of your own story relate to the startup scene during those days?*

I got to San Francisco in 1996 and left ten years later, so I was there for the whole first boom and bust. So some of it was from doing reporting in various contexts. I moved there right out of college, so a lot of it was that my friends were going to startup jobs.

At that time, the thing for a company to do was to spend as much money as you could, as fast as possible, and hire a ton of people. So I knew a lot of people who were getting jobs that they couldn't properly explain, and where I didn't understand what the companies did. There were a lot of parties. It was fascinating and in ways sort of mystifying to me.

By the time I started working on the book, I had become interested not so much in the startup business but in the programming side of things. I had begun reading essays and books by programmers—there was a boomlet of writing about programming in the first decade of this century. That got me interested in programming as a pursuit separate from startups. And that's how I came to this aspect of Eric's character—the idea that he was someone who would enjoy immersing himself in this intensely rational, cognitive activity. In the end, the fact that he makes a bunch of money by founding a startup is, for him, almost an accident or an afterthought.

*There are a number of passages in the book where you seem to appropriate the language of startups in an ironic and dismissive way—for example, there's one sentence that reads "I made myself into the person she needed, and while it wouldn't scale it was at least a proof of concept."*

I think that's because I have ambivalent feelings about it. I learned a little bit about programming in the course of writing the book, and became an intermediate-level programmer, but there is something I very much admire about people who become really expert programmers. They seem to be driven by natural curiosity and a love of making things and a creative impulse, and I find all those things admirable. In particular, a lot of programmers—more then than now—are people who don't care whether it's cool to do or not, they are just fascinated by it. That is the aspect of the classic programming geek that I really admire. I aspire to that quality of focus. There is something monastic about it—these are people who are separating themselves from the world to try and figure something out.

About the people nowadays who come out of business school and decide they want to disrupt the parking meter space, or something like that, I say good luck to them. Maybe they will make something useful, but I don't find myself as sympathetic to that impulse.

In a way, if I see one big difference between the startup-founder-programmers of Eric's generation, around the turn of the millennium, and those of today, it's that the technology has gotten so much better. Nowadays you can build a modern startup website with social features largely by assembling components that have already been developed by other people. You can use a framework like Ruby on Rails and host it on Amazon servers and a lot of the work has been abstracted away. Which is terrific, but the modern startup scene has less of a role for intense programming. So the advantage that somebody like Eric had in 1999 or 2000 would no longer be such a competitive advantage.

*One thing about Eric's biography seemed improbable or at least outdated to me. He's very rich as a result of selling his software startup, and he's still in his early twenties, but he seems totally stalled in life. Today there's a very well-marked-out path for people in that situation—they become angel investors and start putting money into their friends' companies, and eventually they start something new of their own. But Eric isn't doing any of that. He's not even trying to stay plugged in to the startup scene.*

There are more of these guys today than there were ten years ago. Back then, there weren't things like Y Combinator. There weren't books explaining what you need to do to start a disruptive company. It certainly could happen, but it wasn't a known strategy. So there's more of a default path, now that there is a more stabilized startup culture.

But more importantly, I think this is an area where Eric is not representative of anything beyond himself. He is a guy who fell into this by accident—he says at one point that he wasn't even trying to get rich. I could imagine Bill Fleig [Eric's teenage hacker buddy and eventual co-founder] as a successful innovator working on another startup. But for Eric there was this whole other set of problems that he was preoccupied with, even as he was writing the code that would eventually make him very wealthy.

As I thought about "Okay, what would happen to him after he's made all that money and no longer has to worry about a day job?" it did seem like it would be difficult for him. I didn't think he would have much interest in networking with people. There's a scene where he goes to a conference and afterward, people are mobbing him and trying to get him to invest in their companies, and the only interesting thing to him is that maybe being surrounded by these people will elevate his status and help him become what he actually wants to be, which is an attractive person that a girl will love.

*Eric comments early in the book that "some people found social life as obvious as I found computers." How real do you think that dichotomy is? Are there some people who just instinctively understand how other people think, and people who don't?*

I certainly don't think it's a dichotomy. It's not that there are people who get it and people who don't get it. It's a spectrum. People like Bill Fleig are probably more hopeless than Eric is. Eric in many ways is extremely insightful and empathic and understands other people quite well. His problem, in a way, is that his intense self-consciousness makes it difficult for him to respond in an appropriate or natural way, after he has processed the data correctly.

I do think there are people who, for whatever reason, have a natural ability to be likeable, or to act in ways that are socially appropriate, and there are others for whom that comes harder. Adolescence is really the time when that gets sorted out—when people are revealed to have that natural sense or not. Everybody sort of figures it out along a slightly different path, and that can make those four or five years extremely intense and, for some people, extremely uncomfortable. That's why there are sections in the book about Eric's teenage years.

*The core perception that seems to set Eric up for romantic disaster is this idea that it's possible to "hack the girlfriend problem." He's obviously unsuccessful at that with Maya, but what do you think about the impulse itself? Eric seems to be trying to work with the tools he has. Is that so misguided?*

What I sympathize with in Eric is the intensity of his inspiration. He wants it so badly, he is willing to try anything. And he doesn't have a lot to work with. His parents certainly haven't given him much to work with, and nature hasn't equipped him with much to work with, in certain respects. But it has equipped him with this high cognitive intelligence, so he's working very hard with what he's got. I'm really sympathetic to that.

It would be much better if he weren't stuck in his head so much, and if he had a more natural way to act around other people. He would be very fortunate if he had even a slight increase in those things. He doesn't, and so he's in trouble.

*But what about this idea that it's possible to reduce human relationships to algorithms—that a coder's mind-set might actually help you understand other people? You don't have to look to fiction to find people who believe that's actually true.*

Let's say I'm skeptical. I think we should call it "thinking" rather than algorithms. I think that thinking is very useful, up to a point. Thinking about what other people feel and want, and what you yourself feel and want, can be really helpful. But if it's divorced from feeling and emotional insight, then it's hard for me to imagine building a really satisfying relationship out of it.

*Toward the end of the book Eric observes, "We can only know each other the way we know distant stars: by observing years-old light, gathering outdated information, running calculations and making inferences." That seems to be a defense of his original idea that there's a kind of calculus for managing relationships. That passage left me feeling unsure whether Eric has really learned anything.*

Those lines about distant stars feel very important to me, and I read them slightly differently from the way you do. I think what he is acknowledging in that moment is that people are inherently unknowable—that there is a limit to what you can see of other people's minds. And that engaging in a relationship with another person involves dealing with something that is ultimately opaque, and that you have to go ahead in your life and figure out how to proceed with that.

Eric is really good at solving problems of complexity, but the problems in his relationship with Maya aren't just problems of complexity, they're problems of ambiguity or opacity. That is what he has recognized in the end that he didn't know at the beginning. But unfortunately, he has recognized it too late.

*For Eric to be able to hack a relationship, he wants all the variables to be known. But as you've just described, it's important for the arc of the coming-of-age story to have him learn that this just isn't possible. Is that why you gave Maya's character this issue where she's struggling with what may be repressed memories of sexual abuse? That was a big cultural theme in the 1990s, and it still seems like a question that just can't be unraveled.*

I think the answer is yes. Structurally, putting her in that situation is a way of giving Eric a problem to solve that will be the problem that tests him and ultimately breaks him. You want to put your character in a situation that is not just as difficult as possible, but difficult in a way that reveals something about who he is. Giving Maya this aspect that is so important and so entirely unknowable and unresolvable seemed like a good way to do that.

In addition, I think that was an interesting period in our history. It seems to have begun in the late 1980s with the McMartin pre-school case, and to have died out by 1999 or so. After being a central cultural preoccupation for a while, it disappeared just like that. It was something I was interested in at the time, and when I went to study it more thoroughly for the book, I came to think that this was a situation that our culture had gotten itself into where it had raised questions that it was unable to answer. Here was something that was sort of exciting and in a way titillating and psychologically gripping, but suddenly it became too complicated for the culture to really figure out, so we just agreed to stop talking about it. That was interesting to me.

*In the end, you seem to leave it deliberately unclear whether Maya was abused or not.*

I am not going to disagree with that.

*I worried a little about Maya's character. As I made my way through the first third of the book, before you really get into the repressed-memory stuff, I was afraid she might turn out to be a Manic Pixie Dream Girl — the kind of female character that doesn't have an inner life or a*

*story of her own, except to the extent that it advances the male protago-*
*nist's story. It didn't turn out that way, but by the end I felt like she might*
*be another kind of character type—maybe the Manic Depressive*
*Dream Girl. Did you struggle with how fully realized you wanted*
*Maya's character to be? Or was it important for the plot that she stay*
*somewhat opaque?*

Well, let me say first that in a novel like this one, there are some
characters who are intended to be round and some who are intended
to be flat, to use a distinction that E. M. Forster made. There are
some characters in the book who are supposed to be lively and funny
and serve a function, but they are not intended to be fully rounded
humans. My intention was for Maya to be as round a character as
possible. And to the extent that she isn't, that is just my failure as a
writer—that is not to do with intention.

It's difficult, obviously, when everything is so firmly locked into
one character's point of view, to make the other characters round
when you want them to be. You have to do it through their actions
and dialogue, mostly. I had the benefit of getting to do some story-
telling from Maya's point of view when she talks about her childhood, which at least gives the reader a sense of her voice and what
things looked like from her perspective.

At the same time, as you brought up, there are central things about
her that the reader can't know for sure—that are just not resolved.
And that's the way it has to be for the book to work. Maybe that com-
promised my ability to make her a fully rounded character, but anything beyond that is just the result of my shortcomings as a writer.

*Going back to a technology question. At one point Eric says: "With*
*enough calculations per second you can generate the impression of*
*spontaneous compatibility, the way a grid of tiny pixels becomes a*
*photograph." That made me wonder what Eric, or you, would say*

*about the Turing Test. Do you think it will ever be possible for a suffi-*
*ciently advanced computer to fool a human into thinking that it's*
*human?*

I don't know. There are people who have spent long enough thinking about that that it would be dumb for me to venture an opinion. What is interesting about the question is that it is exactly a version of what a novelist is trying to do, and of what we were just talking about. Is Maya a rounded character, or is she a caricature? Well, either way, both are just arrangements of letters and punctuation marks on the page. That is literally all they are. It's a very limited set of symbols—only around a hundred—that you can manipulate, and out of that I have to make real, alive human beings, at least for the duration of the book, and inso-far as you are willing to suspend your awareness that they are not real. Any programmer working on passing the Turing Test is engaged in an activity that novelists have been doing for hundreds of years.

*I've also been reading Scott Hutchins's book* **A Working Theory of**
**Love,** *which is another first novel set in San Francisco, and is also, in*
*a way, about the extent to which relationships can be reduced to algo-*
*rithms. Do you think it's somehow symptomatic of our times that*
*writers such as yourself are driven to explore these questions about*
*technology and human consciousness and emotions?*

I'm aware of the book, but I didn't read it, just out of superstition. But here's what I think, and I sort of suspect this would be true for Hutchins as well. I think novelists in general, and me in particular, are interested in what it's like to be alive. That is a fundamental and only very loosely timely question. What it's like to be alive may change over time, but it changes pretty slowly.

In the end, talking about computers and programming and hav-ing a character who is a computer programmer is not so much out of a theoretical interest in technology or programming. It's more about trying to find a different way of talking about the experience of being alive and the way human beings relate to each other. This material happens to be there, and it hasn't been worked over as much as some other stuff, so that is what I am going to use.

But that's probably the wrong thing to say to make your audience read the book!

*Well, I'm a little surprised to hear you soft-pedal the technology part. It seems like technology actually is changing what it means to be alive, and far faster than in the past.*

And I think there is a ton of interesting stuff to say about that. But much of the interesting stuff points to the future. Already, I can see how life is different from a few years ago, before social media. How will the experience be different for my kid, who is now very little? I have no fucking idea, but it's going to be crazy. And there are novelists using fiction to think about that question—William Gibson is probably the greatest of them—but that is not quite the kind of book I was writing. I don't know that I have the insights to go into those kinds of future-oriented questions.

This interview was conducted by Wade Roush and originally appeared on xconomy.com. Reprinted with permission.

# Questions and topics for discussion

1. In the opening chapter of *The Unknowns* we see adult Eric using his analytical mind to navigate the social stratosphere of a party. How does this set piece change the way you perceive him and interpret his behavior in latter parts of the book?

2. How was your first impression of Eric altered by the chapters that take place during his high school years? If you'd never observed teenaged Eric, would your opinion of him be different?

3. Eric describes his state of being as "stretched across the gulf between my life's twin goals: experiencing uncompromised happiness and not being a loser." Would you say that those are really Eric's goals? How would you describe his goals?

4. Eric's high school notebook—where he catalogs the interests and particularities of the girls in his school—is a perfect illustration of how Eric leads with his heart but executes with analysis and data. What does Eric miss by navigating social situations with logic gleaned from programming and video games? What does this impulse to categorize, label, and define everything tell us about Eric?

5.  If the notebook hadn't fallen into the wrong hands, would Eric have ultimately achieved a greater understanding of his female classmates? Could it have led to a meaningful connection?

6.  How does knowing about the notebook change the way you feel about Eric's impulse to track down Maya's father, and his need to investigate the "unknown" areas of Maya's life?

7.  Both Eric and Maya have complicated relationships with their fathers. How does Eric's relationship with his father affect how he interprets Maya's claims of abuse?

8.  Readers never really find out if what Maya remembers about her childhood is true. Does that matter?

9.  In an email to Maya, Eric writes, "I have no idea how anyone managed to have sex before email." How has technology changed romance and relationships?

10. What kind of unknowns exist in a relationship? Is a certain amount of uncertainty healthy or destructive?